THE WICKED SEX

'The Ottoman suite has been prepared for you,' the hostess continued. 'I shall wait in the hall outside and send in men as required. They will be naked and each will have a number stencilled on his right buttock for identification purposes. Your colour is black, Ms Sales, and yours white, Ms Dominovna. I shall keep a tally of those you exhaust according to the definition you have given me.' She paused briefly and in a matter-of-fact voice inquired: 'Do you require cocks or have you brought your own?'

Valerie Sales and the Russian looked at one another and then down at their briefcases. Both women grinned girlishly.

'I seldom travel anywhere without mine,' said the former. 'High heels, an Italian handbag and a strap-on cock are *de rigueur* for every serious businesswoman.'

'How true,' agreed the Russian. 'Though I would add a fourth item to your list: a personal assistant with a long and flexible tongue!'

THE WICKED SEX

Lance Porter

This book is a work of fiction.
In real life, make sure you practise safe, sane and
consensual sex.

First published in 2007 by
Nexus
Thames Wharf Studios
Rainville Rd
London W6 9HA

A catalogue record for this book is available from the British
Library.

www.nexus-books.com

Typeset by TW Typesetting, Plymouth, Devon

Printed in the UK by CPI Bookmarque, Croydon, CR0 4TD

The paper used in this book is a natural, recyclable product made
from wood grown in sustainable forests. The manufacturing
process conforms to the regulations of the country of origin.

ISBN 978 0 352 34161 7

Distributed in the USA by Holtzbrinck Publishers, LLC, 175
Fifth Avenue, New York, NY 10010, USA

   . . . Adorned
She was indeed, and lovely, to attract
Thy love, not thy subjection, and her gifts
Were such as under government well seemed,
Unseemly to bear rule . . .

Paradise Lost

nexus Symbols key

 Corporal Punishment

 Female Domination

 Institution

 Medical

 Period Setting

 Restraint/Bondage

 Rubber/Leather

 Spanking

 Transvestism

 Underwear

 Uniforms

Contents

1

Bound by a Woman

Gunther's pulse raced and he even felt his cock begin to stir as he watched the first of the disembarked passengers filter through into the arrivals lounge. He pushed himself to the front of the crowd of waving friends and relatives, impatient to get a glimpse of the South Seas girl who would soon be his wife. Hardly able to believe his good fortune, he took one last glance at the photograph in his hand and tucked it inside his jacket pocket. If Bee looked half as pretty in the flesh as she did on her picture, he was set to become the happiest man in all Germany.

He only regretted he had not got himself a mail-order bride ten years earlier. He thought of all the frustration and disappointment it would have spared him. Even in his prime he could boast of few successes with women and now that his body had begun to droop and sag with the onset of middle age his situation had become hopeless. He passed most days in silent despair, a victim of the fashionably dressed and vivacious young women who had become his obsession. His heart beat dangerously fast in their presence, yet they seemed barely aware of his existence – even when he stood at their tables and took their meal orders.

An exotic creature wearing a yellow flower behind her ear and a brightly patterned dress came hesitantly into the arrivals lounge. Her dark eyes blinked nervously at the crowd as she struggled to manoeuvre a heavily laden luggage cart. A smile spread across Gunther's face and he licked his lips. She was a perfect doll! He waved and called out excitedly and she glanced in his direction. But at the same moment another man, some years older than Gunther, stepped from the crowd and embraced the bemused traveller. Gunther reddened at his mistake, but fortunately few people had paid him any attention.

Feeling some affinity with the oddly matched couple, he smiled affectionately as they walked by, the man pushing the luggage, his petite bride-to-be clinging shyly to his arm. Gunther's gaze dropped from the young woman's sleek black hair down to her dainty feet in their pretty silver sandals. What a delectable specimen of a woman, he thought, as he watched the cheeky sway of her round ass: she was the perfect blend of innocence and sex appeal. He couldn't wait to see the faces of the stuck-up *Fräulein* when he paraded his own tropical beauty through the streets of his hometown.

When Gunther turned his head, impatient now for his own fiancée to appear, the sight that greeted him made his jaw drop. Strolling confidently behind a luggage cart and glancing aloofly at the crowd was the most spectacular dark-haired woman he had ever laid eyes on. Men stared at her hungrily as she passed before them and the clinging red dress she wore did little to conceal her extraordinary figure. She walked with a cat-like pertness, rolling her powerful hips, and Gunther began to suspect she was a famous athlete, long used to such keen male attention. Indeed there was something familiar about her features. He squinted, wondering where he had seen those slanting brown eyes and full pouting lips before. A shiver ran through his body – he was staring at his bride-to-be.

Gunther let out a wild cry and rushed out in front of the luggage cart. Bee stopped just in time and looked down at him with narrow and suspicious eyes.

'It's me,' he said. She was at least half a head taller than him and he felt tiny standing before her. 'It's me, Gunther.'

'Gunther?' She pronounced his name with a strong foreign accent.

'Yes, Gunther. Your fiancé.'

She frowned. 'You old. You not like photograph.'

Gunther was hurt by the remark but tried not to let it show. He stepped behind the trolley and put an arm around her waist. 'Welcome to Germany,' he said. 'I promise you'll be very happy here. Now let me take you to your new home.'

Bee made no response but she allowed Gunther to keep his arm fastened around her narrow waist as they proceeded to the exit. They did not speak but Gunther was more than content to walk in silence at his beautiful fiancée's side, savouring the supple movements of her hip against his palm. He relished the envious glances of the men they passed and hugged her possessively. As they left the terminal he had to hobble for several strides while he freed the fierce erection trapped down the leg of his pants.

Bee was disappointed to discover that she would be taking a taxi to her new home. 'You no have BMW?' she said to Gunther as she watched the driver struggling to lift her suitcases into the boot. Gunther, who had never owned a car in his life, quickly changed the subject and after considerable coaxing persuaded her to get into the vehicle. As they pulled away, Bee turned her face towards the window and seemed prepared to spend the whole journey ignoring him.

The small cabin was quickly dominated by her spicy feminine scent and Gunther felt his temperature rise until he became unbearably hot. He loosened his collar and wriggled agitatedly on his side of the seat, casting lustful glances at her breasts and thighs which were

3

teasingly outlined beneath the thin red dress. The driver too, he noticed, was watching Bee in his mirror.

Gunther could hold out no longer. He slid across the seat until his hip was pressed against hers and placed a hand on her bare knee. Her skin was smooth and warm and enticing and his fingers seemed to move of their own accord. They crept up the inside of the silky thigh, seeking the source of the heat that radiated from beneath the dress. Bee snapped her legs shut on his hand but Gunther continued pushing towards her crotch.

'You stop!' she shouted, seizing him by the wrist and twisting his arm away. Gunther fell back against the seat, astonished by her strength. Angrily she pulled the hem of the dress over her thighs. She crossed her legs tightly and placed her handbag firmly on her lap. Gunther slid back to his corner where he sat like a spurned teenager. He was sure the eyes in the driving mirror were laughing at him.

A while later Bee turned to him and spoke as if she had forgotten all about the humiliating incident.

'You have restaurant?'

Gunther nodded stiffly.

'Where?' She peered through the window as the car turned into a busy high street.

'Not far away.'

'Show me.'

'Tomorrow . . . maybe.' It gave him some satisfaction to refuse her request and remind her that he was the one who made the decisions. His feisty bride-to-be needed to be taught who was master. He imagined the things he would do with her when they were alone inside his apartment. The lusty male blood surged through his veins again. The marriage formalities could wait. He would keep her locked in the bedroom for a week. She would soon learn to respond to his advances with a little more passion.

* * *

4

At long last the driver pulled up in front of Burgundy Court, the apartment block where Gunther lived. While the two men heaved the suitcases from the boot, Bee walked nimbly towards the three-storey building, her neat black handbag swinging from her shoulder.

'Just like the picture,' she said, gazing up at the Gothic façade. She clapped her hands excitedly. Gunther paid the driver and then contemplated the two big cases which stood on the pavement.

'Why you don't call your men?' Bee asked, puzzled.

'My men?'

'You have men, yes?'

Gunther thought for a moment. 'I can manage,' he said. He positioned himself between the cases, stooped and gripped the handles. But when he tried to straighten up, the cases seemed bolted to the ground. He grinned sheepishly, stretched his arms, and prepared to try again. But this time, as he attempted to lift the cases, a sharp pain shot through his lower back. He barked a curse and stepped away, gritting his teeth.

Bee shook her head, holding back a smile. 'I tell you to call men.'

'What in God's name have you got in these things?' He stood rubbing his back and looking at the cases, wondering what to do next. Bee walked over to him and removed the handbag from her shoulder.

'Hold,' she said.

Gunther took the handbag and watched her step out of her mules. Bare-footed, she stood between the cases and lifted them without any show of effort. Walking with balletic grace, she crossed the pavement carrying the two cases as if they weighed no more than bags of groceries.

'Bring my shoes,' she shouted when she reached the front door.

Gunther bent down slowly, careful of his aching back. He felt deeply ashamed of what she had asked him to do, but he saw no way to refuse the request since he was not able to carry the cases. Gingerly, he picked up the pair of black mules, which still felt warm from her feet, and limped after her.

'It's an old injury,' he said when he caught up. 'I damaged it lifting weights in the gym.' He could not help glancing at her arms. They were long and magnificently toned. Her smooth biceps looked much stronger than his own, yet they were distinctly feminine, like those of the Norse warrior goddesses he remembered from his childhood picture books. As a boy he had been unsettled by the sight of these mighty women defeating men in battle. Even to his young mind it had seemed wrong and unnatural. Confronted with Bee's powerful physique he felt an odd tingling in his balls.

He took out his key and opened the door. Bee went in first, but she stopped suddenly a few steps beyond the threshold and put down the cases.

'Why you have numbers on doors?'

'Oh ... Don't worry, it's traditional.' He pointed towards the stairs across the hallway but let his arm fall again. He had been holding out the shoes like a buffoon in a comedy. He cleared his throat. 'Those stairs are rather steep. Perhaps you should take one case at a time?' In answer Bee picked up both cases and marched forward, somewhat huffily, it seemed to Gunther.

Just as she reached the foot of the stairs a nearby door opened to reveal the face of Siegfried, Gunther's young neighbour and occasional drinking partner. His eyes bulged at the sight of Bee and his gaze trailed down over her ass and legs to her shapely bare feet.

'So this is the lucky lady,' he said with a grin and stepped out into the hall, never taking his eyes from Bee. 'Aren't you going to introduce us, old man?'

But Bee had already begun to climb the stairs, her long legs bearing her gracefully upwards, the big cases seeming to hang weightlessly from her hands. Nodding in admiration, Siegfried watched her ascend.

'My word!' he said as Gunther reached his side. 'What an amazon you've got yourself there.' Gunther muttered a greeting and tried to slip past his neighbour while keeping Bee's handbag and shoes concealed behind his back.

'What's that you're hiding?' Siegfried asked playfully.

'Nothing.'

'Let me see.' As Gunther twisted away from Siegfried's snatching hands, the heel of a shoe caught on the banister post. Gunther felt the shoe being torn from his grip and watched, gritting his teeth together, as it bounced with a clattering sound across the tiled floor.

Siegfried stooped and picked it up. 'Pretty shoe,' he said, holding it in his broad fingers and rubbing his thumb along the slender heel. Still crouching, he caught sight of the handbag and the other shoe behind Gunther's back. He stared up at Gunther for a long moment, uncertain what to say. Finally he stood up and his blond eyebrows came together in an expression of disapproval.

'My, that young lady has already got you well trained, hasn't she?'

Gunther, who had turned very red, said nothing. He snatched the shoe from Siegfried and proceeded up the stairs, as quickly as his sore back would allow.

Bee was waiting on the top-floor landing, sitting on one of the cases and massaging her toes. The bottom of her foot was filthy from the floor.

'Who that man?' she asked without looking up.

'Him? Oh, nobody.'

She snorted and gestured to the row of doors. 'They also nobody?' She got to her feet and snatched up the cases. 'So, which number your house?'

Gunther had never considered his apartment small. Indeed, as a bachelor who entertained guests only rarely, its kitchen, comfortable lounge and double bedroom with en suite bathroom had been more than adequate for his needs. Bee thought otherwise. She crossed the lounge in a few long strides. Once at the window, she peered through the blinds at the apartment block across the street and shook her head crossly.

'You say this big house yours.'

'A small cultural misunderstanding.'

'You lie to me.'

'Now, look here –' He was about to tell her she should count herself lucky to be in his country at all, but he checked himself. 'You'll get used to it,' he said.

She came away from the window and sat down in an armchair. Gunther took the couch opposite. He stared at her pretty pouting lips and his cock swelled in his pants. He patted the cushion beside him.

'Why don't you sit here?'

She shook her head.

'Listen,' he said and leant forward in his eagerness. 'If you're really unhappy we can find somewhere bigger. I have plenty of savings.' Bee was unimpressed. She sat back in the chair and stretched out her long legs so that her feet with their dirty soles were right under his nose. In places the skin was almost black and Gunther felt offended by the uncouth sight she was presenting to him, apparently in response to his generous offer. He recalled reading somewhere that showing the bottoms of the feet was a deliberate gesture of disrespect in eastern cultures. The idea that he was the target of such a barbaric insult in his own home and that a young woman, his would-be wife, was the perpetrator, felt like an attack on his manhood. Simmering with rage, he glared at the boldly displayed female soles and was about to kick them away when he suddenly remembered that it was in a travel guide to Thailand that he had read about the sole-showing custom. Perhaps it did not apply to the South Seas? He glanced across at Bee who stared back at him boredly. He remained suspicious but decided to give her the benefit of the doubt.

At length Bee stood up and stretched herself. 'I need wash my body,' she said with a yawn. She had not meant to suggest anything by her choice of words, but the prominent reference to her body, though merely the quirk of a non-native speaker, had an immediate effect on Gunther. In his mind he saw steamy water jetting against her naked breasts and buttocks. He squeezed his palms together as he imagined rubbing them over her slippery soap-covered flesh. Forgetting all about his sore back, he jumped to his feet.

'The bathroom is through there,' he said, hoarse with excitement, 'in the bedroom.' Bee went into the hall and Gunther followed her, but his hopes were quickly dashed.

'Leave me,' she said. 'I manage.' She picked up the suitcases and went into the bedroom, closing the door behind her.

Gunther returned to the lounge and paced about restlessly. For a while he sat down and tried to watch TV, but the thought of Bee naked in the shower would not go away. He turned off the TV and threw down the remote control. 'Damn her!' he muttered to himself. 'Whose apartment is this!' He went back out into the hall and walked up to the bedroom door. He knocked softly and waited a moment. Cautiously, he went in.

The glass-panelled door to the en suite bathroom was steamed up and he could hear the sound of the shower as he approached. One of the suitcases stood against the wall; the other was lying open on its side at the foot of the bed displaying a collection of fashionable outfits. He sniffed the air. Bee's distinctive scent had already colonised the room. He caught sight of the red dress hanging over the back of a chair. Unable to resist the temptation, he went over and picked it up. Now that it was no longer stretched over her body, it seemed flimsy, insignificant. He smiled wryly: to think, this slight garment was all that had shielded her from the hordes of panting men she had passed today. He brought the dress to his face and inhaled. As he did so, something dropped lightly onto the seat of the chair.

They were her panties! A thrill crept through him as he stared at the partly rolled-up pair of plain cotton briefs. Black, he thought to himself, the colour of sin. He reached down and took them in his trembling fingers. He lifted them towards his face and was about to press them against his nose when he became aware that the shower had gone silent. He glanced at the door nervously and saw the blurry outline of Bee's body through the frosted glass. He dropped the dress over the back of the chair, stuffed the panties underneath, and quickly left the room. He sat down on the couch and pretended to be engrossed in the TV.

A few minutes passed and he heard Bee shout his name. Her voice sounded more cheerful than it had been and he began to hope that the shower had put her in a better mood. He took a few deep breaths to calm himself. He did not want to appear too keen. Bee called again, louder this time:

'I tell you bring handbag.'

Gunther snatched the bag from the table and headed rapidly to the bedroom.

He found Bee standing before the wardrobe mirror brushing her luxurious black hair. She wore a short silk bathrobe tied at the waist with a belt. In the reflection in the mirror he could see that the front of the garment hung partly open, offering a tempting glimpse of her breasts.

Bee put out a hand. Without needing to be asked, Gunther drifted across to her, beaming like the most hopeful of lovers. He held the bag open while she reached inside and took out a silver hair band. She slipped it over the front of her hair, pulling the dark locks back from her face.

'Take bag over there,' she said, pointing to the chest

10

of drawers. Gunther did as he was bidden – anything to get her into that bed, he reminded himself.

Bee began to rub cream on her legs. Working up from the calves, she bent forward and Gunther was treated to a flash of her tanned ass cheeks. He watched without blinking as her hands moved slowly up one leg and then the other in a gentle caressing action, leaving glistening skin behind them. His mouth watered. His breathing became heavy. When Bee's hand slid beneath the robe, he could restrain himself no longer. He kicked off his shoes, tore off his shirt and trousers, and stood there in his boxer shorts sweating.

Bee continued to rub cream on her legs as if he were not even in the room. He had hoped for a more dramatic reaction – a shriek of surprise or a cry of fear. He had been ready to rip open the robe and thrust himself against her naked body. But her composure deflated him. He sat down on the bed and simply stared at her while she finished applying the cream to her legs. The front of his boxers was pushed up in a crude pyramid shape, and remained that way, making his desire for her plain and obvious to them both.

Bee finally came over to him but stopped just beyond the reach of his outstretched arms. She glanced down at his lap and shook her head condescendingly. Gunther caught sight of their reflection in the wardrobe mirror. He looked like a desperately imploring suitor and she a cold disdainful princess.

'You a liar,' she said. 'I not marry you.'

'I beg your pardon.'

'Where your restaurant?'

'Now just one moment, young lady –'

'You a liar. You not have my body.' And with that she walked to the other side of the bed, slipped under the duvet and turned her back on poor Gunther and his aching cock.

Gunther wrung his hands together in vexation. What kind of fool did she take him for? She was in his apartment, lying in his bed, and his hard-earned money had brought her here. It was finally time she learned who was master. He climbed under the duvet and eased himself across the sheet until his hot trembling body was pressed against his young fiancée.

'I tell you *no!*' she snapped and wriggled away from him, pulling the robe around herself.

But Gunther was not listening. At last, after so many years of longing and frustration, he had his hands on a sexy young woman. Her warm scented flesh drove him into a lustful frenzy and his excited fingers crawled under the robe, seeking her body's most secret place.

'Get off me!' she screamed indignantly.

Gunther could only grunt in reply as he dragged up the bottom of her robe. His bloated cock sprung through the front of his boxers as if it had a will of its own and speared the tight cleft between her buttocks. Bee's struggles became more urgent, but Gunther was not to be deterred from his purpose. Gripping her thighs, he clamped her ass against his crotch and jerked his hips, panting noisily as he did so.

'I warn you!' she said.

But Gunther's mind was bent on one thing only and Bee's lively resistance increased his excitement. The pressure was building up in his balls and he knew he had to get his cock inside her quickly before he exploded over her ass cheeks and disgraced himself. He bit into the warm flesh at the back of her neck and forced his hand into her wriggling crotch.

Suddenly his wrist was seized and given such a sharp twist that he cried out in agony. The next thing he knew he was being dragged from the bed and forced down onto his knees on the carpet. Bee was glaring down at him, face flushed, hair tousled. Gunther could scarcely believe what was happening. He had been bettered by a girl. He tried to pull his hand free and stand up, but she tightened her irresistible grip and mercilessly twisted his wrist.

12

'Let me go!' he shrieked. He swung at her with his free hand but she easily avoided his poorly aimed blows. She stepped around him and before he knew it she had trapped his arm behind his back. They were both still for a moment and Gunther thought this would be the end of the fight. She had used surprise and taken advantage of his injury. He would get even with her as soon as she released his arm.

But Bee was far from finished. She gave him a hard shove which sent him sprawling forward onto his chin. He tried to right himself, but a knee was pressed firmly into his back, pinning him where he lay.

'No move,' she ordered, forcing his arm up between his shoulders. Gunther bit into the carpet and submitted to her completely.

What she did next made him regret not putting up more of a fight. Keeping his arm firmly pinned, she reached around the bed into the open suitcase and lifted out a pair of black nylon stockings. One of these she tied to the wrist she was holding. Gunther fought to save his other wrist but she savagely twisted his captive arm until he surrendered.

'No fight,' she shouted above his cries. Holding his palms together, she calmly and efficiently wound the rest of the stocking around and between his wrists, stretching the nylon so tightly that it bit into his skin. She finished by tying an elaborate knot.

'How dare you,' he raged. 'Untie me at once!'

'I say no touch me. But you no listen.' She spun around so that she was straddling his thighs and set about binding his ankles together, just as she had his wrists. The taut nylon cut through to the bone and his feet began to turn numb. Bee got up and straightened her robe. 'You easy,' she said.

Gunther tried to stand too. He raised himself to his knees only to fall forward, face first, onto the carpet. He howled despondently and rolled back and forth wrestling with his painful nylon bonds. My God, he thought to himself, I've been tied up by a woman!

Bee sat down on the edge of bed and watched him writhing on the floor at her feet. She had a girlish grin on her lips.

'Untie me,' he said, adopting a more pleading tone, despite his inner rage.

She shook her head.

'I promise I won't touch you.'

'You a liar.'

'I give you my word.'

'Maybe in morning . . . If you good.'

He gazed up at her in horror. 'You can't keep me tied up all night.'

Bee simply nodded.

Gunther increased his efforts to free himself. He tugged at his bonds with all his might, but to no avail. What infernal knots she had tied! It seemed the harder he pulled the tighter they held him.

Bee stood up and gave Gunther a rude shove with her foot, rolling him onto his back. She planted her foot on his chest and pressed down just hard enough for him to feel the power of her muscular leg. He lay submissively with his hands crushed beneath him and stared up at her in trepidation. But then he noticed something. Her posture, one leg thrust forward and raised slightly, granted him a partial view beneath the short robe. In spite of everything that had happened, he had not lost his desire for her. He peered up between her thighs, trying to distinguish the outlines of her sex in the semi-shadow. His cock began to stiffen.

Bee was oblivious to the unintended treat she was giving the tethered man beneath her feet. Her eyes had lighted on a curious fixture on the wall opposite. It was a scrolled metal wall hook mounted at about chest height and it curled upwards and outwards some several inches from its base. Put up by the previous tenant, it was designed for hanging plant baskets. Gunther had never used it but had never quite got round to removing it either.

Bee glanced down at Gunther, who quickly averted his gaze from the enticing shadow between her thighs. She considered for a short while, then, mind made up, she lifted her foot off his chest.

'Get up,' she said. Gunther tried to pull himself up to a sitting position, but collapsed onto his back again almost immediately and lay before her, kicking his bound legs in the air.

'I can't,' he protested.

'OK, you roll.' She gave him a shove with her foot, turning him over onto his belly. Gunther yelped as his erect cock was crushed against the carpet.

'Nasty thing,' she giggled and shoved him again, as if she were playing a game with a child.

When she had rolled him to the wall, she crouched down on her haunches, slipped a hand under his shoulders and lifted him up onto his feet. She moved so quickly Gunther was given no opportunity to resist. She seized his bound wrists and jerked his arms up behind his back so that his shoulders and neck were pushed forward to compensate.

'Let me go, you she-devil!' he screamed.

Giving his arms a final jerk, she forced him up onto his tiptoes and slipped his tethered wrists over the hook on the wall. 'Hahaha! Now you be good.' She calmly walked away, leaving him to struggle.

Gunther gave up quickly, realising that he would never be able to lift his wrists off the hook. His head dropped gloomily. He was bound at the ankles and wrists and practically hanging from the wall of his own bedroom, incapable of freeing himself. Arms yanked high behind his back, his straining torso thrust forward, he resembled a swimmer about to dive from the edge of a pool.

Bee sat on the corner of the bed and regarded him coolly. Gunther, who only fifteen minutes earlier had imagined himself her master, began to plead.

'Please, you must untie me.'

'Tomorrow.'

'I won't touch you. I promise.'

She shook her head stubbornly.

'At least take me off this hook.'

Again she shook her head and Gunther began to tug at his bonds again and curse his unreasonable captor. As his cries grew louder, Bee got to her feet, frowning angrily.

'I make you quiet,' she said.

Gunther watched apprehensively as she bent down and rooted around inside the open suitcase. She stood up holding a pair of white ankle socks tucked together in a tight ball.

'No . . . You can't . . .' he stuttered as she came over. He had suddenly realised what she intended to do. 'I won't let you.'

'Open,' she commanded, holding the rolled up socks in front of his mouth.

He clenched his teeth together and shook his head defiantly.

'Open,' she repeated in a sterner voice and, when he still refused to co-operate, she grabbed his nose between her thumb and forefinger and squeezed his nostrils shut. Gunther tried to pull himself free but Bee's grip was unshakeable. His lungs soon began to burn and his jaws opened involuntarily as he gasped for air. Bee fed him the cotton sports socks, stuffing them to the back of his throat with her strong fingers.

Gunther choked and given time might have succeeded in spitting out the socks, but Bee had still to apply the finishing touch to the improvised gag. She lifted up her dress from the back of the chair and found the black bikini panties. She stretched them open around her fingers and then calmly slipped them over Gunther's head, as if they had been made for that very purpose. She covered the front of his face with the crotch section and tugged the elasticated waistband behind his ears. They proved to be a perfect fit. The gusset was pulled tightly across Gunther's nose and mouth and no matter how determinedly he worked his jaw he could not expel the sock gag.

Bee stood admiring her handiwork, and Gunther, suspended from his hook, gazed back at her through the leg holes of his shameful mask. With each breath he drew, he was forced to inhale the musk that Bee's sex and ass had left behind on the panty crotch. The boldly feminine scent made him viscerally aware of his defeat.

'Now you quiet,' she laughed. Certain he would not trouble her any more that night, she turned out the light and climbed back into the big double bed he had hoped to share with her. Exhausted by her long journey, she was soon sound asleep and oblivious to the pitiful struggles and muffled groans of her unlucky captive hanging from the opposite wall.

Gunther's body ached from head to toe and the pain in his back was quite unimaginable. But it was inside his head where he suffered most. Only the Devil's bride could force a man to remain in such a position. He was half-suffocated with her socks, her pungent panties covered his face, and he was bent towards the bed in a grotesque caricature of a bowing slave. Meanwhile she slept peacefully. He stared across at his tormentress, longing for morning and dreaming of revenge.

When morning came, Bee was in no hurry to put an end to his misery. She lay yawning and stretching on the bed and even drifted off into another short sleep before she finally pulled back the duvet, swung her legs over the edge of the mattress and stood up. Gunther began to twitch, anticipating his release, but first Bee went and stood before the mirror. She stretched her neck, shoulders and arms, as if she were warming up for exercise, and Gunther had to wait until even her toes had been wiggled and flexed before she came over and removed the panties from his head.

'For God's sake, get me off this hook,' he pleaded as soon as she pulled the socks out of his mouth. For once she did what he asked. She stepped behind him and jerked up his arms with such force that he screamed for her to stop. But at last his wrists were free of the hook. Gunther's legs wobbled, then gave way and he collapsed at her feet.

'You want drink?' she asked, glancing down at him. He nodded and Bee went into the bathroom and returned with a beaker of water. She started to hand it to him, laughed at his feeble attempt to raise his tethered hands, and squatted down and held the beaker towards his lips. Lying on his side, Gunther gulped it down, despite the shame he felt at being fed like a baby. Bee was not kind in the role of young mother. She made Gunther stretch for the beaker and tilted it at such an angle that much of the water spilled down his chin. When the beaker was empty, his thirst was far from quenched.

'I take shower,' she announced. 'You be good?'

He remained defiantly silent.

'OK, I put you on hook.'

'No, no, not the hook,' he stammered in terror.

She walked towards the bathroom and tapped the carpet with her foot. 'Come here,' she said. 'I want see you.'

Eager to appear compliant, Gunther dragged himself forward on his belly until he reached her toes. She lifted her foot and patted him on the back of the head with the sole. 'You stay here,' she said. 'Like my little dog.'

She kept the bathroom door open while she showered and every once in a while she pulled aside the shower curtain and looked out to make sure he was still in his place. The hazy outline of her body was visible behind the translucent white sheet and, from where he lay, Gunther could distinguish her darkly pigmented nipples and the black blur of her bush. He watched with guilty fascination as she soaped herself, turning her front and then ass towards the jet of water. He knew he should be using this opportunity to try to escape but his gaze was held fast by the spectacle. Her body seemed to encourage his attention, brushing against the wet nylon drape and turning it transparent when it clung briefly to her golden flesh.

She emerged from the shower wrapped in a short towel and stepped briskly across the room to the other side of the bed. By the time Gunther had turned his aching body around and dragged himself to a position from where he could see her, the towel lay discarded on the bed and she was fastening the clasp of a bra behind her back.

'When are you going to untie me?' he asked, trying to sit up.

She seemed not to hear him and walked over to the mirror in her matching bra and panties. They were made from a sheer black material, delicately patterned and trimmed with lace. Feminine to the point of being frivolous, it was not the kind of underwear Gunther expected to see on a woman who had proved to be as tough as any man he had met.

Bee posed for herself before the mirror, first admiring her sexily cupped breasts and then turning her back to the glass and gazing over her shoulder at her firm round ass, split by the enticing black triangle of her panties.

Still ignoring Gunther, she opened her second suitcase and selected an outfit to wear. She decided to dress more formally than she had the previous day and put on stockings, a narrow black skirt and a plain white blouse. She tied back her hair and but for the absence of a pillbox hat and cravat, she could have passed for a hostess from an east Asian airline. Finally, she stepped into a pair of open-toed mules with sharp heels, which gave added definition to the fine muscles in her calves.

Gunther watched her warily as she faced the mirror and made a minor adjustment to the skirt.

'Where are you going?' he asked.

'Shopping.' She walked across to the pants he had thrown on the floor the previous evening and searched through the pockets until she found his wallet. She opened it and plucked out his bank card and credit card.

'Put them back!' he shouted, struggling to lift himself off the floor.

'Tell me numbers.'

Somehow he managed to raise himself up onto his knees. He shuffled across the carpet towards his young fiancée as she stood inspecting his credit card.

'You tell me you rich man,' she said and laughed at the comical movements of his fettered legs.

'I won't allow you to steal from me.'

'You promise me beautiful ring.'

'Put those cards down now or –' He cut his sentence short, realising how impotent any threat would sound from a man forced to creep towards a woman on his knees.

'Tell me numbers,' she repeated as he reached her legs.

'Never.'

Calmly she lifted her foot and pressed the heel and sole of her shoe against his chest. 'You like me hurt you again?'

Gunther saw in Bee's dark slanting eyes the wicked glimmer they'd had the night before. He tried to back away from her foot but lost his balance. A gentle push from Bee's powerful leg sent him sprawling backwards onto the carpet. She stepped over him and held him down with a foot on his chest. The more he wriggled, the more pressure she applied. Gunther squealed in pain as the sharp heel of the mule dug into his ribs.

'No fight,' she commanded.

He obeyed at once and lay whimpering under the cruel pressure of her heel. Only when she was satisfied he had wholly submitted to her will did she slowly lift her shoe from his chest.

Once again Gunther lay on his back, his tethered hands pinned beneath him, completely at the mercy of his imperious young fiancée. He gazed up as she stepped over his prone body. She stood with one foot placed beside each of his shoulders, her ass turned towards his face. He could see up into the half-shadow beneath her skirt, but this time the view gave him little pleasure. Instead, the sight of her curvaceous cheeks jutting triumphantly above him made him aware how truly humiliating his position was – beaten easily by a girl less than half his age and forced to lie in submission beneath a round womanly ass that should be his to possess. Little did he imagine that she was about to subject him to a far greater humiliation.

Without a word of warning, Bee nonchalantly squatted down as if she were lowering herself onto a seat, only in this instance the seat was Gunther's startled face. Her ass descended so quickly that he did not even have time to cry out before the heavy cheeks landed on his open mouth and trapped his breath beneath them. She showed him no consideration and sat on his face with her full weight, crushing the back of his skull into the carpet, as if his head really were just a cushion for her ass.

Gunther feared his skull would crack open. Never had he felt so helpless in his life. His hands were trapped under his back and his puny neck muscles were no match for the might of the thighs and buttocks bearing down on him. It took all of his strength to nudge his nose out from between the cleft of her ass and snatch a breath of precious air.

Bee heard him snorting frantically beneath her and wriggled her ass so that it settled even more snugly over his face. His nostrils were once again wedged inside the skirt-lined furrow between her overpowering buttocks and his air supply was instantly cut off. Unable to breathe, he was seized by a terrible panic. He felt his lungs begin to collapse and his body jerked involuntarily. He thought he was about to suffocate and that his last memory of the world would be of a woman's smothering rear end.

At the last moment, Bee lifted her buttocks a fraction and allowed him a few gulps of air. While he gasped like a drowning man, she spoke to him in a stern voice. Her words echoed high above him, as if they came from another world.

'Tell me numbers,' she said.

'Never,' he answered foolishly.

The invincible ass bore down on his face again. Once more he snorted for dear life as the suffocating cleft imprisoned his nostrils. She buried his nose and mouth so deeply he could feel the warmth of her crotch through the skirt. On the verge of blacking out, he even imagined he could smell her musky sex. During what he believed were his last moments on earth a single idea tormented him: he would never make himself master of that proud pussy resting on his face.

With perfect timing, she granted him another mouthful of air. The sustained lack of oxygen had left him too weak even to attempt a struggle and his head lay motionless on the carpet, completely at the mercy of her ass.

'Tell me numbers.'

He was quick to oblige her this time. He spluttered out his precious pin numbers to the tightly clad buttocks that hovered threateningly above his nose.

Excited at the prospect of a shopping trip, Bee bounced her heavy ass up and down on Gunther's face, ordering him to repeat both sets of numbers until she had them memorised. Gunther lay there half-unconscious and took it all. She was amusing herself with him, using him as if he were a toy. But what could he do? She was stronger and fitter than him. When she finally stood up and walked back to the mirror to put on her make-up, the only sign she had exerted herself was a slight rumple in the seat of her skirt.

The day, like the previous night, passed slowly and painfully for Gunther. Before she left to go shopping, Bee reattached him to the hook and put on the hateful socks-and-panty gag. He felt like a dog locked indoors waiting for its mistress to return, only he was not even allowed to curl up in a basket or help himself to water and biscuits.

Bee did not come home until late afternoon. Gunther could hear her walking about the apartment, though it was some time before she entered the bedroom. When she switched on the light, he immediately noticed something sparkling on her middle finger. He was certain it was a diamond, a large and very expensive-looking one. He grunted weakly in protest, but quickly suppressed his anger. He had a much more urgent need at the present moment and tugged at his bonds to get Bee's attention.

She walked over to him. 'What?' she said in an impatient tone. She lifted off the panties and pulled the socks from his mouth.

'I need to use the toilet,' he gasped.

Bee rolled her eyes at this most inconvenient request. She moved behind him and jerked his wrists up off the hook. Gunther's knees wobbled and she held him by the elbows until he had found his balance. 'Go,' she said and guided him as he hopped across the carpet towards the bathroom.

Gunther was positioned with his knees against the toilet bowl. All that remained for him to do was pull down his boxer shorts and empty his aching bladder. But with his wrists still bound, even this simple task proved too difficult for him. Bee sighed with exasperation and dragged his underwear down to his ankles.

'You like big baby,' she said and walked away.

Gunther managed to aim his stream into the toilet bowl. He even twisted around and flushed the chain after he had finished. But he was unable to pull up his boxers. Too embarrassed to ask for help, he hobbled slowly out of the bathroom with the shorts hanging around his fettered ankles. He felt shamefully aware of his nakedness in the presence of his elegantly attired fiancée. His shrivelled cock and balls were on full display.

Bee was standing before the mirror and tying back her hair. 'You want eat?' she asked, turning her head to reveal a pair of glittering earrings. Gunther felt a tightness in his chest and had to fight back the urge to curse her. 'Come,' she ordered and strolled out of the bedroom, leaving him to follow as best he could.

Shuffling on his bound feet, the boxer shorts dragging around his ankles, Gunther made his way through the hall and into the lounge, where he found the table laid with a mouth-watering selection of food. Bee was already seated, breaking a bread roll between her fingers. As he approached the table, she kicked out a chair for him. With some difficulty he managed to sit down.

Now he was faced with a further problem. How was he supposed to eat with his wrists bound together behind his back? Bee showed little sympathy for his predicament. She let him stare helplessly at the food spread before him while she buttered her roll and fussily selected ham, cheese and pickles to place inside. She ate without any sense of modesty, relishing every mouthful and licking the crumbs from her fingers.

'You want food?' she asked.

He nodded dumbly.

Bee picked up a slice of salami and dangled it in front of his lips. 'Open,' she commanded. 'Open or I take away.' Gunther's hunger overcame his pride and he opened his jaws and accepted the morsel of meat from her fingers. Bee fed him several more pieces of salami in the same demeaning fashion. But her begrudging indulgence of him was soon exhausted. She took a plate, piled it indiscriminately with food and slid it in front of him. Gunther stared down at his untidy meal. The only way he would be able to eat it was by lowering his face to the table. He sat for some moments until once more hunger got the better of him and he bowed his head like a dog at its bowl.

Bee ate her fill, then lay down on the couch and switched on the TV. She flipped through the channels, yawning contentedly, while across the room Gunther laboured at his plate. The salty food soon gave him a thirst and he glanced with increasing need at the bottle of water standing in the middle of the table. He had no choice but to twist around in his chair to ask Bee for assistance.

Bee was engrossed in the TV and when he called to her she raised a hand to silence him. She had discovered a cable channel devoted to travel and a feature about the South Seas had just begun. Gunther, who rarely tuned into anything other than the sport and adult channels, watched resentfully as images of blue oceans, white sand beaches and swaying palm trees washed across the screen to the sweet strains of an Hawaiian guitar. A mellow male voice enthused about the warmth and hospitality of the natives, who were shown surfing and dancing the hula in traditional dress. However, the commentary suddenly lost its light-hearted tone when Bee's own island was featured. Healthy native girls with shining hair and long golden limbs appeared on the screen wearing revealing skirts made from dried grass and shells. They performed a lewd hip-shaking dance to wildly beating drums. '*But don't let appearances deceive you,*' the voice warned. '*The ladies over here know a thing or two about girl power.*' Suddenly the image of an attractive young woman filled the screen. Blessed with the same voluptuous yet athletic physique as Bee, she sprinted barefoot across the sand gripping a long spear which she launched in a high arc, releasing a loud, almost sexual grunt as she did so. '*In former times a male suitor was required to beat his intended bride in a trial of strength and prowess . . . If he failed he would lose his life. However, a generous lady would often spare the man she'd defeated on condition he became her slave for a year and a day.*'

Gunther's blood turned to ice. He stared at Bee, who lay stretched out on the couch, and wondered what type of demoness he had brought into his home. Her long feet hung over the armrest and she flexed her toes with a teasing rhythm as she continued to watch the enchanting scenes from her native land, now represented by jubilantly dancing women. Gunther contemplated his future and the room seemed to darken and echo with the primitive sound of beating drums. Surely she did not intend to treat him, a citizen of Germany, like one of her defeated countrymen?

The travel show came to an end. Finding nothing else to interest her, Bee swung her feet off the arm rest and stood up. Gunther cringed in his chair as she came towards him, but she walked by without a glance and went along the hall into the bedroom.

Gunther's heart began to pound. This was his chance to act. His first instinct was to make for the front door and he pushed back the chair and tried to stand up. But he quickly realised that with his wrists tied behind his back he would be unable to reach the latch. He slumped down again. He had been released from the dreadful hook, but in reality he was just as much her prisoner as before.

Then an idea came to him. He got off the chair and hopped towards the end of the couch where the phone lay. He squatted down, lifted the handset with his teeth and placed it on the side table. He waited a moment, catching his breath. His naked balls trembled as he listened for any sound of Bee. He hardly dared think what the punishment would be if she caught him.

He had intended to call the police but he changed his mind. The police would ask too many questions and there would be the indignity of the official investigation and perhaps even a trial. It was better, he decided, to call somebody he knew and keep his domestic humiliation a private matter between friends. He immediately thought of Siegfried on the ground floor and the image of his neighbour's strong and manly face filled him with hope. Praying he had remembered the number correctly, he bent his head and began pressing the buttons with his nose. His heart pounded as his neighbour's phone began to ring, and he placed his mouth against the handset, urging him to pick up.

But Siegfried was not at home and a long and rambling recorded message greeted a despairing Gunther. As he waited for it to finish, he sensed his time was running out and that Bee would return at any second. 'Siegfried,' he gasped finally, his voice quaking. 'This is Gunther ... Something terrible has happened. Please help me –' He stopped short. The TV had gone quiet for a moment and he thought he could hear the bedroom door open. He grabbed for the receiver with his mouth but it slipped from his teeth and fell to the floor. God help me! he screamed inwardly as he bent down to retrieve it.

Bee strolled into the living room just as he laid the handset back on its base. She glared at him suspiciously.

'What you doing?' she demanded to know.

Stuttering something about wanting to watch TV, he backed away from the phone, but so clumsily that his knees gave way and he collapsed on the carpet in front of the couch. Bee stepped over his body and sat down heavily on the cushions.

'You like watch TV?' she said.

'Yes,' he muttered, trying to pull himself up from his belly.

He could scarcely believe what happened next. His young fiancée lifted up her feet and placed them rudely on his back, as if he were not a man but a footrest. He squirmed away indignantly but she stretched out a long leg, hooked him with her heel and used her superior strength to drag him back into position.

'Get off me!' he protested.

She jabbed him in the kidneys with her foot, making him yelp.

'Lie still or I hurt you.'

Gunther, who had little fight left in him, gave up struggling and became the lifeless object she demanded. Once he had acquiesced, Bee shifted her feet around on his back until they were comfortably positioned. He found himself lying with his face buried in the carpet, a heavy heel pressing down on his neck.

'Now we both happy,' she said, sitting contentedly on the couch. 'You see TV. I got place for my feet.'

Gunther lay obediently on the floor beneath his young fiancée's feet, longing for the moment when Siegfried would arrive at the apartment door to rescue him. He prayed it would be soon. As if to increase his torment, Bee switched to a dubbed American sitcom. It was a show he loathed, full of bitchy suit-wearing actresses who played at being lawyers. They reminded Gunther of the young professional women who came to the restaurant on Friday evenings dripping with money and their own self-importance. Bee laughed at every joke though he was sure she could not follow the quirky castrating humour.

When the credits played she turned down the volume. Gunther hoped she might at last lift her selfish feet off

28

him and let him return to the table. But all she did was arrange them in a new position, crossing them at the ankles so the weight on the back of his neck suddenly doubled and his face was pressed even deeper into the carpet. He heard her pick up the phone and after a few moments she began talking in a loud animated voice.

Bee forgot all about the man lying under her heels as she chatted to one relative after another in her own strange language. But Gunther was always aware of her cruel and demanding feet which weighed down more heavily with each passing minute. She even bounced them up and down on him during those moments when the conversation became especially lively, which happened often in the course of that long phone call. Gunther grew weary and began to doubt that Siegfried would ever come to his aid. Demoralised by the constant pressure of the feet on his neck, he imagined he would spend the rest of his days crushed beneath this overbearing virago whose strident voice filled the room.

Gunther must have passed out because he suddenly felt Bee rudely rocking his head with her foot. 'Time for bed,' she announced. And she switched off the TV and stood up. Gunther raised himself onto his knees and followed her through to the bedroom, grimacing every inch of the way.

Bee was waiting impatiently by the hook when he came through the door. He felt his muscles wither when he saw her. Surely even she would not be so callous as to make him spend another night hanging from the wall? He pleaded with her, almost breaking down in tears, but to no avail. The indomitable woman came over and grabbed him by the elbow. She raised him onto his feet and steered him towards the wall.

'You won't get away with this,' he protested as she lifted his stocking-tied wrists up over the hook. 'There are laws in this country.' He pulled against his nylon bonds and made impotent threats about the punishment she would receive unless she released him at once.

Bee shook her head. 'You so noisy,' she said and picked up the socks and panties from the chair. She grinned smugly as she brought them towards his terrified face.

Once she had fitted the gag and mask, she left him to sob to himself while she put away the jewellery she had bought that day and prepared to undress for the night. But just as she started to unfasten her skirt the bell to the apartment rang. Gunther's heart leapt for joy. It was the most uplifting sound he could ever remember hearing, like the bugle call of approaching cavalry. Siegfried was young and strong. He would teach this girl-bully a lesson in respect. The bell rang a second time and was followed by loud knocking.

Bee looked puzzled, though not at all perturbed. She went out into the hall, closing the bedroom door behind her. A moment later Gunther heard the click of the latch and then a deep male voice, unmistakeably that of Siegfried, demanding to speak to him. He waited, scarcely breathing, the sense of relief almost too much to bear. Siegfried's voice grew louder and Gunther was sure he must be standing directly outside the bedroom door. He even fancied his brave neighbour had taken hold of the door handle and begun to turn it. Energised by the thought of release, he rose up onto his tiptoes. Any second now, he told himself, and this nightmare will be over.

Suddenly there was silence. Gunther strained to hear, but not a whisper came from the hallway. The lull before the storm, he thought, and scenes from the fight about to break out played in his mind. He saw the two opponents: Bee delivering ineffectual blows to Siegfried's mighty chest; Siegfried seizing her in his invincible arms; Bee screaming and struggling helplessly against his superior male strength; Siegfried crushing

30

her into breathless submission. The last image caused his balls to throb pleasantly. Once Siegfried had defeated Bee she would lose her fiery spirit, he was certain, and the thought of having his vengeful way with her docile body thrilled him beyond words.

Gunther was so absorbed in his fantasy that he did not even notice the bedroom door open, and Siegfried and Bee were halfway across the room before he became aware of them. What a surprise he had when he opened his eyes. Bee was leading Siegfried by the hand and he was following her somewhat reluctantly. Gunther stared with dumb incomprehension. Siegfried did appear shocked, but there was nothing in his expression to suggest the outrage that the sight of a fellow male bound and gagged in such a perverse fashion should have provoked. It was as if he had been prepared for the dreadful spectacle. Gunther tugged at his bonds and moaned beneath his mask.

Siegfried smiled at him weakly, his face conveying the same disappointment he had shown the previous afternoon upon catching Gunther with the shoes and handbag. He took a quick glance down at Gunther's cock, which stood erect and dribbling, and nodded solemnly.

'All right,' he said, turning to Bee, 'I believe you.'

Bee smiled brightly and clutched his arms like an excited schoolgirl. 'Now you do fuck with me?'

Siegfried blushed at the boldness of the request. Gunther was standing – or rather, half-hanging – right beside them, staring at him through the leg holes of the panties with round unblinking eyes. He felt doubtful that Gunther could possibly gain any pleasure from what Bee had proposed. But Bee was insistent and began to caress Siegfried's sturdy thigh.

'Give me dick,' she pleaded. 'I need big cock inside me.'

Siegfried's jaw trembled. The quaint way she spoke aroused him almost as much as the fingers massaging his crotch. Her lips looked sweet and innocent and he wondered where she could have learned such filthy German words if not from Gunther.

'My pussy so hot for you.'

'Well, I suppose –'

'Oh, you make him so happy!'

Gunther watched in despair as Bee led Siegfried into the middle of the room and pressed her mouth hungrily against his. She ran her hands over his muscular frame and in no time she had unbuttoned and removed his shirt. She planted noisy kisses all over his bare torso, starting at his chest and working downwards until she was resting on her knees before him. Eagerly, she set to work unfastening his belt and flies.

Siegfried shot a guilty glance at Gunther, who was tugging frantically, if uselessly, at the hook which held him in his place. The younger man put up a token resistance, pushing away Bee's busy hands half-heartedly. But as she dragged down his pants and briefs, freeing his burgeoning erection, a change swept through him and he no longer took any heed of Gunther. His heavy cock raised itself into a stiff salute and Siegfried became the hot-blooded male animal that he was.

Bee rose and stripped off her clothes without cere-mony, at last revealing in all of its naked glory the body that Gunther had seen only in patches and in shadow. Even in his humiliating bondage he could not help being aroused by the glorious sight before him. She was as perfect as any statue or painting of a goddess: a golden Artemis with a flowing mane of dark hair and high round breasts capped with ripe, thrusting nipples. The muscles in her buttocks flexed as she pressed herself between Siegfried's arms and rolled her hips against his broad thighs and bloated cock.

Gunther felt sick to the very core of his being, yet his eyes remained riveted to the maddening spectacle. Bee dropped to her knees again, wrapped her full red lips around Siegfried's enviable erection, and began to suck with a passion. Gunther felt annihilated as he watched. That same mouth which had spat at him so contemptuously, almost from the moment she had arrived, now attended worshipfully to another man's cock, giving the owner unimaginable pleasure. Somehow she managed to swallow the whole formidable length and slurped it in and out of her throat, wringing wild grunts and exclamations from the owner. Siegfried's eyes rolled to white and he pulled out his spoilt cock, which glistened and dripped with saliva, and begged for a respite.

Bee climbed onto the bed, crouched on her elbows and knees and smiled invitingly over her shoulder. With the attention of the two men fixed upon her, she wiggled her ass in a vulgar circular motion, waving a dark fur-lined channel and wet pink slit at them. The blood drained from Gunther's cheeks, leaving them white, and rushed down to his cock, pointing it like a quivering purple spear at the delectable target. He strained frantically at the hook until the taut nylon was cutting through his flesh. His laboured breathing behind the smothering panties could be heard across the room.

Siegfried too was reduced to a brute by the crude display. He stepped briskly up to the bed, seized Bee by the hips and uttering only a throaty growl plunged his cock deep inside the proffered orifice. Within moments he was thrusting himself between her buttocks in such a fury of lust that his pale thighs became a blur.

Gunther witnessed every detail of the crushing act of betrayal that took place on the bed where he had hoped to consummate his marriage. He tried to force his eyes closed but Bee kept him watching in envious wonder as she threw back her head, flailing her dark hair behind her, and spread her knees ever wider on the mattress, arching her buttocks wantonly to meet the thrusts of the frenzied beast pounding at her rear.

Siegfried strove valiantly to satisfy his wild and exotic partner. Never had a woman responded to his cock with

33

such shameless abandon and the cries that came from her throat spoke to the most primitive part of his manhood. He roared in response, squeezed her juddering ass cheeks between his clawing fingers and drove himself with ever-greater vigour. Outrageous thoughts raced through his mind as he stared down at the glossy sex that gripped his pumping cock and the dark star of her asshole which promised unspeakable delights. He wanted to go on forever: this room, this woman, this enthralling cunt, was all that now mattered to him. But Bee was too much even for a man with his stamina and all too soon his balls were ready to surrender. He yelled out in joy and anguish and extracted his cock just as a mighty spasm tore through his body. The muscles in his legs went rigid as his balls erupted, hurling thick wads of foamy seed onto Gunther's duvet.

Once he had recovered, Siegfried was overcome with shame at what he had done. He stood blinking apprehensively at Bee and dared not look around at Gunther, whose snorting was audible in the tense silence. Bee turned away from him and stretched her body restlessly on the bed. Siegfried opened his mouth to speak to her but, noticing a faint scowl on her face, thought better of it. He quickly retrieved his shirt and pants and, covering his dwindling manhood, crept out of the room.

Bee rolled onto her side and twisted a lock of her dark hair between her fingers, examining it distractedly. Her skin glowed and her still-hard nipples quivered on her heaving breasts. She stretched a leg into the air and flexed the muscles like an athlete warming up, treating Gunther to a lingering view of her sex, which remained swollen and red within its nest of ebony hair.

Suddenly she glanced across at him like a tigress whose eyes had caught sight of her prey. She sprang off the bed and swayed over to him with a hungry and determined look on her face. Gunther shook his head in dread as her naked body approached – the swinging breasts and the rolling hips that he both desired and feared. She ripped away his mask and gag and he started to scream for help, but she silenced him with a hand over his mouth. He fought with every muscle as she jerked his wrists from the hook and wrestled him down to the floor, but she seemed ten times stronger now than before and effortlessly beat him into submission. Once more he found himself lying on the carpet with his head between her feet and staring up at her ass – only this time no garments concealed the arrogant mounds of her tanned buttocks.

'Do like pig,' was all she said as she spread wide her cheeks and lowered them over his face.

For Gunther, nothing existed beyond the smothering confines of her hot, insatiable sex. She rode him pitilessly, using his nose and mouth and chin as a substitute for the cock that had let her down. For a time, Gunther did grunt and snort into her sex just like a furrowing swine. But soon her pleasure-seeking ass cut off all the air to his lungs and the frightful animal noises ceased. Gunther slipped into black unconsciousness as Bee rode on his face towards a moaning climax.

The following morning Bee stood at the mirror putting in her sparkling earrings. Gunther hung behind her on the wall in his accustomed position, motionless and silent, as if he were a figure made from wax – a hideous effigy of a bowed and broken man.

A car horn sounded from the street below and Bee took a final look at her reflection before picking up the house keys. 'Good bye,' she said to him like any sweet young fiancée leaving for the day, and she even blew him a kiss with her freshly glossed lips.

Gunther, of course, could do no more than groan beneath his stale-smelling mask. With the eyes of a dead man he watched her carry the suitcases out of the room and listened to the clatter of her high heels in the hall.

The door to his apartment opened, closed, and there was silence.

Bee disembarked from the plane at the only airport on her native island. Her family were there to welcome her, all wearing their bright costumes and waving excitedly. Her sisters pawed at the jewellery she had brought back and tore open the gifts she bestowed. Bee gave her youngest sister the honour of carrying her new designer handbag. As they rolled home along the coastal road in the old family jeep, this inquisitive young girl, who had been rooting in the handbag throughout the journey, suddenly began to jingle what for her was a most exciting toy. Bee glanced over and, recognising Gunther's house keys, a shadow fell across her face. She had forgotten to post them through Siegfried's door as she was leaving the apartment block. But the natural brightness soon returned to her golden skin. The image of poor Gunther, still bound and gagged and hanging from his hook, dissolved against the sunny background of that tropical afternoon. And his muted groans for help? They were drowned out by the joyful voices in the car. 'Keep them,' she said to her little sister and bent over to kiss her soft cheek. 'They will bring you good luck.'

2

Teen Tease

People always tell me I remind them of Christina Applegate. They mean when she played Al Bundy's airhead daughter, Kelly. I take it as a compliment ... well, kind of. But I only pretend to be a bimbo. Hey, and my butt is like way cuter than Christina's! As for *my* daddy – or stepdaddy, I should really say – he's a big shot at City Hall with some scary Italian friends, not some loser who works in a women's shoe store. When Stepdaddy says jump, you say how high ... Hmmm, unless you happen to be his little princess!

He's old – at least fifty – and gross looking. He wears the thickest glasses I ever saw and he's got more hair growing out of his ears than on his head. He's really fat too and in summer he breaks into a sweat just walking from the front porch to his car. But, hey, I can deal with a butt-ugly stepfather with a belly like a walrus, just so long as he keeps his greasy hands off of me ... OK, maybe I do let him touch my feet sometimes. But nowhere else. Ewww! Never!

I can't stop him from looking at me though – and he does, *all the time*, even when Mommy's around. She gets really pissed. 'Stop looking at her!' she tells him twenty times a day. 'You're always looking at my daughter.' But he can't keep his eyes off my teenage goodies. They get into fights about me whenever I'm home from school. I can hear them yelling at each other in their bedroom at night. Usually Mommy ends up smashing a vase against the wall. All because of me. That's sooo cool!

But who is she to get all pissy and uptight? She knew what kind of man Stepdaddy was before she married him. He first saw her in a Vegas club when she was up on stage shaking her butt in a teensy silver G-string . . . Mommy, hellooo! Do you think Stepdaddy was attracted by your personality?

She sent me away to boarding school right after they were married – a Catholic one with nuns and priests so I wouldn't turn out a hoochie like her. But my education didn't go quite the way she'd planned. It was her own fault. She should have visited Magdalene College herself instead of jetting off to Europe to spend Stepdaddy's money. If she'd seen the uniforms the senior girls were wearing, she'd have driven me straight back home. Their little plaid skirts were as short as the ones she put on for her stage routine. And they all wore heels at last three inches high. But that's all in the past. I turned eighteen last year and I can do whatever I like now. If I decide to tease Stepdaddy, nobody's going to stop me – not Mommy, not my teachers and especially not Father John.

Father John is the main point of this story. He's the only guy I've ever been really really crazy about. I've got a boyfriend – two actually – and they're both keepers, but Father John . . . well, let's just say I want to have his babies. He started taking our Divinity class after our other teacher, Father Anthony, was sent away to a monastery for playing with his pecker under the desk. He's a total Jesus freak and talks like he ate the Bible for breakfast. But he's sooo handsome! I mean drop-dead George-Clooney gorgeous! When he speaks I get butterflies in my tummy, even if he's just reading out a verse by some boring old apostle.

38

I've never met a man like Father John before. He must be aiming to be a saint or something. He has a class of horny eighteen-year-old girls and every one of us is wet between the legs for him. But what does this hot guy do? Stands at the board and talks about sin and forgiveness. Go figure. Like we could care less! He never even lowers his eyes. Never. And there we are, me, Jessie, Christina, Charity and Maria, all of us sitting in the front row with our knees apart, showing off our white panties beneath our tiny skirts. Father Anthony used to get so steamed up when we flashed at him he'd leave the room in a sweat. But Father John goes right on with the lesson, looking into our faces and not once, *not even once*, sneaking a peep below our desks, where our gleaming white crotches are screaming for his attention.

After he'd been our teacher for about a month, he asked me to stay behind at the end of class. The other girls were sooo jealous. I loosened my tie, popped open another button on my blouse and sat on the edge of his desk with my legs crossed, the pleats of my skirt barely covering my panties.

'Shelly,' he said in his serious but totally sexy voice, 'your mother is a fallen women but you can still be saved.'

'Oh, Father John,' I replied, 'are you volunteering to save me?' His dreamy blue eyes were gazing into mine and I gave him one of my cutest smiles. God, you're sooo hot, I kept thinking. Just put your big hand on my knee and slide it up under my skirt. I'm not usually such an easy slut, but I will be for you.

'Shelly, I know there is good inside you. Open your heart to the Lord and you will receive his love.'

'Just my heart?' I pulled a sulky face.

'Your thoughts are impure, my child. Impure thoughts lead to sin and sin leads to damnation.'

'Can you really read my thoughts, Father John?' I wanted him to pounce on me. I imagined him ripping

39

open my blouse and squeezing my titties with his strong hands. I could feel my nipples pushing against my bra. 'So what am I thinking now?'

Without taking his eyes from mine, he got up from his chair. 'Shelly, I will not let you fall into sin.' Then he walked out of the classroom leaving me all hot and bothered.

A few weeks later I found out that he'd started calling on Stepdaddy. It seems like he just walked into the house and said, 'Sir, your wife is a whore. But I can save your daughter.' And would you believe it, Stepdaddy agreed! I figure it's because he's getting scared about what's going to happen to him after he dies. He's got a real murky past and wants to get on the right side of God before it's too late. Mommy is totally freaked out over Father John. She throws a fit whenever he calls around. But what can she do? He's got Stepdaddy all worked up about the fiery pit and he comes and goes as he pleases.

Stepdaddy stopped loving Mommy years ago and they've both had affairs. But after I turned eighteen, I became his number one, his little princess. I think I remind him of how Mommy used to look when she was a Vegas showgirl. I've got the same long legs, awesome butt, super-flat tummy – and my boobs are totally natural! This summer he couldn't take his eyes off me. It was sooo much fun to tease him.

I came back home from school still wearing my uniform because I knew he had a thing for them. He'd quizzed me on the subject before I went away at the start of the semester.

'Shelly, your school skirt is a respectable length, isn't it?'

'What do you mean, Daddy?'

'I've seen some girls wearing them very short. You don't expose your legs above the knee, do you?'

'But Daddy, it's the fashion now.' We were on the deck eating breakfast. It was a cool morning, but the talk of schoolgirls and their uniforms was making him sweat. He wiped his flabby face on a table napkin.

'And do you wear those little white ankle socks too?'

'Yes, Daddy. The ones with the lace ruffle around the top. They're so cute.' I was trying hard not to laugh at the goofy expression he made as he pictured my toes wiggling inside the tight white cotton. 'Gee, I must have a whole drawer full of them.'

'What type of shoes do you wear?'

'Black Mary Janes, of course. They're part of the uniform.'

'And I suppose your Mary Janes are the new style with high heels?'

'The heels are not *that* high, Daddy. Mine are only three inches or so.'

He coughed as he tried to swallow his coffee and it dribbled from the corners of his mouth. He cleaned his lips on his napkin and apologised.

'Be careful, Daddy, or you'll make yourself choke again.' I calmly sipped my papaya juice and looked out across the garden.

'I hope you fasten up your blouse decently,' he said when he'd recovered.

I gave him one of my baby-cute looks. 'But, Daddy, it gets so hot and stuffy inside the classroom with all those excited girls. I'm pink and sweaty even before the lesson starts. If I didn't open up my blouse and fan myself I'd probably pass out.'

The image of me as a trashy blonde schoolgirl was more than he could handle. Excusing himself, he pulled his body up from the chair and waddled into the house to look for his blood pressure pills.

So anyways, this summer I arrived home from school dressed like one of those schoolgirl sluts he fantasises about. I had my hair in pigtails and my pleated skirt was

41

so short that the chauffeur kept stumbling and dropping my bags as he followed me from the car to the porch. Mommy scowled at me, but I forgave her. Stepdaddy was standing beside her and grinning like a drunken hillbilly. I clipped over to him on my four-inch Mary Janes and puckered my shiny red lips close to his cheek. But I didn't kiss him. Ewww! No way! I just made a kissing sound and let him smell my Tommy Girl perfume.

All through dinner he kept leaning across in his chair to get a look at my legs. It was so funny. Mommy was getting really bugged.

'Shelly darling, school's over,' she said bitchily. 'Why don't you change out of your . . . uniform?'

Stepdaddy snapped at her. 'Leave her alone. She's old enough to dress however she chooses.' As a reward for him I parted my knees a few inches. And don't you just know, he 'accidentally' dropped his fork on the floor. The maid stepped over to pick it up but he waved her away.

'I can get it, I can get it,' he said, half-rising and pushing back his chair.

Holding onto the table corner, he leaned down and pretended to reach for the fork with his chubby fingers. But all the while his head was twisted around so he could see my legs. Awww, too slow, Daddy. No panties for you. All he got for his trouble was the sight of my knees snapping shut. He groaned in disappointment and then banged his head as he tried to pull himself up.

Mommy threw down her knife and fork. 'Pathetic!' she yelled. She stood up from the table and stormed out of the room. Stepdaddy finally managed to get himself back up on his chair. His glasses were crooked on his nose and his face was flushed red.

'Has Father John been upsetting Mommy again?' I asked in my most innocent voice.

'Father John is a good man. If only all men had his strength.'

'But you're strong, aren't you, Daddy?'

He sighed and straightened his glasses. His eyes looked small and worried behind the thick lenses. 'I am strong but not in the way Father John is strong ... unfortunately.'

I pretended not to understand and sucked some cranberry sauce off my finger.

'Are you still dating Brad Taylor?' he asked.

'Yes, Daddy.'

'Does he take good care of you?'

'Of course he does. You took him into your den and spoke to him, remember?'

'I know, but sometimes young women feel they have to –'

'Have to what, Daddy?' I was dying to laugh.

'They drink and –'

'And what?'

'Some of them dance in front of men.'

'But what's wrong with dancing?'

'... They don't just dance. They get their tops wet and lift up their skirts ... You've never done anything like that, have you, Shelly?'

I raised my cute little eyebrows. 'Daddy!'

He stared down at his plate, ashamed of his own thoughts. A minute later he excused himself and left the table.

I guess I should say something about Brad at this point. I think I called him my boyfriend, but really he's more of a bedbuddy. I know he wants us to get serious, but that's too bad. One man just isn't enough for me – unless his name happens to be Father John! Stepdaddy gets so jealous when I go out with Brad and I love to torment him. I dry my hair and paint my toenails in front of him. I even ask his advice on what I should wear: 'Do you like this skirt, Daddy? Does it go with my heels?' I say, posing in front of him. Or I turn around and show him my perfect butt: 'How do my shorts look from the back, Daddy? Do you think they're a little too tight?' When I get into Brad's Lexus wearing my sexy little outfit, he watches from the front porch with a broken heart and a stiff pecker. In your dreams, old man!

The last time was the most fun of all and you would never believe how the night ended. I spent most of the afternoon getting myself ready. First I had the maid set up a chaise longue at the bottom of the garden so that I could lie in the sun and get a glow to my skin. I wore the cutest bikini bathing suit. It was red with white polka dots and, if I'm honest, the top was a size too small.

Stepdaddy came out after less than ten minutes. That was a record! He puffed and panted his way across the lawn, wiping his sweaty face on his shirt sleeve and pretending to be interested in the plants and things.

'Beautiful day, isn't it, Shelly?' he said when he got close to me. I was lying on my front reading *Vogue*. My legs were bent at the knee and my little tootsies were rubbing against each other. I looked up at him over the rim of my sunglasses and smiled. His eyes were crawling all over me.

'That's a very pretty bathing suit you're wearing.'

'Thank you, Daddy.'

'It reminds me of the fashion when I was a young man.'

To tease him, I said: 'Brad brought it back from Florida for me.'

He frowned. He was already imagining what my handsome young man would be doing to me later that evening. I picked up my lemonade and sipped it through the curly straw. He watched my lips the whole time.

'You tan very well for a blonde.'

'Do you think so?' I rolled onto my side, revealing my perky titties squeezed into the tight bikini top. His eyes travelled the whole length of me, from my smiling face down to my flexing toes. I ran a fingertip along the inside of the bikini cup. 'The problem is,' I said, glancing down at my precious titties, 'I always get tan lines and tan lines suck.' I had him riveted to my teasing finger. His eyes urged me to push back the cup another inch. Not so fast, old man! You don't get to see boobs like these so easily.

'But tan lines are fashionable now. I've ...' He stopped suddenly, realising he had already said too much. Oh, Daddy, were you about to tell me about those little sluts you watch dancing in front of their webcams showing off their hard teenage bodies?

'Well, I don't care about other girls. I think tan lines are trashy.'

He looked at his watch. Mommy wasn't due back from shopping for a few more hours.

'If you really don't want tan lines, you could ...' It was so funny watching him struggle to get the words out. 'Shelly, you could take off your bathing suit. This is your own garden.'

I formed an O shape with my mouth to show him how shocked I was by his suggestion. 'But, Daddy, somebody might see me.'

'I'll tell the maid to pull down all the blinds and I won't let anybody into the garden until you're done.'

'You'd do all that for me?'

'Of course, you're my princess.'

'Thank you, Daddy.'

He plodded back across the lawn and went into the house. A few minutes later the blinds came down over each of the windows. I laughed to myself. He really thinks I'm the ditzy blonde I pretend to be. After a little while the blinds behind his bedroom window began to shake. That was even quicker than I'd expected. The old man must have been panting like a dog from having climbed up the stairs so fast. A good way to make you lose some weight, hey, Daddy!

I kept on my bikini bottoms, obviously, but I unfastened my top. Making sure my titties stayed hidden from his peeping eyes, I lay down on my front. All poor Stepdaddy got was a view of my lovely bare back as I sipped lemonade and read my magazine.

Before long he came out of the house again. His shirt was hanging loose and one of his shoes fell off because he was in such a hurry. I sat up on the chaise and held the bikini top over my titties as he approached.

'What's wrong, Daddy? Has something happened?'

'I was worried about you.' He tried to catch his breath as he spoke. 'The sun is very strong. You might burn.'

'Oh, Daddy, I'm fine. But you look ... What's that you're carrying?'

He held out a tube of sunscreen. 'Perhaps you should put some on?'

'You ran all the way out here to bring me sunscreen? That's sooo sweet.' I reached for the tube with one hand and the bikini top slipped, almost revealing my pointy pink nipples. His eyes popped forward in their sockets. It was lucky for him his shirt was hanging over the front of his trousers because I know his pecker had jumped to attention. And just think, he needs Viagra to get it up for Mommy!

'If you want, Shelly, I could rub some on your back.'

'Would you? You're so kind to me.'

'It's no trouble at all.' His fingers were already twitching. He was just dying to get his paws on my young body. I made him stand and wait while I studied the instructions on the tube.

'But, Daddy, this one is no good for me.'

'Why not?' he whimpered.

'It doesn't use natural ingredients. I don't want nasty chemicals on my skin.' His mouth drooped like an unhappy clown. He had come so close to touching his stepdaughter's sexy ass and now the chance was slipping away.

46

'But Shelly, I'm sure it will be all right.'

I shook my head stubbornly, enjoying making him suffer. If his big-shot friends could have seen him then. Totally under my control.

I smiled brightly. 'Hey, I think Mommy's got some Body Shop sunscreen I could use . . . But gee, it's all the way up in the bedroom.'

He looked across at the house and gave a tired sigh. 'I'll get it for you, Shelly.'

'Oh would you, Daddy?' I passed him the tube and lay down on the chaise, wiggling my cute butt excitedly. 'You're so kind to me.' He could hardly tear his eyes off my body, but he had to go back for the sunscreen if he wanted the chance to touch me. He dragged himself away and trudged across the lawn. What a good little man!

I enjoyed the sun for a while longer and pictured him rooting around in Mommy's vanity cabinet, pulling out tubes of sunscreen and carefully reading the ingredients. But when he finally reappeared carrying three different tubes, he had an unpleasant surprise waiting for him. I was sitting up on the chaise with my bikini top back on. He came across the lawn, doing the nearest thing he could to a run, but by the time he reached me I'd slipped into my robe and was fastening the belt around my waist.

'I thought you wanted to get an all-over tan?' he wheezed.

'I did, Daddy, but there isn't time. I've still got to do my hair and my nails and I haven't even decided what I'm going to wear yet.' He watched me slip my feet into my beach sandals and stand up. He reminded me of a dog that's had a juicy bone snatched from his bowl.

'If the weather stays good, maybe I'll come out again tomorrow.'

I walked away, leaving him standing by the chaise holding his tubes of sunscreen and cursing himself for the chance he'd missed. I could feel his eyes following me all the way to the house. I had him just where I wanted him. He'd crawl around me for the rest of the day and do pretty much whatever I told him.

Sure enough, twenty minutes later he tapped on my bedroom door.

'Yes, Daddy?'

He twisted the handle but the door was locked.

'I'm about to take a bath, Daddy.' He knows what I'm like. I can soak in the bath for hours. He couldn't stand not being able to see me for so long.

'I've got something important to tell you, Shelly.'

'You have?'

He rattled the handle desperately. Awww, poor Daddy! Locked out again.

'You can have the new car you've been asking for.'

'Oooh, can I! The same as Paris Hilton's?'

'Yes . . . What model is it? You didn't say.'

'I don't know, Daddy. I just saw a picture of it in a magazine. Some kind of sports car, I guess.'

'Princess, there are many types of sports car.' I could hear a teensy bit of irritation in his voice. The locked door was getting to him. He hates it when he can't see me.

'I've got an idea,' I said excitedly.

'Yes, Shelly, tell me.' He so couldn't wait to get in my room he was scratching the door with his fingernails. 'Tell me your idea.'

'You could do a search for Paris's car on the internet while I'm taking my bath?'

As Stepdaddy crept away to complete the assignment I'd given him, I tied up my hair and climbed into the bath. I relaxed in the warm water and closed my eyes. As usual, I began to think about Father John. My thighs were parted and I gently teased myself with my fingers. I was missing him already. I almost wished I was back at school where I got to see him every day.

He used to run on campus each morning and his route took him past our dorm block. All of us got up early to watch him and I'm sure he knew. How can you not see a hundred girls standing at the windows in their night clothes? But he never looked up. He mostly wore sweat pants to run in, but in summer he put on shorts. What a butt that guy has! I want to dig my nails into it while he's lying between my legs and pounding me like the world is going to end. God, I could scream just thinking about his big cock pumping in and out of me.

And I do *know* his cock is big. OK, so I haven't actually seen it in the flesh, but me, Maria and the other front row girls are pretty good at judging what a man's carrying between his legs. It helps a lot if they're stiff and we've had so much fun giving the teachers woodies during lessons. Father Anthony was the easiest to get excited. All we had to do was slip off a shoe and flex a set of toes inside a frilly white ankle sock and, in less than ten seconds, he'd have a tent in the front of his slacks. We could keep him hypnotised for the entire lesson by dipping our feet in and out of our shiny black Mary Janes or letting them dangle from our toes by the strap. What a scene. A whole classroom of girls chatting on their cell phones and listening to their iPods, while their teacher is staring down at their feet and playing with himself under his desk.

Father John was a different story. No matter what we tried, we never got a rise in the front of his pants. But that didn't matter because we could see what he was carrying anyway, the whole meaty length of it tucked down the right side of his crotch. Father Salami, Maria named him. That's why I don't believe in God. If God really did exist, he'd never let that guy be a priest. No way!

For an old man, Stepdaddy has good computer skills. It's not surprising though, considering the amount of time he spends on the internet. He tells Mommy he's in his den catching up with work, but really he's checking out pictures and video clips of teenage girls. I know because I've seen his bookmarks and private folders.

He was waiting for me as I came down the stairs after my bath wrapped in my silky house robe.

'I found the car, Shelly.'

'Did you, Daddy? You're so clever.'

'There's still time to get to the dealer's if we leave right now.'

'But Daddy, I'm going out with Brad, remember?' I brushed past him and crossed the hall to the living room. Yes, Daddy, your stepdaughter will be doing the nasty all night long with her handsome young stockbroker. Brad's not hung like Father John, but he knows how to use what he's got and he'll do anything to please me. I usually have him start off by eating my freshly shaved cookie. He even presses his tongue into my butt hole sometimes.

I sat down on the couch and tucked my legs under me. My hair was still damp and I played with a strand between my fingers. Stepdaddy took the couch opposite, his fat ass spreading over two cushions.

'Where is Brad going to take you?'

'A nightclub probably.'

'You're only eighteen, Shelly.'

'I won't drink anything. I just like to dance.' His eyes lit up at the word 'dance'. He was imagining drunken coeds in Cancun flaunting their sexy bodies on stage for the chance to win a few hundred bucks. They never did spring break like that back when he was at college.

'Are you a good dancer?'

Still toying with the strand of hair, I shrugged my shoulders. 'Brad says I am.' If only he knew how I shook my ass out on the dance floor.

I soon got bored of talking to him and switched on the TV. While he sat and ogled me, I flicked between MTV and a rerun of 8 Simple Rules, which is a seriously funny show. Stepdaddy likes my booty best of all but, when it's covered over, he stares at my feet instead. So I made myself comfortable, lying on my back with my feet resting on the armrest. Now and then I wriggled my toes to keep him hooked, while I laughed out loud at Kaley Cuoco who can do sassy better than anybody. Stepdaddy really does have it bad for me. He pulled himself up from the couch and moved to another chair so he could be closer to my tootsies. He had a perfect view of my creamy wrinkled soles and was near enough to have reached out and touched them. But he wouldn't dare do that without permission. He just sat and stared at them for an hour like a good little doggie.

When Mommy came back from her 'shopping trip', she stood in the doorway and scowled at us both.

'Take your feet off the couch!' she yelled at me.

What a bitch! Her date must have let her down. I swung my feet off the armrest and stood up. It was time for me to decide what to wear for Brad anyways. Stepdaddy looked so disappointed, like a kid whose favourite game had been interrupted. I could hear them fighting as I climbed the stairs to my room. Mommy was screaming the same thing as always. 'Stop looking at her! You're always looking at my daughter.'

I don't blame Mommy for being jealous of me. Once upon a time she was Stepdaddy's princess, but now he has to take pills to get his pecker hard for her. She's still in her thirties and keeps herself in great shape. A whole bunch of guys have got the hots for her, including the chauffeur who she flirts with like crazy, crossing and uncrossing her legs on the back seat so he can hardly concentrate on the road. But Stepdaddy doesn't notice her $500 hairstyles or big fake boobs anymore. He's only got eyes for me.

Mommy needs a lot of sex – like at least once every day. She's the one who buys the pills and she forces

Stepdaddy to take them. She'd kill him inside a week if he was the only man she had and that's why he turns a blind eye to her affairs. I saw him outside their bedroom one night bent over the stair rail. He was the colour of a ripe plum and I thought he was having a heart attack. Mommy was standing in the doorway with her arms folded and a real sour expression on her face. Her hair was done up and she was wearing a gorgeous silver-and-black basque and high-heeled mules with feathers on the front. I didn't see Stepdaddy for the whole of the next day, but Mommy came down early and got the chauffeur to take her 'shopping'.

She showed me her true colours back in the spring when Stepdaddy hired two Canadian contractors to resurface the drive. Before they had even unpacked their tools she was standing at the window licking her lips. She told the maid to take some cold beers out to them. Then she thought up an excuse to get rid of me.

'Shelly,' she said, 'I've got some dresses I want you to take to the cleaner at the mall.'

'Awww, Mommy, can't the maid take them?'

'Silvia's got work to do in the house.' She opened her purse and gave me one of her precious credit cards. 'Why don't you buy yourself those shoes you keep pestering me for?'

'Can I get a new spring outfit too?'

'Yes, whatever, but hurry up!'

She paced around the room looking out the window while I finished my breakfast. She was trembling all over and kept stroking her hips.

I set off in my car but I didn't drive out to the mall. I parked at the end of the street and walked back. Awww, I'm sorry, Mommy, but the engine cut out. Hehehe! Well, I *have* been asking you for a new car for sooo long.

She hadn't wasted a moment. As I walked up the drive I saw the contractors' tools lying on the ground and their big work boots were standing in the front porch. The maid practically dropped dead when she saw me. I put my finger over my lips and smiled. Little Silvia knows all about Mommy's men friends and Mommy slips an extra something into her wages each week to keep her quiet.

Mommy was so hungry for her young studs she'd taken them straight up to her bedroom. She hadn't even bothered to close the door properly and I could hear her cries as I came up the stairs. I always knew she was a slut, but it was still a shock to actually see her fucking two strange men on the double bed she shares with Stepdaddy.

She was on all fours with her bare butt raised in the air and her classy lace panties were hanging from her ankle. One of the contractors was kneeling in front of her and squeezing her titties while she sucked him off. She had his whole length stuffed in her mouth and she was gagging as she tried to swallow his balls. The other contractor was behind her, holding her hips steady with his big hands and spearing her pussy with his cock. With each hard thrust his thighs slapped against her butt and made the flesh wobble. He spread her cheeks with his hands and stared down between them like he'd never seen a cookie before. It must have given him a real thrill to watch his cock going in and out of a rich old man's slutty wife. He treated her roughly and Mommy loved it. Her eyes were half closed and she moaned and slobbered like a porn star, keeping the other fat cock sucked halfway down her throat.

Watching Mummy being fucked got me totally horny and the dark-haired contractor who was pounding her from behind reminded me a little of Father John. I went into my bedroom, lay on the bed and started rubbing myself through my panties. I imagined Father John bursting into my dorm, all hot and sweaty from running, and taking me on the bed doggy style while I was still half asleep. I was already wet and I brought myself off just by pressing my thighs together and stroking my tingling clit. The pleasure was intense but as it flowed away I was pissed off that I'd had to use my own fingers.

Mommy's door was shut when I came out of my room. And the two contractors were back at work. They stared at me as I walked along the drive in my fresh panties and white skirt and I could feel them undressing me with their cheeky eyes. One of them even had the nerve to blow a kiss at me. No, guys, I don't think so! You're both kind of cute, but hard dicks are easy to find when you're young and beautiful and you two don't have anything else to offer me.

It's sooo cool choosing what to wear for a night out. You can turn every guy into your slave if you dress right. The secret is to put on something that'll make 'em drool, but at the same time don't come across like you're a hoochie straight from the projects who'll give it up for a five-dollar cocktail. I usually go for the spoilt brat look – if I decide to show off my legs in a mini, then it's got to be a chic and expensive little number. I'm saying to all the guys who look at me: I'm dressing like this because I can. I've got the money and I've got the body. The dorks and spoogers are way too intimidated to approach me. Hehe! Most of them are too chicken even to look me in the eye. They stare at my legs and feet while the hunky guys crowd around and try to impress me. High heels are essential for the brat look and I generally wear sandals to show off my freshly pedicured toes.

Just before the end of the semester Christina, Maria and I sneaked out of the dorms and went to a nightclub with our fake IDs. We looked so A-list guys sent champagne to our table the whole night long and we were asked to dance about a million times. It's so much fun to be a tease out on the dance floor. I shook my titties and brushed my butt against an army of excited dicks. But I wouldn't let anyone touch me – except my girlfriends of course! Christina and Maria are great teasers too and every guy around us had a lump in the front of his pants as we danced together, kissing and pretending to be lesbian lovers. It turned me on to see them stiff and ready for us, but it was real funny too. Once you've got a guy worked up like that you can do anything you like with him. Christina looked the hottest of us all that night in a backless dress which showed off her tanned skin right the way down to the sexy dimples just above her butt. She had a swarm of guys trailing after her wherever she went, even when she was only walking to the restroom. By the end of the night there was a silver-haired lawyer on his knees massaging her pretty feet, while a property dealer was leaning across the table showing her pictures of his yacht on his cell phone. We were treated like celebrities all night and got a luxury ride back to the dorm. But we gave nothing away . . . OK, Maria did make out with a hot Italian actor for about one minute, but he had totally sexy lips and she is kind of a slut.

Anyways, back to the main story. I made up my mind I would dress for Stepdaddy that evening. While I was out with Brad, I wanted him to be shut up in his den eating his heart out over me and thinking of all the fun he was missing. I decided to go for the Barbie doll look – his favourite. Old men just can't resist a teenage bimbo. And if you know how to pout your lips and flutter your eyelashes, you can twist them around your little finger. I tried on a few combinations in front of the mirror. I have so many outfits sometimes it's impossible to decide what to wear. In the end I chose a tight denim mini and a glittery red top which left my shoulders bare. I tied my hair in pigtails and put cherry-red gloss on my lips. Last of all, I selected my shoes: black spike-heeled sandals.

Stepdaddy is obsessed with thongs, so I made sure to wear my raunchy Brazilian G-string with the jewelled back which my other boyfriend bought me as a Valentine's gift. In Stepdaddy's day only strippers wore thongs and now he sees them everywhere he goes. The female staff at City Hall wear them to work and let them peep above their skirts as if they were competing for a show-your-thong award. Poor Daddy. No wonder he can't get thongs off his mind.

He took me and Mummy to a restaurant a few months back. When the pretty Chinese waitress leant over to clear a nearby table a leopard-print triangle rose above the waist of her neat black skirt. The sight made Stepdaddy cough up his wine. Mommy jabbed him with her elbow and snapped a bitchy remark loud enough for the waitress to hear, then she got up and went to the restroom in a huff. Stepdaddy was wobbling with excitement in his chair and couldn't resist talking to me about the waitress and her pretty underwear.

'Your mom's got a point, Shelly. Why does a girl need to wear a thing like that when she's waiting tables?'

'Oh, Daddy,' I said sweetly, 'it's the fashion now. Panty lines are sooo ugly.'

'But why show the whole world what you're wearing under your skirt? It gives men the wrong idea.'

I shrugged, but I was ready to crack up laughing. Well, Daddy, I thought, there's no need to ask what ideas our waitress gave *you* just now, is there? I could read it in your eyes. You wanted that Chinese cutie to lift up her skirt and sit on your face wearing her tiny leopard-print thong. You wanted to press your big pug nose deep inside her hot little crotch. Yes, I know all about your fantasies. I've seen the pervo pictures you've got hidden on your hard drive.

'It can be very distracting,' he said. 'And it's a safety hazard. There was a traffic accident last week because a truck driver was filming a group of college girls strolling along the sidewalk with their underwear on show.'

I shook my head. 'That guy must be a dork. Didn't he ever see panties before?'

Stepdaddy swallowed some water and dabbed his face with a napkin. He loosened his collar and glanced over at the waitress who was taking orders at another table. I wondered if he could detect the faint outline of her thong beneath the tight black skirt. I could, but I've got eyes for that kind of fashion detail.

'Even so,' he said, tearing away his eyes from the waitress's perky little ass, 'women do have a responsibility.' He coughed nervously. 'Shelly, you would never expose your underwear in public, would you?'

'Daddy!' I blushed and looked around me as if I was embarrassed someone might have overheard him. 'How can you ask me such a question in a restaurant?'

'I'm sorry,' he whispered, 'I didn't mean –'

'Anyways, if all the other girls are showing theirs, why shouldn't I?'

His eyes sparkled behind his glasses at the thought of me showing off my thong in public.

'Do you wear thongs often, Shelly?' He tried to pretend it was just an ordinary question, but his voice was trembling and he stared down at his plate while he asked it.

'I guess.'

He made a loud gulping sound. 'Are you wearing a thong tonight?' He slowly lifted up his eyes as he waited for my answer. They looked small and guilty and I almost felt sorry for him. But I couldn't resist teasing him. I puckered my lips and sucked some noodles from my chopsticks.

'Please, Shelly, tell me.'

I stared back at him, pretending to be just a little disgusted by his question. I wanted to make him feel low-down and dirty. But Mommy returned from the restroom and I had to stop the game.

Stepdaddy's face fell. He'd plucked up a lot of courage to ask that question and now he'd never find out what his sexy stepdaughter was wearing under her pink ruffle skirt. Mommy looked at us both suspiciously as she picked up her chopsticks. She knew something had been going on. She can always tell when Stepdaddy's got an itch in his pecker.

So, I came downstairs wearing my cute denim skirt and shoulderless red top. Mommy had locked herself in her bedroom and was playing her Tammy Wynette CDs. I felt kind of sorry for her but she had to realise that her reign was over. I was the queen of the house now. Stepdaddy must have been listening out for my footsteps because he opened the door of his den as I walked across the hall. He gawped at my body like a goofy teenager.

'Shelly, I'm on the dealer's website now. Come and see.'

I kept a serious face as I followed him in. He wanted my approval but I wasn't going to give it to him *that* easily. He sat down in his chair and I stood beside him, my titties just inches from his face. He could hardly keep his eyes on the monitor.

'I like the blue one,' he said. 'But Paris Hilton's car is silver-grey.'

'But, Daddy.' I sounded like the sulkiest little bitch you can imagine. 'This is her *old* car. She drives a different model now.'

He was hurt. He wanted to snap at me like he does all the time at Mommy and his staff. He turned his head and opened his mouth, but all he saw were my juicy young titties pushing out the spangly red top. He was helpless.

'OK,' he said with a sigh. 'Let's find the car she drives now.' He turned back to the computer and started searching for Paris's car. I waited with my hands on my hips, doing my best to look impatient, while he clicked away on the mouse. It was so funny watching him surfing the celebrity websites checking out the actresses and models in their sexy little outfits. He'd sell his soul to be young again and hang out with those shiny party girls.

'Oh my God!' I said suddenly and put my hand over my mouth.

He jumped. 'What's wrong, Shelly?'

I stared down at my feet in the high-heeled sandals. 'I forgot to put polish on my toenails.'

Stepdaddy looked down too and I know his eyes followed my feet as I quickly walked away.

'Where are you going?' he said in alarm.

'I've got to do my nails before Brad gets here.'

'But . . . but . . . what time is he coming?'

'In less than an hour.'

'Wait,' he said as I reached the door. 'You could polish your nails down here, couldn't you?'

'I guess . . .' I sounded reluctant and it had the effect I wanted. He was scared I wouldn't come back into the den. With a loud creak, he got up from his chair.

'I've just found a picture gallery. Come and have a look.'

'But Daddy, my nails!'

He wobbled towards me. 'You stay here. I'll get the polish for you.'

'Are you sure?'

He didn't answer. He had already left the den and was plodding across to the stairs.

I sat on the chair, crossed my legs and looked at the gallery of sports cars. I couldn't wait till I was driving my own. My girlfriends would be so jealous. For a moment, I wondered what colour nail polish Stepdaddy would bring down. He was so desperate to keep me in the den he'd forgotten to ask the obvious question. Oh well, Daddy, it's your own fault if you have to run back up to my room and get the colour I want.

When he returned after about ten minutes, he was cradling my entire collection of nail polish in his chubby hands.

'I forgot what colour you wanted,' he said breathlessly. Carefully he put the bottles down on the desk so I could choose. I picked up two or three and examined them in silence, before selecting a Maybelline Water Shine in cherry red to match my lips.

'Have you decided about your car?' he asked hopefully.

'Not yet. I guess I'll have to look again some other time.' I uncrossed my legs, ready to stand up.

'No, keep looking. There's still time.'

'But, Daddy, I've got to polish my nails.'

'I can do that for you.'

'Don't be silly!'

'I'm not being silly. I'll polish your nails while you choose the colour of your new car.'

I settled back in the chair. 'Are you sure?'

'Yes, princess.'

'And do you know how to paint toenails?'

'Of course.'

'I don't want you to make a mess of them.'

'You'll have the best-looking toenails in the whole state.'

Crossing one leg over the other, I swivelled around the chair so that I was half turned towards him. I held out the bottle of polish between my finger and thumb. He took it from me and slowly got down onto his knees, his bones creaking beneath his weight.

'You'll have to take my sandals off first,' I told him.

He put the bottle down on the floor and began to fumble with my dainty sandal buckle, while I sat on his chair glancing at the sports cars on the computer screen. He released the strap and gently pulled the sandal from my foot. His bald head was bowed and he seemed transfixed by the pink crisscross patterns the straps had left on my instep. I flexed my long toes right under his nose.

'You must be quick, Daddy.'

He opened the bottle and brought the tiny brush towards my big toe. Very carefully he started to paint the nail, bending his head over my outstretched foot like a jeweller working on a precious stone. I waited for him to finish the first nail and then held my foot up to inspect his work.

'Very good, Daddy.' I lowered my foot again for him to continue. He had done a super job and I was sure this wasn't the first time he'd painted a woman's toenails. I have a feeling he used to pamper Mommy's feet once upon a time.

When he'd finished, I recrossed my legs so that he could remove my other sandal. As I did so, he lifted his eyes and tried to peep up my skirt. What a pervert! He'd kneel in front of me all day if I let him, just for the chance to see my panties. Men get more and more desperate as they grow older. Father Anthony was over sixty and used to steal our stinky socks from the laundry room. How gross is that!

While Stepdaddy worked on my foot, I tried to decide which colour car I should have. They were all so gorgeous I couldn't make up my mind. The red one looked cool. It was exactly the same shade that Stepdaddy was painting my toenails. But I also liked the shiny sapphire blue because the colour matched my eyes and I always get complimented on them.

I glanced down to see how Stepdaddy was getting on, just as Mommy poked her head around the door. The expression on her face was priceless. She was facing the truth at last. Her husband was down on his knees attending to my toenails while I sat in his chair with my legs crossed like the queen of bitches. Our eyes met for a few seconds, then hers dropped and she went away. Stepdaddy didn't even see her because his face was bent over my foot.

When he was done, I stretched out my legs and lifted my heels off the carpet to check both sets of nails. He remained on his knees as if he needed my say-so before he could stand up.

'You did a good job, Daddy. You should paint my toes more often.'

He beamed up at me, his mouth hanging open.

When the polish was dry, I held out one foot at a time and told him to put the sandal back on. His hands were trembling with excitement and felt clammy against my skin. If he'd touched me above the ankle, I'd have probably screamed. I rested a foot on his thigh while he fastened the buckle. His belly hung over the front of his pants and hid his crotch, but I knew one hundred per cent that he was stiff. I slid my foot further up his thigh, almost to his crotch and, sure enough, my toes found a hard lump under his pants. I pretended not to notice and kept my foot where it was, poking his nasty old cock with the tip. His fingers were shaking so much that he couldn't thread the strap through the buckle.

'Are you OK, Daddy?'

A deep grunt came from his throat and he nodded his head.

I nudged my sandal further into his crotch and trapped his cock beneath the sole like it was a big fat worm. His fingers went limp and his eyes closed as I pressed down on it. It reminded me of stepping on the gas pedal in my car and Stepdaddy's breathing rose and fell like an engine revving, depending on how hard my foot squeezed his cock. All the while I had my head turned to the computer screen, as if I had no idea what I was doing to him. He began to moan. I'd have made him cream in less than a minute if the maid hadn't come in.

'Miss Shelly,' she said, 'Brad Taylor has arrived.'

'Be quick, Daddy!'

He whimpered as I eased the pressure on his cock and, like a horny dog, he jerked his crotch against my teasing sandal sole.

'Come on, Daddy, hurry up! Brad's waiting for me.'

He tried to rub himself against each sandal as he buckled it up, but I wouldn't let him. As soon as he'd finished, I pulled away my foot and got up off the chair.

I went out into the hall where Brad was waiting holding a bouquet of red roses. I kissed him on the lips and gave the flowers to Silvia to put in a vase in my room. Stepdaddy appeared behind us, looking old and miserable, and gave Brad's hand a stiff shake. While they talked I bent down to readjust one of my sandal straps. Of course, the silver clasp of my thong 'accidentally' peeped above the waist of my low-rise denim skirt. Stepdaddy immediately began to stutter and lost track of what he was saying. Yes, Daddy, I'm wearing a teensy thong tonight because I like the effect it has on men like you. When I'm strolling through the mall they get so distracted they collide with each other. And once, when I walked though the parking lot with my tight black straps clinging to my hips, a cyclist crashed into the hedgerow.

Brad and I walked out to his car while Stepdaddy stood in the light of the porch and watched us. I waved goodbye to him from the passenger seat as we pulled away, enjoying the sad and hopeless look on his face. My other hand was on Brad's crotch squeezing his cock, which had already grown big and hard for me.

Brad was dying to get his hands on me that night. I let him stroke my thigh while he was driving, but I pushed him away if he tried to go under my skirt. I like it when he's worked up over me because he's always so sweet and attentive. In the restaurant he listened to everything I said and I rewarded him by stretching my leg under the table and gently prodding his rigid cock with the heel of my sandal. I wanted sex as much as he did but I was still going to make him beg for it. That's how you keep a man wrapped around your little finger.

When we got back to his apartment, I put on the TV and started to watch an old film. He brought me a drink and slid up next to me on the couch. He couldn't sit still because he wanted to fuck me so bad.

'You look gorgeous,' he said.

'Do I?' I spoke without taking my eyes off the TV screen.

'I want to make love to you.'

'Oh, Brad, I'm watching this film.'

'Please, Shelly, I'll be so good to you.'

I said nothing. Just sipped my drink and continued to stare at the TV.

'Please, Shelly. Don't make me beg.'

I could have made him kiss my hands and feet like the time before. But I was too horny to play that kind of game tonight. I let him take me through to the bedroom and sat down on the edge of his bed. I leant back on my palms and crossed my legs.

'I don't know if I'm in the mood,' I said.

He knelt down beside me and put his arm around my waist. With his other hand he gently stroked my leg. He looked up at me with puppy-dog eyes.

'I'll do it just the way you like it.'

While he begged me for sex, I couldn't help admiring my toes. The glossy red polish looked great on my nails. Stepdaddy hadn't done a bad job at all.

'All right,' I said finally. 'Take off your trousers.'

He jumped to his feet, unfastened his belt and almost fell over as he tugged off his pants. The head of his cock was so red and swollen I thought it would burst. I sooo wanted to feel it stuffed inside me, but I remained cool and in control.

'Would you like me to suck it for you?'

'Oh God, yes!' He shoved it in front of my face. Brad has a nice-sized cock. It's smooth and as straight as a ruler and he's really proud of it. I watched it bob up and down an inch from my painted lips.

'What do you say?'

'Please, Shelly. Please suck it for me.'

I stretched out my tongue and flicked it lightly across the bulging head. 'Say it like you mean it, you naughty boy.'

'Please, Shelly. Please put it in your mouth.'

'Put what in my mouth?'

'My cock. Please put my cock in your mouth.'

I parted my lips and closed them softly around the head, barely touching the hot bulging flesh. It drives him crazy when I hold him in my wet mouth without sucking. I looked up into his eyes, knowing what a sexy picture I made with a stiff cock stuffed between my shiny red lips.

'I love you, Shelly.'

I rewarded him with a long hard suck and rubbed my tongue underneath the head where all guys are so sensitive.

'Oh yes,' he moaned. 'Just like that.' His eyes were watering.

I swallowed him deeper into my mouth and tickled his balls with my fingers. I could have sucked him off in seconds, but I wanted to use that solid meaty cock for my own pleasure. I was going to ride my handsome stud like a cowgirl and watch myself in the big mirror on the wall.

'Get on the bed,' I said. 'Lie on your back.'

He did as I told him. He stretched out on the mattress and started to stroke his cock, keeping it stiff for me while I undressed. He watched me without blinking as I slowly unfastened my skirt, eased it over my hips and let it drop to the floor. Next I peeled off my clinging top and shook my fat boobs at him as they sprung free. Last of all I rolled the teeny-weeny thong down my legs, bending over and letting him feast his eyes on my ass.

I usually have him eat my pussy first, but that night I just couldn't wait to feel his cock inside of me. I climbed onto the bed, gave him a sloppy kiss on the lips, then turned around and straddled him, my ass pointing towards his face. Watching my reflection in the mirror, I lowered myself onto his big purple erection. I was so wet, I slid all the way down on top of it without any help from his hands.

Resting on my knees and pressing down on his thighs for support, I rolled my hips in a circle, squeezing and stretching his cock with my tight pussy. He'd never felt so thick and hard before and every nerve in my body was tingling. As I rode him, I glanced at the mirror at the end of the bed. The reflection showed only me and the bottom half of a male body trapped between my thighs. Brad's face was hidden behind my ass and it could have been any man's cock I was enjoying. I began to imagine it was Father John's cock inside me. Oh yes, his huge trouser salami! The thought made my pussy melt. I bounced up and down on Brad, slapping my butt cheeks against his crotch and moaning like I'd never moaned before. I felt mean and dirty and I loved it. I lifted up my hands and squeezed my titties together. I was wild with excitement and had to bite my bottom lip to stop myself shouting out Father John's name. Not even a saint could have resisted my pounding pussy. It was too much for Brad.

'Oh fuck! I'm going to come,' he shouted and grabbed my hips. His body arched and his toes curled as he erupted inside me. When he'd emptied his balls, he sunk down on the bed beneath my thighs like a worn-out runner.

'I'm sorry,' he said in a weak voice.

I did not reply. I climbed off him and looked down at his shrinking dick. Father John would never have done this to me.

* * *

It was way after midnight when I got back home but Stepdaddy was still up. He heard me come through the front door and called me into his den. He must have been staring at the computer the whole time I'd been with Brad because his eyes were red.

'I've found the perfect car for you, princess. Come and see.'

I was tired and really wanted to sleep but I decided to take a quick a look at the car before I went up to bed. I could smell drink as soon as I entered the den and on the desk next to the monitor was an almost empty bottle of liquor. Stepdaddy dropped down onto his chair and clumsily reached for the mouse.

'Wait till you see her,' he said, slurring his words. 'She's a beauty.' He clicked open a window and a webpage sprung up. But instead of my new car appearing, a noisy video clip started to play. It showed a group of girls, stripped down to panties and T-shirts, dancing on a stage surrounded by cheering, beer-waving men. Their oily wet bodies glistened in the bright lights and the white T-shirts, damp and half-transparent, clung to their titties and showed off their dark nipples. Stepdaddy jerked forward in his chair and shoved around the mouse, clicking it like crazy. But he couldn't get rid of the clip. Each time he closed the page it popped up again, and he got himself in such a fit the mouse slipped from his hand and fell to the floor. All the while, the girls on the screen continued to shake their sexy butts as if they were making fun of him.

'Daddy! What have you been looking at?'

He swivelled around in his chair. His face was burning and he wiped away the sweat with his sleeve.

'I don't know where it came from ... It was an accident ...'

While he stuttered his lame excuses, the girls went on dancing to the music and the wild cheers. One of them was teasing her thong down over her hips as hundreds of men chanted, '*Take it off! . . . Take it off!*'

'You're lying, Daddy.'

'But, Shelly –'

'Pervert!' The word had a strange effect on him. Instead of getting angry, he whinged like a child.

'What's wrong with a guy looking at attractive women once in a while?'

'They're just college girls!'

'But see how they show off their bodies? Everywhere I go teenage girls are showing off their bodies. At work. On the street. In the mall. Everywhere.'

'Nobody forces you to look at them.'

'It's not my fault, Shelly. I can't help myself.' He picked up his glass and swallowed what was left at the bottom. His gaze dropped to my legs and I could almost feel his eyes trying to creep up under my skirt. I pity him in a way. It must kill you to want something so bad and not be able to get it. But that's just nature making things even. Old men like Stepdaddy have all the money and we girls need something to bargain with.

'Shelly, will you dance for me like these girls?'

'Daddy!'

'I promise I won't touch you.'

I backed away from him, shaking my head and pressing my pretty lips together.

He reached out his hands to me like a street bum begging for a dollar.

'Please, Shelly, I'll give you anything you ask for.'

At that moment Mommy came in. She had just gotten out of bed and without her make-up on she looked kind of old and worn out.

'My daughter will not dance for an old porn hound!' she shrieked from across the room.

'Go back to bed, you whore! This is none of your business.'

'She's *my* daughter. This is *my* business. Shelly, go up to your room now!'

Stepdaddy dismissed her with a wave. 'Ignore her, Shelly. Dance for me and you can have whatever you ask for.' He tipped the rest of the liquor into his glass and swallowed it in a gulp. Mommy became hysterical as the cheering crowd grew louder: '*Show some bush . . . Show some bush!*'

'Turn that filthy computer off! Turn that filthy computer off!'

'Dance for me, Shelly!'

'Go to your room, Shelly! He's out of his crazy old mind.'

'I want her to dance for me.'

'You're a beast!'

'And you're a low-down whore!'

Their fighting brought the maid into the room. She stood in the doorway behind Mommy with her mouth wide open.

'Dance for me, Shelly, and I'll give you half of everything I own.'

I'd already decided to accept his offer. Mommy, you flashed your cookie on stage and got yourself a husband, so why shouldn't I?

'Do you promise to give me whatever I ask for, Daddy?'

'Up to half of all my possessions.'

Mommy couldn't take anymore. She ran from the room screaming and waving her hands, almost knocking over poor Silvia. 'My own daughter! My very own daughter! Dancing like a slut for a dirty old dog.' But a few seconds later she put her head around the door to watch.

Stepdaddy didn't even notice her. He only had eyes for me. And I'd never seen such a hungry look in them before. If he wasn't so fat I'm sure he'd have jumped up from his chair and ripped off my clothes.

'How shall I dance for you, Daddy?' It was a dumb question, but I wanted to tease him first and make him admit all the dirty thoughts that were sloshing around inside his head.

'Like those bitches on the screen.'

'Show you my butt, you mean?'

'Yes, Shelly, I want to see your butt. I want to see you shake it.'

I began to move my body to the beat of the music. 'Gasolina' it sounded like, or some other Latino dance number – just right for shaking your booty to.

'Like this, Daddy?' I said, swaying my hips.

He nodded his head, grinning like a giant toad. 'Let me see your ass.'

Rolling my hips, I turned around teasingly until he had the view he wanted. I shook my rump for him. There you go, old man, feast your eyes on that!

'I always knew you could dirty dance, Shelly.'

I flipped up the back of my skirt and flashed him the thong he'd been dying to get a peep at earlier.

'More! Show me more!' he shouted repeatedly as I wiggled my butt, his words blending with the chants of the men on the video clip. I gave him another flash of my thong and looked over my shoulder. I was shocked by what I saw. Stepdaddy had his fat legs apart and was massaging the crotch of his trousers with both hands. Mommy and the maid were staring at him as well, and now Mommy had her mouth wide open too. Stepdaddy rubbed and squeezed his imprisoned cock regardless. He really had lost his mind. His gaze was totally focused on my swaying ass.

'Come closer, Shelly,' he begged.

I could read his thoughts. He wanted me to grind my ass on his lap like a club dancer and feel my pert butt cheeks squeezing his cock. No way, Stepdaddy! You can't touch, remember? Just look and dream. I moved back a step but kept out of reach of his hands. I flipped up my skirt again and shook my bare ass right in front of his face.

I was actually kind of enjoying myself. I love dancing and I carried on as if I had no idea that Stepdaddy was rubbing his cock though his trousers and getting off to me. I tried a move that one of the Puerto Rican girls at school showed me. It's kind of cool. I pulled up the back of my skirt and, keeping my legs perfectly still, I made my butt cheeks quiver. My hips aren't as heavy as the Puerto Rican girl's, but I've practised in the mirror for hours and I know I look good. I can even make my cheeks jiggle one at a time. That drives Brad crazy when we go dancing.

'Oh yes, Shelly! More! More!'

If I'd looked at him I'd have probably fallen down laughing. I mean, how lame. Getting off to an ass. An ass you can't even touch. I spread apart my legs, so that I was halfway to doing the splits, and put my hands on my hips. I let the hem of my skirt drop down again but it barely covered my cheeks as I thrust them out and jerked them to the music. I learnt this awesome move from being a cheerleader. Every man in the auditorium used to point his camcorder at us when we did our routine. No wonder we had to wear shorts under our little red skirts! I forgot all about Stepdaddy as I worked my glutes and thought how sexy it would be to dance like this for Father John.

Suddenly Mommy screamed. I glanced around and saw that Stepdaddy had unfastened his pants and pulled out his cock. The big purple head was bobbing under the roll of his belly as he pumped it with his hand. He was panting so much I could feel his breath.

'Keep dancing, Shelly!'

I was more disgusted than afraid as he wanked himself to my body. His old cock looked like a poisonous mushroom and there was white juice leaking from the end onto his pants.

'Keep dancing!'

I gave him what he asked for. I stayed in my cheerleader position, thrusting back my ass and bouncing my cheeks up and down just above the carpet. He looked hilarious as he peered down at my thong-covered crotch, jerking himself senseless because of a strip of white cotton. His face was screwed up on one side, his glasses were hanging off his nose, and he was making the creepiest grunting noises I ever heard.

'Oh yes, Shelly! Yes, Shelly! Shake it! Shake that tight young ass, you cock-teasing bimbo slut!'

He didn't want the moment to end. He slowed down his rhythm and tried to fight back his orgasm, but the sight of my quivering booty pushed him over the edge. He let out a curse and a sticky white mess oozed over his fat fingers. He slumped back in his chair with a groan.

I stood up and straightened my skirt. Like how easy was that!

Stepdaddy watched me without speaking. The sexual excitement and alcohol had both gone to his head and put a retarded grin on his fat old face. His cock was poking from his trousers, still swollen and dribbling.

'You said I could have anything, Daddy?'

'Be my new queen, Shelly.'

I hid my disgust at the suggestion and calmly gave him my request. 'I want the cock of Father John.'

The smile instantly vanished from his face. I repeated my request.

'Daddy, I want the cock of Father John.'

'Ask me for anything but that, Shelly.' There was fear in his eyes.

Mommy walked over from the door. She was laughing heartlessly.

'You old fool!' she giggled. 'You heard what my daughter asked for. Now give it to her. You made a promise. The maid and I are both witnesses. She danced for you and you did your filthy business in front of us all. Now give her the cock of that miserable priest!' She pressed her lips hard against each of my cheeks. 'My daughter! My beautiful daughter!'

Standing side by side we both stared down at Stepdaddy. He had sunken into the chair and his dick had shrunk back inside his trousers. But the naughty girls on the computer screen next to him were still waving their sexy young assess and the crowd was screaming for bush.

'I want the cock of Father John,' I said again.

A year into married life, John Michael Abelard came home from work, even more tired and disheartened than usual. Sitting in an office at City Hall didn't suit him and to add to his woes he had just been informed in an anonymous email that his young wife was having an affair. He felt humiliated, disgraced. He of all men, married to a jezebel. He went into the lounge and poured himself a large bourbon. He swore he would drink only one glass and vowed to get up an hour early in the morning and go running. But he knew he was lying to himself. He had made the same promise every evening for the last six months.

'Home already, darling?'

It was his young wife. She was standing in the doorway, dressed-up and ready to go out. She was a stunning woman, he had to admit, and she did everything to draw attention to her spectacular body. He'd had impure dreams about her even when she was his student. But there was surely a limit to a man's conjugal duties? God decreed women should bear children for a good reason. Husbands needed some time out.

'How's my cock?' she asked.

He smiled weakly and his hand shook as he drained his glass. He hated it when she used that crude word and she used it all the time. She liked to remind him how close he had come to losing his cock before he would agree to marry her.

'Take it out for me,' she ordered, walking over to him. 'I've got ten minutes before I have to leave.'

3

The Land of Giant Supermodels

Jack Dolman was sitting on board a charter flight admiring the shapely legs of the fashion company rep as she strutted towards the front of the plane on her elegant high heels, when all at once everything started to spin . . .

The next thing he knew he was lying on his belly on a hard surface. He rolled over groggily onto his back and opened his eyes. High above him were small circles of bright light gathered in clusters. He squinted to bring them into focus and tried to get his bearings. Something felt wrong. He jerked up into a sitting position and wrapped his arms around his body protectively. He was naked – his clothes had disappeared. And he was not alone. Sprawled around him like battle causalities were other naked men. Some were beginning to stir and lift their heads. Through the dimness, he could recognise the faces of passengers from the plane.

Soon all the men were awake and talking in loud angry voices. They quickly reached a consensus that they had been drugged and most of them blamed the champagne they had been served shortly after take-off. But they could not decide who was responsible for imprisoning them or what the motive might be. Some were adamant they had been kidnapped for a ransom, others argued they had been taken as hostages by terrorists, while a few believed they were participants in a secret psychological experiment. The discussion degenerated into a bitter argument as those with opposing viewpoints strove to assert their position: insults were hurled, threats were made and two men came to blows and had to be dragged apart.

Jack retreated into a corner. He knew that survival depended on keeping a clear head and conserving energy. He began to analyse the events leading up to his blackout. He recalled arriving at the airport and being greeted by the fashion company rep. Instinctively he knew she was in some way responsible for what had happened to them. She was an exceptionally good-looking woman and he had been immediately attracted to her; yet right away he had sensed something cold, disdainful even, beneath her charming professional smile. True, she had not actually done anything to justify his suspicion: her presentation was flawless, slick in fact. But that was the very thing. He and the other men were prize-winners – selected by the fashion company from hundreds of thousands of hopeful male contestants to be photographed with some of the world's most beautiful models. Yet she had behaved towards them like a school mistress chaperoning a group of boys on a day trip, her manner subtly imperious, her tone faintly condescending. There were forty of them and when Jack had expressed doubts that they would all have the opportunity to pose with a model she had sneered at him.

'Don't worry your little head,' she had said. 'I guarantee we'll use every one of you in our new poster campaign. But, of course, you don't *have* to come.' And she had flashed him one of those plastic bitchy smiles that say: We both know you'll do exactly what I want because you can't resist me.

The room rose suddenly, as fast as an express elevator, then lurched sideways. Men cried out as they were shaken from their feet. Jack braced himself in a corner. The light through the portholes in the ceiling dimmed briefly and then grew very bright, sending down long golden shafts. It was not a room they were in, Jack now realised, but a container of some kind and they were being transported by a crane or lifting apparatus. One side of the chamber dipped for a moment and men were sent hurtling against a wall.

They dropped again, as rapidly as they had risen, and everything was still once more. Shouting and cursing, the men staggered to their feet. They thumped on the walls demanding to be released and one man dropped to his knees in the middle of the floor and started to pray out loud.

A flood of intense light forced them all to shield their eyes. Squinting upwards from beneath his palm, Jack saw with amazement that the entire ceiling had been ripped away. There had been no sound of tearing or wrenching prior to its removal – it had simply disappeared noiselessly, inexplicably, and he was gazing up at what looked like a bright white sky.

Nothing could have prepared Jack for what happened next. In the space where the ceiling had been a giant female face suddenly appeared, stretching across his whole field of vision. It was as if the face from a roadside hoarding advertising lipstick or mascara had come to life. Jack's gaze traversed the monstrous visage, taking in small sections at a time. The sparkling hazel eyes were as big as windows, the grinning red mouth large enough to swallow him whole. But the features were familiar, unmistakable: the gigantic face belonged to the rep.

'HELLO, BOYS,' she said. Her voice blasted down at them and they pressed back against the walls, covering their ears. A giant hand came into view. The fingers held a huge trough-like vessel, which they lowered into the middle of the cell. The hand descended to within a few feet of the cowering men who watched, frozen with terror. The fingers were as thick as logs and a long red nail curved from the end of each one as wide and as shiny as the bonnet of a sports car. A second hand appeared clutching a can of Coke bigger than an oil drum and above the heads of the men the giantess pulled open the tab with an explosive hiss. She poured a foaming torrent of liquid down into the vessel.

'DRINK UP,' she said, placing the empty can in the corner of the cell. 'I'LL BE BACK IN FIVE.'

None of the men moved or spoke. It was as if they had been participants in a mass hallucination and they continued to stare up out of their cell into the space where the giant-sized rep had been. Then, driven by thirst, a few of them moved towards the trough and dipped in their hands. They began to mutter among themselves. Some wanted to believe they had witnessed an optical illusion created by lasers and mirrors. The deafening voice which had knocked them off their feet, they said, was the product of amplifiers and speakers embedded in the walls. But they could not explain the gigantic Coke can standing in their midst.

Jack went to the trough and slaked his thirst but kept out of the debate. He knew he had nothing useful to contribute. Not even ten years in the US Special Forces had prepared him for a confrontation with a giantess. Yet there had to be an explanation, a simple, straight-forward and scientific explanation for what they were experiencing. Real women simply did not grow to thousands of times their former size. It was a physical impossibility. If the rest of her body had expanded in proportion to her fingers she would stand close to two hundred feet tall and weigh in at six million pounds – the equivalent of four hundred African bull elephants.

His calculations were interrupted when the giant woman returned and peered down into the cell. The men backed away from the trough and huddled against the wall again, trembling and shielding their naked bodies with their arms.

'I NEED THREE VOLUNTEERS,' she announced curtly.

None of the men dared move.

'WHAT HAPPENED TO THE MALE SPIRIT OF ADVENTURE?' she joked. 'OK, I'LL CHOOSE MY OWN VOLUNTEERS.' She lowered her index finger and used it to point, her long polished nail hovering an inch above each man's head as she made her selection. 'YOU WILL DO ... YOU ... AND YOU ...'

None of her volunteers stepped forward and the rep frowned menacingly. She pushed the trough aside and jabbed her fingernail against the floor with a thud. 'HERE, NOW!' she barked in a thunderous voice which made the walls of the cell vibrate. Two of the men sloped forward, their bodies quaking as they approached the massive hand. The third volunteer attempted to conceal himself in the press of bodies.

The giant woman reached for him. She moved so quickly that the men around him scarcely had time to drop to the floor as the snatching fingers passed over their heads. She seized her victim between thumb and index finger and lifted him screaming and kicking into the air.

Jack stared up at the awful scene, his stomach tight with fear. She was holding the man by the waist in front of her enormous face and glaring at him with dark and angry eyes. He continued to struggle, beating against her finger and thumb, but his efforts to free himself were futile. She could have popped his body like a grape had she felt like it.

'THE ARE TWO WAYS YOU CAN DO THINGS AROUND HERE,' she boomed at her tiny captive. 'MY WAY OR THE HARD WAY.' She glanced down at the other men quailing on the floor. 'AND THAT GOES FOR THE REST OF YOU PUNY LITTLE CREATURES.'

There was no doubt in Jack's mind that she enjoyed belittling and terrorising them. He felt the stirrings of despair as he imagined what it would be like to live the rest of his life under the tyranny of this big cruel woman.

Still squeezing the screaming man between her fingers, she lowered her other hand and commanded the other two volunteers to climb onto her palm. They obeyed at once and she lifted them out of the cell. A moment later the ceiling was replaced and Jack and the remaining men were plunged into dungeon gloom.

The situation seemed hopeless and the men broke down in tears or became hysterical. Jack observed them from his corner. There was a man he nicknamed the Fanatic who ranted that the giantess was a punishment visited upon them by God for their sins against womankind and that only prayer could save them. Another he christened Muscle Man: a 250-pound body builder who had gone through life relying on his physical strength and could not accept that somewhere outside was a woman who could crush him beneath her little finger without even chipping a nail. The big man shook his head in denial and swore that everything was an hallucination caused by a drug they had been fed on the flight. Two younger men tried to reason with him. Jack took them to be brothers, both military, he decided, judging from their buzz cuts and lean physiques.

'She's no giantess,' said a voice nearby. Jack turned his head and saw a man, perhaps forty years old, sitting a little further along the wall.

'She sure did a damn good impression of one.'

'She's no bigger than she was on the plane. We've been shrunk. That's what's happened.'

The idea had already occurred to Jack, but he said nothing. He wanted to get the measure of the man before he ventured his own opinion.

'How is that possible?' he asked. 'To shrink forty grown men?'

The older man shrugged. 'I don't know. I'm a scientist and I've seen nature manipulated and transformed in ways that would astonish you. But size change on this scale is a phenomenon that belongs to science fiction. It defies all known physical laws. Judging from the dimensions of her hand I'd say we are between two and three inches tall. But I can't explain how it happened.'

'Could it have been caused by a chemical in the champagne?'

'It's a possibility. But it's equally possible that we were shrunk by a mysterious gas filtered through the onboard air conditioning, or by a magical ray in the scans we passed through before boarding. Days, weeks or even longer may have passed between our being on that flight and waking up here in this prison. Our bodies could have been subjected to any number of processes during that time. That seems the most likely scenario to me.'

Jack felt he could talk to the scientist. 'For me, the most important question is not how we were shrunk but why.'

'Judging from the lady's behaviour so far, I doubt it's for our benefit.'

'That's for sure. She regards us as little more than bugs and ladies hate bugs. You know what they do to them.'

'She hasn't gone to all this trouble just to crush us under her fancy shoes.'

'I'm relieved to hear it,' said Jack. He smiled grimly.

The scientist gave him a gloomy look. 'There are worse things than being crushed.'

As the hours passed the captive men grew weary of arguing and each retreated into his own dark thoughts.

The heavy silence thickened the air and Jack felt himself succumbing to its demoralising influence. He stretched out on the hard floor and tried to sleep, but his instinct for survival kept him nervously alert.

For a second time, the ceiling was lifted away and light blazed down on the torpid men, rousing them in an instant. Shielding his eyes and once again overcome with awe, Jack watched the giant female hand descend from above. Dangling between forefinger and thumb like a chess piece was one of the volunteers. He was lowered to within a few feet of the floor and then casually dropped, landing with a soft thud. The hand abruptly withdrew, leaving the man in a naked heap in the middle of the cell. Cautiously, fearing the giantess might return at any moment, the other men gathered around him. For a long while he sobbed uncontrollably, but little by little he managed to describe what had happened to him. Jack listened closely to his every word.

They were inside a box, he told them, on top of a coffee table in a room of unimaginable dimensions. The rep had carried him and the other two men out of the room and onto a terrace. There was a pool on the terrace the size of a small lake and playing in the pool were more giant women. As soon they saw what the rep had in her hands, they scrambled to get out. The men were passed from one set of fingers to another and held up in front of huge inquisitive eyes.

A busty blonde giantess claimed the storyteller for her personal pet. She sat down in one of the chairs and gently stroked his quivering flesh with her big fingers. 'LOOK, MY PINKY IS NEARLY AS TALL AS YOU,' she said, measuring him against it. She giggled at the demeaning comparison. 'I BET MY TITTIES LOOK LIKE MOUNTAINS TO YOU, DON'T THEY?' She shook her breasts proudly, then popped one of the massive things out of the clinging bikini top.

It tumbled towards him, a monstrously large nipple jutting from the tip. 'GEE, MY NIPPLE IS BIGGER THAN YOUR HEAD.' She rubbed his face playfully against the fearsome protrusion, knocking him half senseless and laughing all the time. 'COME ON, TRY TO SUCK IT.' Dizzy and confused, he stretched apart his jaws and gnawed uselessly against the hard mound of rubbery red flesh. 'AWWW, TOO BIG FOR YOU, IS IT? WELL, THEY SAY MORE THAN A MOUTHFUL IS A WASTE.' She spoke down at him in a girlish sing-song voice that almost burst his eardrums. When she'd had enough of her game, she put him inside the cup of her bikini, leaving just his head peeping over the top. And there he had remained for the rest of the evening, crushed in the humid space between the tight Lycra and her warm breast.

The two other men had been less fortunate. The rep took special delight in tormenting the 'bug', as she called him, who had dared to disobey her earlier. For a finale, she made him hang from the base of her glass while she sipped her champagne. After a minute or so his fingers lost their strength and he plummeted, screaming, some eighty feet to the flagstones below. The other man had come to an even more inglorious end, though it was not the result of deliberate maliciousness. Aroused by the enormous female bodies, he had sprouted an erection which had made him the favourite of the giant women. They were so eager to play with his tiny stiff cock that they started to fight for possession of him, snatching him from one another's hands. The unlucky man had been torn in half.

The giantess did not return to replace the lid but night fell and it became dark inside the box. The men lay down and tried to sleep, all except Jack, who sat in a corner looking back and forth between the trough, the Coke can and the walls. He calculated. The can was at least twelve feet tall and using the trough as a base would add another two feet. A man standing on top could reach up and pull himself over the wall. It would be a long drop down on the other side with a risk of injury, but a few casualties would be acceptable. He estimated the coffee table would be the equivalent of forty feet or more above the ground, so jumping would be out of the question. But they might discover another means of descent once they were out of the box. He reflected long and hard and decided his plan was the best chance they had of survival.

The other captives were difficult to persuade. Many of them believed they should try to placate the giantess and were terrified of being caught by her during their escape. But Jack's reasoned arguments finally prevailed and they agreed to his plan.

The sun was already rising as the men hoisted one another up onto the Coke can and climbed over the wall. Before long more than thirty escapees stood on top of the coffee table.

Jack peered over the edge. They were even higher above the floor than he had anticipated and the only object on the table was the black plastic box which had been their prison. Anxiously, he walked around the table perimeter until he reached the furthest corner. A little distance away was a couch and lying on a cushion next to the armrest was a leather handbag, big enough to be a house.

Jack made up his mind in a moment. He took a long run-up, launched himself off the table and made a safe landing on the edge of the cushion. From the couch, he beckoned to the others to do the same. He knew some would not make it across, and the very first man to try jumped short and spun to the ground with a desolate cry. Jack did not even glance back. Sunlight was already pouring in through the windows. Time was running out.

He bounded across the cushion to the handbag, pulled himself up the strap and climbed through the partly open zip. It was dark inside and the air was saturated with a musky sweet feminine scent that burned his lungs and made his eyes sting. Blindly, he clambered over cold hard objects in search of something that could aid them getting down from the couch. He fell often, grazing and bruising his naked body. Everyday items of female adornment became deadly hazards to one so tiny: he smashed his head against lipstick cylinders, got his leg caught in a hair slide as big as a mantrap and almost impaled himself on the sword-sized teeth of a plastic comb.

He was beginning to despair when at last his luck changed. In the deepest recesses of the handbag he found what to him felt like a huge elasticated net, gathered into a dense heap. Clutching a handful, he started to pull. It required all his strength but the compact bundle slowly unfurled. Dragging the expanding length behind him, he climbed up towards the light. He poked out his head and called to the others for assistance.

A minute later, two dozen tiny men stood on the cushion, lined up like a tug-of-war team, stretching the sheer nylon stocking out of the handbag. A cheer went up when the reinforced toe sprang free of a snag and they all fell onto their backs, covered by the soft and fragrant mesh. A group of them helped Jack attach the toe to the handbag strap, then others heaved the heavier welt end over the cushion. Without delay, the men climbed down the dangling black stocking like a team of mini-commandoes.

But no sooner had the last man dropped from the stocking to the floor when the thud of heavy footfalls sounded from beyond the door at the other side of the vast room. The blood drained from every face. Discipline gave way to wild panic, comradeship to the selfish

85

instinct to survive. The men scattered in every direction like insects discovered under a stone. Their injured comrades were left lying where they had crashed to the floor from the table.

Jack hid himself behind one of the table legs and watched the giantess come into the room. She crossed towards him with enormous strides. The colossal size of her made him dizzy. She was too immense for his eyes to take in whole and all he saw were fragments of a vast vertical panorama of flesh and fabric as she approached.

'OK, YOU LITTLE CREEPS, I KNOW YOU'RE AROUND HERE SOMEWHERE.' A huge naked foot moved towards the broken and immobile men curled on the floor between the table and the couch. 'THAT WILL TEACH YOU,' she bellowed, prodding one of them with her big toe. He tried to squirm away from her, pathetically pulling himself forward with his one good arm. She laughed and held her bare sole a few inches above him, covering his naked body with an ominous shadow. 'SHALL I LET YOU SUFFER A LITTLE LONGER, WORM? OR DO YOU WANT ME TO PUT YOU OUT OF YOUR MISERY?'

Jack could see faces peering out from under the couch. They too were hypnotised by the dreadful sight. The giantess had lowered the tip of her big toe onto their comrade and she was slowly pressing him into the parquet floor. Her toes flexed with a lazy indifference as she squeezed the breath from his lungs. Jack watched the man's feeble attempts to drag himself free. He knew that any one of them could have been her victim, pinned like a worm beneath an invincible female foot. The thought made him burn with shame and rage.

Suddenly one of the men beneath the couch began to yell abuse at the giantess. His comrades threw themselves upon him and covered his mouth. But it was too late –the rep had been alerted to their presence.

'COME OUT FROM UNDER THERE,' she shouted down. 'YOU'VE GOT THREE SECONDS.' As she began to count, a few of the men crept out and stood trembling before her feet.

'I KNOW THERE ARE MORE OF YOU,' she snarled and suddenly pushed back the couch, exposing half a dozen startled men. They did not even try to run and seemed paralysed by the sight of the colossal figure looming over them. Crouching down, she plucked them up with her fingers as if they were her tiny pets and returned them to the box.

Jack saw his chance. While the giantess was preoccupied with the others, he ran from under the coffee table and sprinted across to a cabinet by the wall. When he reached it the giantess had already begun to search beneath the cushions on the couch.

'JUST WAIT TILL I FIND YOU,' she shouted. 'YOU'LL BE SORRY YOU EVER CRAWLED OUT OF YOUR BOX.'

Using furniture for cover, Jack made his way swiftly to the door where he was joined by three other men who, like him, had been bold enough to take their chances and flee. Together they left the room and the raging giantess who was now rolling back chairs and throwing cushions onto the floor. A hallway lay before them as broad as a highway and they ran along it in single file, keeping close to the wall. But Jack knew they were vulnerable. There was no place to hide. Were the giantess to follow she would see them at once. He made a quick assessment of their position and led them through a door that had been left partly open.

They entered a bedroom. At the far side, bathed in the diffuse light of half-open blinds, was a colossal bed. Jack decided that the safest place for them was in the dark space beneath it. Giving the signal to follow, he started across the room, wading through the deep-pile carpet which came up above his knees. Magazines, shoes and discarded clothes lay across their path, huge obstacles which they had to clamber over or laboriously trudge around.

Jack paused in sheer wonder before a black stiletto which lay on its side. It was longer than a bus and he could have climbed inside it, even crawled into the long pointed toe. He rubbed his hand over the shiny leather at the front. The creases left by the flexing toes were like ripples. He pressed the cool surface and felt it give a little when he applied his full strength. He walked towards the back of the shoe and put both palms flat against the inside sole. He leant forward and pushed from his legs. But try as he might the shoe would not budge. He stood up, aching from the exertion. Once again he was sickeningly conscious of his puniness in this house of giant objects and giant women. What chance did he have against a creature who could casually slip her foot into this enormous shoe which he, with his whole body's strength, could not even move?

At that moment a light came on in the room. The men scrambled for cover. Jack's first thought was to hide inside the shoe, but a gut feeling told him it was a bad idea and he ran, stumbling though the knee-deep carpet, towards a nearby hill of clothes. Two of the other men got there at the same time as him and together they burrowed into the pile of soft fabric. Deeper and deeper they dug until they squeezed through an opening into a cave-like chamber where light no longer reached them. They collapsed, panting with exhaustion. The air was thick with a pungent and unmistakably feminine odour.

They could hear and feel the giantess pacing about the room. Sometimes she stepped right over the heads of Jack and his comrades and they cringed at each heavy footfall. Jack began to wonder if it might have been safer inside the shoe after all.

Suddenly the shelter was torn away from around them and they were exposed to the light. The giantess screamed when she saw them and jumped back, protecting her scantily clad body with her hands. Then, realising what it was she had uncovered, she bent down, holding her long blonde hair away from her face and smiling.

'SO YOU LIKE MY DIRTY UNDERWEAR! YOU MEN ARE ALL THE SAME WHATEVER SIZE YOU ARE.' Carefully, she lifted up a lacy red bra, in one cup of which Jack and his comrades were huddled like baby birds in a nest. Holding them aloft, she laughed cheekily. 'JUST THE RIGHT SIZE FOR YOU, ISN'T IT?'

She hung them from the handle of a drawer while she quickly wriggled into a skirt and slipped on a T-shirt, then she carried them through to the kitchen. As they entered, Jack caught sight of another giantess. Her silky black hair flowed halfway down her back.

'LOOK WHAT I FOUND, SATSUKO,' cried the blonde giantess, holding out her bra and showing off the men as if they were her little pets. 'DON'T THEY LOOK SO CUTE IN THERE?'

Satsuko glanced over her shoulder and wrinkled her nose without much interest.

'BE A HONEY AND TAKE CARE OF THEM. I'M GOING TO LOOK FOR MORE.'

'PUT THEM ON TABLE,' said Satsuko and turned back to the stove.

The blonde lifted the men out of the bra cup one at a time and lined them up on the kitchen table like toy soldiers. She wagged her finger at them playfully. 'BE GOOD FOR SATSUKO,' she said and then left them in the charge of her sister giantess.

The men stood in the middle of the table and waited, too ashamed even to look at one another. Eventually the Japanese giantess came across from the stove bearing a bowl and a cup. Barely glancing at them, she sat down, picked up her chopsticks and began to eat. Yards of noodles disappeared through her pursed lips with each noisy slurp.

'YOU HUNGRY?' she asked abruptly. She moved the flagpole-sized chopsticks towards the group of men and dangled a noodle above their heads. 'HERE,' she said, waving it like bait, 'EAT.' The man on Jack's right could not resist the temptation and reached up with both hands. But the noodle was lifted just above his fingertips. 'JUMP,' commanded the giantess and a sinister grin spread across her sweet face. He began to jump, half-heartedly at first, but soon he was leaping up into the air and snatching desperately at the dangling noodle. Satsuko's dark eyes sparkled with glee. 'JUMP HIGHER,' she boomed, jerking the morsel up and down. 'YOU MUST JUMP HIGHER.'

Grudgingly, she released the noodle and the hungry man fell upon it. It was thicker than his arm and with some difficulty he tore off chunks, passing one to Jack and his other comrade. No sooner had he done so when he was seized between the giant chopsticks and swept up into the air.

'I NOT SAY YOU TO SHARE.' She twisted him slowly in front of her huge golden face and glared at him with narrow, reproachful eyes. The man kicked and tried to pull himself free, but she held him fast between the tips of the chopsticks like a rare titbit. Then she lowered him again, suspending him over the cup of steaming tea.

'YOU LIKE TO TAKE BATH?'

'No! Please!' he screamed.

'HAHA, MAYBE I BOIL YOU LIKE SHRIMP.' She slowly lowered her tiny victim until his bare feet made contact with the surface of the scalding liquid. His knees sprang up to his chest.

'God have mercy!' he cried out.

The unreality of it all made Jack's head feel light. Before him was a man his own size, pinched between chopsticks and kicking frantically to keep his legs out of a cup of steaming hot tea. High above the table top and looking down was the complacent face of the giantess who, without effort, controlled the extent of his suffering. She watched through big feline eyes as she toyed with him, twisting him this way and that and threatening to plunge him into her drink. Her power was absolute and it was only female capriciousness that saved him from a slow and agonising death. She deposited him on the table beside her bowl, where he collapsed in a fit of sobs, and she resumed eating her noodles as if nothing had happened.

'BRING ME SOY SAUCE,' she said, chewing a mouthful, and she pointed with her chopsticks to a bottle standing at the other side of the table. Jack ran to do her bidding. The bottle was more than twice his height and fatter than a tree trunk but fortunately it was almost empty. Combining their strength, he and the man who joined him were just able to slide it over the smooth table surface; but their progress was hopelessly slow and the giantess grew impatient. She reached down with her chopsticks and lifted up the weeping scrap of manhood that lay beside her bowl.

'YOU HELP,' she ordered, dropping him in front of Jack.

Backs bent and straining like a pharaoh's slaves, the three naked men pushed the bottle towards the waiting giantess. Sucking a noodle lazily into her mouth, she watched them approach,

'HERE,' she said as they came nearer, and she put a hand down on the table ready to receive the bottle. She made them manoeuvre it into the curve of her palm and then lifted it effortlessly up above their heads. She poured a stream of black sauce into her soup, stirred and tasted it, and then her catlike gaze fell on the exhausted men.

91

As quick as a flash she reached down with her chopsticks, snatched up the man closest to Jack, and dropped him into the bowl of soup. Jack started running even before he heard the screams. But he knew it was futile. There was nowhere to go and nowhere to hide. He was trapped on a barren plateau more than ten storeys above the ground. He'd covered scarcely half the length of the table when two thick wooden planks crashed against his body, knocking all the wind from his lungs. His knees gave way and he was hoisted up into the air at such a speed he lost all his bearings. The next thing he knew he was falling head first towards a dark brown liquid.

Satsuko played with the shrimp-sized men, chasing them around the bowl with her chopsticks and dunking them under the soup. She laughed out loud as they struggled to the surface entangled in noodles, spluttering and gasping for air. Through stinging eyes Jack caught glimpses of her huge hand and grinning face. She was watching them intently, like an engrossed child. Seizing the man beside him, she lifted him from the bowl and held him in front of her nose. The heat of the soup had turned his body bright pink and a long train of noodles dangled from his shoulders.

'YOU LOOK LIKE KING PRAWN,' she said. 'NOW I SEE HOW YOU TASTE.' She opened her enormous mouth, exposing two rows of massive white teeth, and brought him kicking and screaming towards the cavernous orifice. Gripping him firmly between the ends of her chopsticks, she set about trimming and sucking away the trailing noodles, brushing his flesh with her soft lips and hard teeth. Then she stretched out a wet pink tongue and laid him flat upon it. His head was hidden inside her mouth and she seemed about to swallow him.

At that very moment the blonde giantess strolled into the kitchen. 'SATSUKO!' she screamed, rushing to the table. 'WHAT ARE YOU DOING?'

Satsuko quickly removed the tiny man from her mouth and held him aloft in her chopsticks. 'I ONLY TEASE HIM. SEE, HE NOT HURT. JUST VERY FRIGHTEN.'

The blonde shook her head in good-natured reproach. 'BE CAREFUL. WE'LL RUN OUT IF WE CARRY ON BEING SO ROUGH WITH THEM.'

'HOW MANY WE HAVE LEFT?'

The blonde held out her hand guiltily and showed her sister giantess something resting on her palm. From down in the soup bowl Jack saw Satsuko's narrow black eyes spring open.

'WHOOAA! HE A REAL MESS,' she cried. 'WHAT YOU DO TO HIM?'

'I DIDN'T DO IT ON PURPOSE, SATS. HONEST-LY. THE SILLY LITTLE THING WAS HIDING INSIDE MY SHOE. HOW WAS I SUPPOSED TO KNOW?' Sighing, she went over to the corner of the kitchen, brushed the battered body off her palm into a pedal bin and washed her hands at the sink.

The casualties were beginning to mount. Jack wondered whether the scientist or Muscle Man and the two brothers were still alive. The giant women seemed unconcerned about the gruesome deaths they had caused. Flattened inside a shoe by a colossal female foot, torn in half by excited hands, made to drop from the base of a champagne glass – how long would it be before he met a similarly inglorious end?

An idea came to him. He took a deep breath and lay face down in the soup, his arms floating limply in front of him.

'OH NO! NOT ANOTHER ONE,' the blonde groaned tiredly. A moment later he felt a blunt heavy blow between the shoulders and he was pushed around the bowl.

'THEY SO WEAK,' Satsuko whined. 'I NOT EVEN TOUCH THIS ONE.' Jack stifled a cry as the chopsticks closed like pincers around his waist. He was swung through the air and then dropped onto a soft sloping surface. 'SEE, THERE NOTHING WRONG WITH HIM.'

Opening his eyes briefly he saw that he was lying in the palm of the blonde giantess. Her other hand was descending towards him. He lay passively as a finger stroked his naked body and nudged his head almost gently. 'HE PROBABLY DIED OF FRIGHT,' she said with a trace of girlish compassion in her voice. 'IMAGINE BEING SO TINY. IT MUST BE TERRIFYING FOR THEM. POOR LITTLE THINGS.' The hand closed around him and he felt himself accelerate. Through the gap between two fingers he saw a dizzying rush of chrome, pinewood and tiles. Then the hand descended and he was cast into the garbage. Down he spun, his body ricocheting off a cardboard box and finally coming to rest in a pile of discarded sandwiches. The lid came down above him, landing with a thud on a protruding object and leaving a narrow band of light.

Outside, the giantesses continued to talk in their booming voices.

'AT LEAST THE OTHER TWO SEEM TO BE ALL RIGHT,' the blonde was saying. 'GIVE THEM TO ME. I'LL RINSE THEM UNDER THE TAP.'

'YOU NEED BOTH?'

'YES, SATS, WE DO. THE PHOTOGRAPHER IS ALREADY HERE. SHE WANTS TO START SHOOTING MY SET.' Excited about the photo shoot, the two giantesses soon departed, taking their tiny male props with them.

Jack wasted no time. Strengthened by the piece of sandwich he had eaten, he clambered to the top of the rubbish and peered out from under the lid. The kitchen floor was seventy dizzying feet below him. Other men would have sunk in despair at the sight but Jack remained focused and determined. He searched through the contents of the bin and found some used paper napkins. He tore them into long strips which he knotted together to form a single length. Aware that every second was precious, he worked quickly and did not even pause when he stumbled across the crushed remains of his unlucky comrade. Pulling the napkin rope behind him, he climbed to the top of the refuse heap once more and attached one end to the handle of the plastic milk carton that was propping open the lid. He cast the other end down towards the kitchen floor.

He descended swiftly and, when he reached the bottom, he allowed himself a moment of triumph. But he had taken only the first step to freedom. He now faced the greatest challenge of his life: to escape from the giant-sized house and its cruel inhabitants. It was not just his own survival that was at stake but the future of men everywhere. He had to alert the world to this monstrous regiment of women who could shrink men to the size of insects. He had a nightmarish vision of a future in which the entire male population was miniaturised and forced to creep and crawl around the feet of women who had become tyrannical with power.

The kitchen led to a living room and he entered it warily, gazing up at armchairs and couches. Though they were unoccupied, he felt intimidated by their monumental dimensions. They seemed to belong to a different order of being and impressed upon him the formidable size of the house's occupants – those towering women who extended upwards to the limits of his vision and covered thirty of his strides with a single step of their own.

A male voice called out to him softly and shook him from his trancelike contemplation of the furniture. At the base of a couch, a mere speck before its vastness, stood the scientist waving his arms. Jack's spirits rose and he ran towards his comrade. Yet as he drew nearer he became uncomfortably aware of his own wretched appearance: his matted hair, his filthy naked body, the stench of the rubbish bin that he carried with him. The scientist appeared to have fared better and even had a scrap of white fabric fastened around him like a toga.

They greeted each other with brotherly affection, each glad to have found a companion and, under the shelter of the couch, they took stock of their situation. The scientist confirmed Jack's own pessimistic view that the giant women regarded them as mere playthings. They were obeying a fundamental law of nature, he told him, a law which compelled the strong to dominate and exploit the weak. Given unlimited power over males by virtue of their gigantic stature, the women were expressing the darkest and most primitive side of their femininity.

He told Jack about his own narrow escape. He and four others had managed to stay hidden from the rep – though she had rounded up at least a dozen escapees and put them back into the box. After she left the room, they made their way out into the hall. But they had scarcely covered half its length when they heard a loud clatter of heels coming from the other direction. They squeezed under a door they were passing and found themselves inside a steamy bathroom.

To their horror the approaching giantess entered the bathroom too, closing the door behind her. Unaware of the men's presence, she almost trampled them beneath her fluffy mule house slippers as she stepped across to the bath. From the cover of a discarded towel they watched as she leant over to mix scented oils into the water. It was not the rep but an exotic woman with tanned skin and dark wavy hair that flowed over her shoulders.

She rose to her full height again and casually kicked off her footwear, revealing long cream-coloured soles. Then she stepped over to the toilet. Scooping up the bottom of her robe, she sat down heavily on the seat with her knees apart. One huge tanned foot, the nails polished bright red, was planted just in front of the towel which hid the men.

A moment passed and then a mighty torrent was released inside the toilet bowl. It was as if a dozen fire hoses were being blasted against the interior wall and the sound of gushing and churning water filled the room. The hissing built to a crescendo as gallons of liquid were discharged each second, then slowly subsided until all that could be heard was an irregular sequence of drips deep inside the bowl. It was at this point that the giantess happened to glance down at her feet and caught sight of the tiny gawping men.

'YOU LITTLE CREEPS!' she shrieked.

Half-standing up and clutching the front of the robe against her crotch with one hand, she reached forward with the other and snatched at the men as they scurried away from the towel. She grabbed two of them in a single swoop and stretched her foot after the third, kicking him to the ground. He lay on the carpet, stunned by the force of the blow, and she calmly leant down and plucked him up. Holding all three of them captive in her hand, she got off the toilet.

'HERE, HAVE A CLOSER LOOK,' she roared and held them low over the bowl. Their puny cries echoed against the walls but this only excited her rage.

'IS THIS WHAT YOU WANTED TO SEE? MY PISS? MY GOLDEN PISS? FANCY A SWIM IN IT, DO YOU?' And so saying she opened her fingers and let them tumble into the water at the bottom of the bowl. Her eyes smouldered with sadistic contentment as she took in the unimaginable sight of men struggling to keep afloat in the noxious yellow pool of her urine. 'THE FIRST ONE OF THE MORNING IS ALWAYS A BIT STRONG,' she said tartly. 'BUT WHAT DID YOU EXPECT, NECTAR?'

Then she flushed them away as if they had been nothing at all.

The scientist had crept behind one of her discarded mules while this was taking place and when she was relaxing in the bath he had squeezed out under the door.

'It's a disturbing phenomenon,' he said to Jack glumly. 'These women treat us with contempt because to them we are no bigger than insects. Yet we cannot help but feel a sense of awe in their presence. Their colossal size makes us regard them as superior beings. Our subjection to them is as much psychological as physical –'

He suddenly stopped talking and he and Jack peered out from under the couch. A group of naked men was running across the open floor towards them. They were driving themselves forward like road racers and their faces were haggard. Some way behind the men strolled a pair of giant feet strapped into towering high-heeled sandals. They pursued their quarry lazily, yet each resounding step halved the distance between them and the hopelessly out-paced men. In a few strides the giantess had caught up with the breathless runners. She swung a sandal-clad foot over their heads and stomped it down on the floor in front of them.

'HALT!' she ordered. 'GET DOWN ON YOUR KNEES.'

The men sank to the floor around the shiny red sandal, bowing like primitives before a monstrous idol. But one of the worshippers proved to be less obedient than the others. Seizing a chance, he darted under the arch of the heel and began to run again. Jack watched him puffing and panting towards the couch and for a second he thought the man had escaped unnoticed. But a giant foot suddenly sailed after him. It followed him, almost mockingly, and his ignorance of its looming presence just behind him gave his frantic flight a farcical character. The first he knew of the pursuit was when the rim of the sole rammed into his back, sending him sprawling across the floor. But still he would not give up. He raised himself onto his hands and knees and crawled forward determinedly, until the smooth sole came down on top of him, pressing him flat on his belly.

'YOU DESERVE TO BE CRUSHED,' she said, raising her heel slightly and flexing her toes to increase the pressure on him.

Jack was just able to see her face. Peering down from a vertiginous height, she was using a hand to hold her light-brown hair away from her face. Her green eyes were focused on her foot and her glistening pink lips curved meanly as she spoke.

'WOULD YOU PREFER TO DIE UNDER MY SOLE OR UNDER MY HEEL?' She lifted up her sandal and released her victim from the crushing weight that had turned his face beet-red; but before he could even attempt to slither away, he was trapped beneath the ten-foot high heel. The circular tip covered his back and his naked body curled and stiffened under the cruel pressure she exerted. Jack's head reeled – the force that could be concentrated into the tapering stiletto defied calculation. She could grind the man out of existence with a single twist.

'HEEL OR SOLE? WHICH IS IT TO BE?'

The man grovelled for mercy as she increased the pressure on his back.

'WHEN I SAY STOP, YOU OBEY ME INSTANTLY. DO YOU UNDERSTAND, LITTLE MAN?' Twisting her heel, she turned his conquered body around on the polished wooden tile. Words gurgled from his mouth between cries of pain.

'I CAN'T HEAR YOU.' She lowered her head and scooped a strand of hair away from her ear. 'YOU'LL HAVE TO SPEAK UP.'

Using the last of his strength, he screamed his desperate apologies, and gradually, begrudgingly, she reduced the pressure upon him until he was able to worm out from beneath her deadly heel.

'LINE UP WITH THE OTHERS,' she commanded, pointing with her toes. He crawled quickly into position like a beaten dog. She roared down, addressing them all: 'THE NEXT LITTLE SHIT THAT EVEN RAISES HIS HEAD TO ME WILL BE A STAIN ON THE FLOOR.'

She crossed to the other end of the room and the troupe of naked men ran breathlessly behind her imperious red heels. She sat down in a chair and stretched out her legs indolently.

'TAKE OFF MY SHOES.'

She looked down with amusement and made fun of their desperate but ineffectual attempts to carry out her simple command. To give them a sporting chance, she unbuckled the ankle straps and dangled one of the sandals from her toes. The men gathered around the tip of the dipped heel and together they managed to lift it. But they were too minuscule to nudge the front straps over her unhelpful toes.

The scientist turned to Jack. 'I can no longer believe that we have been shrunken. These women are simply too inhuman to belong to our own species.'

Jack listened to him but continued watching the giantess as she flexed her toes and flicked off the sandal. It crashed to the floor, knocking over half of the tiny slaves.

'What other explanation is there?' Jack asked bleakly.

'I think we have been taken through a portal into an alternative universe where women grow to Brobdingnagian proportions. The worst traits of the female sex have increased proportionately. These giant captors of ours are supremely capriciousness, spiteful, indolent and vain.'

'And the rep? She was once our own size, remember?'

'I don't know,' the scientist conceded with a sigh. 'Maybe she is able to pass back and forth through the portal and change size accordingly? From a scientific standpoint it's just as probable as her having the power to shrink us.'

Jack listened to what the scientist had to say but saw little use in further speculation. For him, all that mattered was to find a way out of the house.

The giantess had kicked off both sandals and the men were kneeling in an arc before her bare feet which were crossed at the ankles. She flexed her toes sensually and deep wrinkles rippled over the sheer surface of each pink sole.

'NOW, MY LITTLE FOOTMEN, IT'S TIME TO MAKE YOURSELVES USEFUL.' She reached down with a lotion dispenser and squirted a stream of white goo at each man in turn. It oozed down their faces and chests and the sudden chill of it against their naked flesh made them shiver; but they remained on their knees and kept their heads bowed. The giantess shook with laughter at the sight of them and her round heels bounced up and down.

'GOD, I CAN DO ABSOLUTELY ANYTHING I WANT TO YOU, CAN'T I?' Then, regaining her composure, she said: 'YOU ONE-INCH WONDERS KNOW HOW TO MASSAGE FEET, RIGHT?

A timid murmur rose from the men.

'THEN GET TO WORK!'

Leaning back in the chair, she folded her arms behind her head and watched them with a languid expression. Lotion dripping down their bodies, the men approached the feet, gazing up at their mammoth task. The pink soles curved high above their heads and at the summit a set of long toes wiggled impatiently. Like a bizarre priesthood they gathered around a heel and began to anoint it with the lotion. They worked diligently, but even stretching their arms to their fullest extent they could reach no higher than the bottom section of the foot.

'PUT MORE EFFORT INTO IT,' she snapped. 'OR I'LL MAKE AN EXAMPLE OF ONE OF YOU.'

Jack and the scientist slipped out from under the rear of the couch and crept along the skirting board towards the door. They could hear the brusque commands of the giantess as they made their way. She ordered the men to climb up onto her feet and cursed their ineptitude when they slipped and fell. All the while she threatened them with savage punishments.

Just before the doorway, Jack took a last look across the room. Some of the men were balancing precariously upon the giantess's angled feet and kneading the flesh with all their might.

'IN BETWEEN THE TOES AS WELL.'

She sighed, clenching and flexing her toes as they did her bidding. One man, who was climbing up her big toe, was flicked from the slick skin and fell somersaulting to the floor. He landed heavily and lay groaning and clutching his head. Those who were standing nearby instinctively ran to his aid.

'LEAVE HIM,' she said with a quick glance down at the floor. 'AND GET BACK TO MY FEET.'

Jack and the scientist crept out into the hall. They went forward at a jog, hugging the cliff-high white wall. With every step they felt their smallness and vulnerability.

'Which way?' Jack asked as they neared the end of the hall.

But before the scientist had any chance to consider, an ominous thud echoed from around the corner. Both men froze like mice caught by a sudden light. Another thud followed and then another, each one louder and closer than the last. The men stared at each other for the briefest instant, their faces expressing a shared consciousness of a single terrifying concept – a giantess in high heels. They turned and raced back towards a plant stand they had just passed. Squeezing under the inch-and-a-half gap between its base and the floor, they waited, heads bent, hearts thumping in their chests.

A man their own size came panting around the corner. He was running, but not because he was trying to escape from the giantess. That was impossible for him. He was bound to the giant woman like a toy dog to its mistress. A white thread, the thickness of gallows rope, had been knotted around his neck and this crude leash extended upwards at a steep angle. It ended some hundred feet above the ground between a set of dark fingers tipped with long brightly coloured nails.

Rising almost as high as the leash, but vertically, like satanic ebony towers, came a pair of slow-moving stiletto-heeled boots. Each reverberating step sent a tremor through the parquet floor. Jack crouched down and his gaze climbed up over the warm brown flesh of the thick upper thighs and bare midriff until it reached the face of a black giantess. Set beneath a fringe of Cleopatra-style hair were two bewitching dark eyes. Wide angular cheeks sloped towards a sharp chin above which a pair of fleshy pink-frosted lips were pressed into a self-contented grin. Glancing down at the man scurrying before the tips of her boots, she lifted a mobile phone to her ear. All at once her eyes lit up and her mouth opened wide.

'HI, JAMILLA! OH-MY-GOD! I'M HAVING THE TIME OF MY LIFE OVER HERE.' As she chatted, the leashed man continued to run, just managing to keep ahead of her strolling boots. 'MOVE YOUR CHEAP ASS,' she boomed down at him.

Phone pressed to her ear, she took two lazy steps and stopped in the centre of the hall level with the plant stand. She lifted her boot and pointed with the tip towards where Jack and the scientist were hiding. 'GET UNDER THERE AND DO YOUR JOB,' she ordered. Her tiny slave ran towards the plant stand and the giantess continued her conversation. Her musical voice trilled with excitement. 'GIRLFRIEND, I'VE NEVER HAD SO MUCH FUN IN MY LIFE. I'M GONNA

GET ME A WHOLE ARMY OF THESE FREAKY LITTLE GUYS.'

Jack and the scientist retreated into the darkness at the very back of their hiding space. Scarcely daring to breathe, they stood with their backs to the wall. A moment passed and the leashed man dipped his head and came in. Out of sight of his giant mistress, he bent forward, resting his palms on his thighs, and tried to catch his breath.

Jack ran at him. The startled man raised his hands in a show of appeasement. 'It's all right,' he said in a rasping voice. 'I won't give you away.' The thread was wrapped so tightly around his throat that the effort to speak made him choke. A crude knot bulged at the back of his neck from which the leash extended out into the light. Jack began tugging at it, looking for a way to free the man. But the man pushed away his hands.

'It's no good. I'm done for.'

A noise like the report of heavy artillery made them all jump. The pointed toe of a leather boot came into view, almost penetrating their tiny sanctuary.

'WHAT'S TAKING YOU SO LONG, SHORTY? ... JAMILLA, YOU'VE GOTTA GET YOUR ASS OVER HERE. YOU'LL FEEL LIKE A GODDESS.'

'Go in the direction you saw me coming from,' croaked the man. 'That's your way out.'

Jack nodded, trying to ignore the menacing sight of the shiny black boot just beyond them.

'And promise me you'll take care of these bitches.'

Jack placed a hand on the man's shoulder. 'I swear to God I will, if it's the last thing I do.'

As Jack finished the sentence, the man staggered backwards clutching at the heavy rope around his throat. Jack watched helplessly as he was dragged on his heels out into the open. Spluttering and gurgling, he was hoisted into the air. Jack came to the edge of the hiding pace and gazed up

'YOU'RE TESTING MY PATIENCE,' the giant woman scolded, dangling her captive by the neck in front of her big face. 'EITHER YOU FIND ME SOME MORE OF YOUR LITTLE FRIENDS OR I'M GONNA WASTE YOU LIKE THE LAST ONE.' She lowered him to the ground again. 'NOW GET YOUR LAZY ASS TO WORK!'

The man picked himself up and began to run, heading across the hall towards a doorway. The giant boots came after him, calmly, effortlessly, never more than a step behind, beating their thunderous tattoo on the wooden floor.

'HI, CHANELLE! OH-MY-GOD! I'M HAVING THE TIME OF MY LIFE OVER HERE . . .'

As soon as the giantess disappeared through the door, Jack and the scientist sprinted to the end of the hall and followed the leashed man's directions. Cautiously, they entered a bright room. At the far side was a wall of shimmering glass and through it they could see blue sky. Their spirits lifted and their tired legs gained new strength. But as they drew nearer it dawned on them that they were not yet free. The towering glass plane which stood between them and the bright world outside was at least half a foot thick. They placed their palms against it, breathing heavily. Freedom was only a step away, but it was a step they could not take.

Jack heard something. It sounded like the call of a small bird. He looked over at a pile of magazines stacked thirty feet high in the corner of the room. He could hardly believe his eyes. Muscle Man and one of the brothers were standing at the base of it and beckoning frantically. The four men came together and despite their nakedness embraced each other joyfully.

'It's not safe in the open,' said Muscle Man and led Jack and the scientist behind the magazines.

Scarcely were they out of sight when the sound of female voices boomed across the room. The familiar thunder of heels followed and two giantesses stepped up to the glass door. Their sandal-clad feet were planted where Jack and the scientist had been standing only moments before.

The sight made Jack's stomach knot. 'I owe you one,' he said to Muscle Man.

The door slid open with a terrific roar and the giantesses went onto the terrace.

'They're setting up for a photo shoot,' explained Muscle Man. 'One is the photographer and the other her assistant. But they always close the door when they come back inside. They must know there are a few of us they haven't rounded up or killed yet.'

'Can't be many,' said Jack darkly.

'Until I saw you two guys I thought it was just me and soldier-boy here.'

Jack turned to the young man. With some difficulty he asked: 'What happened to your brother?'

'A giant bitch of a Latina got him. She picked him up like he was a toy and stuck him in the top of her stocking. I never saw him after that.'

The giantesses reappeared, absorbed in a loud conversation. The last one in was giggling and left the door partly open behind her.

'Now!' said Muscle Man as soon as the women had crossed the room. He dashed towards the door, calling to the others to follow. The young soldier went after him, his limber muscles bearing him swiftly across the floor. Jack thought the risk was too great: to him the unclosed door signalled the imminent return of the giantesses, or even worse – a trap. Muscle Man called again and the scientist began to run, his strange toga billowing behind him. Caught in the rush of the moment, Jack went too.

His fears proved unfounded. The men passed safely through the opening and climbed down onto a paved terrace. Ahead of them was a lake of blue water and along its edge stood massive deckchairs and sunloungers like towering avant-garde structures. From their ground-level perspective they could see no obvious path leading from the terrace and they crept forward, uncertain of the direction they should take. A forest of shrubs on the opposite side of the pool seemed the most promising destination, but it would have taken them many minutes to reach it and they felt dangerously exposed under the bright afternoon sun. A cluster of potted plants provided one of the few hiding places on the bare terrace and they took advantage of its cover to plan their next step.

It was a fortunate decision. One of the giantesses reappeared, strode to the pool and proceeded to set up a reflective screen. A moment later, the other giantess stepped out, a camera swinging at her hip. In her wake came a third giant woman and Jack and the other men tilted back their heads as she sauntered towards them on her Perspex high heels. Their gaze swept up her tanned legs towards a white triangle of material moulded tight around her crotch, more than a hundred feet above their heads. Her bulbous breasts were supported in two white hammocks of the same bright material and rocked with each step she took.

'The Latina,' murmured the young soldier and his body tensed.

Muscle Man laid a strong hand on his shoulder. 'You'll get your chance. I promise you.'

The model began to pose and the photographer approached her from behind, cooing appreciatively and firing off shots. She crouched down on one knee and aimed the lens at the broad-hipped girl's ass.

'HOW DOES IT LOOK?' asked the model, turning her head over her shoulder.

'BEAUTIFUL, HONEY, LIKE A DREAM. WHEN THEY SEE THE POSTER EVERY GIRL WILL WANT A THONG LIKE YOURS. NOW PUSH OUT THOSE BOOTILICIOUS CHEEKS ... MMM!

THAT'S THE WAY ... BEAUTIFUL ... HEAVEN-LY.'

The model bent forward, placing both hands on her knees and squeezing her breasts together between her upper arms. Above the deep valley of her cleavage the men could see her rosy lips and dark eyes. The photographer stalked closer, the camera lens zooming in and out excitedly at the playfully wiggling ass.

'LET'S GET SOME SHOTS AGAINST THE POOL, HONEY.'

The model straightened her skimpy bikini top and thong bottom, turned around and tottered after the photographer on her tall heels. From their hiding place among the pots the men stared up at the quivering mass of ass flesh; but these huge gravity-mocking globes were not the only thing she displayed to them. Where the white crotch section of the thong emerged from the ravine between her buttocks and would usually rise to join the waistband to form a T, there was no strap or decorative clasp. Instead, a naked man had been fixed there like the victim of a crucifixion. The vertical section of the thong had been attached to his legs, and his arms were stretched outwards by the ends of the waistband which were fastened to his wrists. Every time the giantess took a step and swung her hips, the straining male body was pulled in three directions at once.

The model performed for the camera again, smiling affectedly and sticking out her ass to show off her living thong clasp. She seemed unaware that with each con-trived pose she was torturing the tiny man strapped above the deep cleft of her swaying and flexing cheeks – or else she simply did not care. She pranced about playfully, hands on hips, pointing her buttocks to left and right, stretching his body without mercy. Then she squatted down, her mountainous cheeks hovering just above the ground. The man's legs were dragged down into the gulf of her ass and his arms were all but ripped from their sockets.

They saw him clearly now, stretched across the tanned buttocks like a heathen sacrifice to a voluptuous earth mother. His features were distorted with pain and his face barely recognisable, but there was no mistaking his distinctive buzz-cut.

The young soldier hurled himself forward. Jack and Muscle Man barely managed to restrain him.

'What are you planning to do?' asked Muscle Man, fighting to control his own rage. 'That giant bitch would take you out with her little toe.' Held fast by four strong hands the young man watched his brother being tortured by the gigantic female ass.

'I'm gonna kill her! Somehow I'm gonna kill her!'

As if she were making fun of his threat, the squatting model began to clench and release her buttocks rhythmically so that each one bounced up and down in a lewd dance above the flagstones. The men watched with a revolted fascination as the juddering gluteal muscles set tons of soft ass flesh in motion.

The photographer shouted encouragement. 'YEAH, HONEY, SHOW ME HOW YOU WORK THAT BOOTY.'

'JUST USING WHAT MY MAMA GAVE ME,' the model giggled.

Her antics caused the thong to lodge in her deep cleft and she stood up to pull it loose. Her index finger slid up along the crotch section and in between her cheeks until she located the tiny man. She nudged him free, dragged him back into place at the top of her buttock cleavage and then tugged the waist band high over her hips.

'YOU WANNA TAKE FIVE?' asked the photographer.

'SURE, I COULD USE A SODA.'

'GIVE ACTION MAN A BREAK AS WELL. DON'T WANNA FINISH HIM OFF TOO SOON.'

The model slipped off the thong, rolling the tiny man over her ass and down her thighs. Her bald pink sex was exposed and glistened in the sunlight as she bent and hung the thong from the arm of a deckchair. She went over to the table where the photographer's assistant was pouring drinks.

The man attached to the thong was left dangling face-down some thirty or forty feet above the ground. His eyes were shut and he did not move.

'We've got to save him,' said his brother, holding back tears. 'He can't take any more.'

Jack opposed the idea but Muscle Man was swayed by the young man's emotion and the two men sprinted towards the deckchair. Jack watched them with a sinking heart. The giantesses were standing around the table, drinking, talking and laughing, oblivious to the rescue attempt. But for how long?

The men reached the deckchair and quickly shinned up the legs. Strong and fit, they pulled themselves up onto the seat without difficulty. But they could not agree on the best method of freeing their comrade from the thong. The minutes passed and Jack signalled to them anxiously that they should abandon their attempt. In a fury, the young soldier moved towards the dangling thong, seized it in his two hands and began to drag it towards the end of the armrest.

But it was too late. The model was on her way back to the chair, striding on her skyscraper legs, swinging her huge hips. As she approached, she cast a long shadow over the tiny men who froze as they caught sight of her. She turned her head to joke with the photographer and did not even glance down as she lowered her mammoth ass onto the chair.

Jack held his breath as he watched. At the last moment the young soldier leapt from the corner of the seat, an expression of terror frozen on his face. Arms flailing, he fell towards the ground. In the same time frame, Muscle Man staggered backwards across the seat, gazing up in awe at the descending ass. His arms were held above his head in a futile attempt to defend himself. Then his whole body disappeared beneath the enormous brown buttocks.

The model crossed her legs and continued talking. The man beneath her ass seemed never to have existed and she was oblivious to the young soldier rolling in mute agony just a few inches from one of her enormous Perspex heels.

She lifted the thong from the armrest and briefly examined the unmoving tiny man. She shook him and then flicked him with her finger, but he made no response.

She wrinkled up her nose. 'THEY DON'T LAST LONG, DO THEY?'

Suddenly she jumped to her feet with a shrill girlish scream. Jack saw Muscle Man tumble from her buttocks and land on the seat of the chair. Rubbing her ass with her free hand, she spun around and caught sight of the nuisance.

'LOOK, I FOUND ANOTHER ONE,' she yelled. 'I WAS SITTING ON HIM AND HE BIT ME ON MY ASS.'

'I BET YOU SQUASHED HIM FLAT,' shouted over the photographer.

'I SQUASHED HIM A BIT, I GUESS.' She picked up the unconscious man and rolled him between her fingers. 'BUT HE'S ALL RIGHT, I THINK. JUST DAZED.' She clipped across to the table. 'SPRAY SOME SODA WATER ON HIM. THAT'LL WAKE HIM UP . . .' Her voice trailed off and she looked at the photographer quizzically. 'WHAT'S UP? WHAT DID I DO?'

The photographer pointed towards the chair and grinned sheepishly. 'HONEY, I HATE TO TELL YOU THIS, BUT I THINK THERE WERE LIKE *TWO* OF

THEM.' The model turned around and saw the messy red trail stretching from the chair to her heel. She pouted and scraped the sole of her shoe clean on a concrete slab.

'ALWAYS GETTING UNDER MY GODDAMN FEET,' she complained.

Jack slumped to the ground with his back against the earthenware pot. He had lost the will to do anything. The scientist lowered himself down beside him and sat deep in thought.

Muscle Man was revived by the cold soda water and sewn into the thong as a replacement clasp. Wearing him proudly above the cleft of her ass, the model went through her repertoire of sexy poses. Bending, twisting and crouching, a knowing smile on her lips, she presented her plump buttocks to the camera lens and displayed the miniman, stretched grotesquely across her tanned cheeks. His trained muscles flexed, taking the strain, and his manly face fought to express defiance.

'NOW SHAKE IT, HONEY, SHAKE THAT BOOTY!'

The model shook her rump with full Latina abandon. The landscape of juicy flesh vibrated with seismic intensity and not even the champion body builder was able to withstand its violence. The living thong-clasp was ripped apart by the hills of juddering ass meat and the thong slid down the massive legs to the ground.

'OOPS, I DID IT AGAIN,' she giggled.

'LET'S CALL IT A DAY,' announced the photographer, lowering her camera.

Behind the pot the scientist jumped to his feet. 'I've got it,' he said. 'This is all a dream.'

Jack looked up at him doubtfully. There was a wild gleam in the older man's eyes.

'Science always opts for the simplest explanation of any phenomenon. You must have heard of Occam's razor?'

112

'This is no dream,' said Jack firmly. 'These women are as real as anything I've ever seen.'

'Real beings the size of these women would collapse under their own mass. Conversely, if we had been shrunken, then we'd be starving to death by now: we'd have metabolisms like mice. Either hypothesis posits an alternative universe, a place where Earth's physical laws do not apply – a clumsy, long-winded explanation. But a dream is simplicity itself. A communal dream induced by a mind-altering drug. Don't you see, our very first instincts were right?'

More giantesses were coming out to the pool. Jack held onto the scientist's toga, keeping him behind the plant pot.

'If this is a dream, then we'll all wake up unharmed,' he urged. 'But in the meantime, let's act as though this nightmare is really happening.'

There was a commotion and both men peered from behind the pot. The giantess with the green eyes and red sandals had appeared and she was carrying a man on her palm. She put him down on the ground and rose to her full height before him.

'WORSHIP YOUR GODDESS,' she commanded.

The man was the Fanatic, Jack now saw, the believer in divine retribution for male sins. Lying prostrate before the huge painted toes, he raised and lowered his arms in shameless obeisance. An idolatrous chant rose from his throat. The women towered around him in a circle, giggling at the grovelling praise he offered up to their sister. Some of them broke into uncontrollable laughter.

'Don't you see?' said the scientist. 'We are being tested in an inhumane psychological experiment. These women are hysterical projections of our deepest fears and desires.'

He broke free, leaving Jack clutching his makeshift toga, and charged towards the group of giantesses believing they were no more real than images on a drive-in movie screen. Jack slid back behind the pots, unable to watch.

Shouts descended and heels clattered across the concrete. Jack covered his ears but still he heard the ensuing furore as the women fought for possession of his last comrade and brought about his pitiful end.

As evening fell the giantesses drifted back indoors. Wrapped in the toga, Jack remained slumped against the pot until he was sure they would not return. At last he stood up and began the long trek to the other side of the pool. He felt numb at the prospect of escape – too many dreadful scenes replayed in his mind for him to feel any positive emotion – but he walked forward steadfastly, determined to avenge every one of his fallen comrades.

It was several minutes before he reached the shrubbery. He scaled up the brick border and walked along the top looking for the best place to descend. The plant growth was thick, like a jungle, and he was worried about the creatures it might harbour.

A sound came from across the pool. Jack turned his head to see a giant figure step out through the doorway. Heels clicking on the concrete, the woman strolled about the empty terrace with an easy, contemplative air. In her dark skirt suit, she looked like a young executive enjoying a private moment after a hectic day, only she was taller than a tower block. She stopped and lightly kicked something on the ground by one of the chairs and then went on towards the edge of the pool.

'CONGRATULATIONS, YOU'RE THE LAST ONE LEFT,' she said, standing with hands on hips and staring ahead, smiling.

The light from the pool caught her face and, even from his low perspective, Jack recognised the distinctive features of the rep. Her voice too was unmistakable, that cultivated blend of charm and iciness. He felt his heart expand into his throat. Yet she could not be addressing him, he thought: he was tiny, far away and concealed in the darkness beyond the pool. It would take the eyes of an owl to pick him out.

'DO I REALLY HAVE TO WALK ALL THE WAY OVER THERE AND GET YOU?'

She was looking at him now. Her enormous face was turned in his direction. The smile on her lips was red and devilish.

Jack did not waste a second. He dropped down from the wall and began to push his way through the dense forest. In reality it was only a narrow herbaceous border and the progress he made could be measured in inches.

The steady report of heels on concrete grew louder and louder and in no time at all, it seemed to Jack, the tops of the trees were pulled apart by huge fingers tipped with long red nails. A laughing face beamed down at him through the foliage. Jack drove on, tripping over roots and crashing into stems, but the clever hazel eyes discovered him whichever way he turned. Out of breath, he collapsed and the fingers swept down like vultures taking their prey.

'How?' he screamed, kicking wildly as he was hoisted from the shrubs. 'How did you know I was here?'

Laughing, the rep held him in front of her face and ripped off his toga. 'LOOK AT THE SIZE OF YOU AND ALL YOU CAN ASK ME IS HOW DID I KNOW YOU WERE HIDING IN THE PLANTS . . . MEN!' She walked with him back around the pool. 'TINY, I SET THE WHOLE THING UP. I EVEN ARRANGED YOUR ESCAPE FROM THE BOX.'

'Why did you do this to us?' he howled in despair.

'WHY?' she repeated mockingly. 'JUST BECAUSE WE CAN. OH, AND BECAUSE IT'S SO MUCH FUN. BUT MOSTLY BECAUSE IT MAKES THE PICTURES LOOK MORE AUTHENTIC.'

Her pace increased. Her arm swung at her side and so did Jack, whom she carried closed in her palm like a car key or a phone. Between her fingers he saw trails of light and colour. Then there was a jerky montage of other giant women, winking, grinning and waving as he was whisked through the rooms of the house. He heard laughter and shouting and music, but it never quite drowned out the relentless clack-clack-clack of the rep's heels on the wooden floor.

At last she stopped. A door was slammed closed and suddenly he was spinning through the air. He braced himself for the smash of impact. He seemed to fall a long way, down and down and down, spinning head over heels. But the landing, when it came, was soft and painless. He rolled over dizzily, but he was unharmed. He was lying in the middle of a smooth white sea.

'I PROMISED WE'D USE YOU ALL, DIDN'T I, MR DOLMAN? PREPARE TO STAR IN YOUR VERY OWN FASHION POSTER.'

Without ceremony she undressed, kicking off her shoes and levering her skirt and panties down over her hips. Her jacket and blouse came off next and then she unhooked her bra, freeing two earth-shaking breasts.

Climbing onto the big bed she almost crushed Jack in her eagerness. She grabbed him in her hand as he tried to run away.

'I SAW YOU STARING AT MY ASS ON THE PLANE. I KNOW YOU WANT ME.' Ignoring his cries, she lay on her back and held him against her breast. 'MAKE THE MOST OF THESE BECAUSE YOU'LL NEVER SEE ANOTHER PAIR LIKE THEM.' She dropped him in their valley and squeezed, trapping him between walls of warm smothering flesh. Gasping for air, he battled in vain to escape. 'SOME MEN WOULD DIE TO BE IN YOUR PLACE,' she laughed. 'NOW SHOW SOME APPRECIATION.'

She set him to work on her big fat nipples, pressing his face against one and then the other and ordering him to suck and lick them and squeeze them with both hands.

Jack did all he could to stimulate the engorged pads. Wrapping his arms around each one, he tugged and twisted them as if he were wrestling a stubborn opponent.

'YOU'RE NOT MUCH USE FOR FOREPLAY,' she complained. 'LET'S CUT TO THE CHASE.' She held him between two fingers and lifted his cock and balls with the tip of a red-painted nail. Despite himself Jack had become aroused by the touch and scent of the gigantic female body and his swollen manhood sat on the hard polished surface like a tiny offering.

'THAT TIDDLER WON'T BE MUCH USE WHERE YOU'RE GOING.'

She lowered him between her parted thighs, where her shaved pink sex waited like a narrow cave on a cliff face. The uneven lips glistened with moisture and twitched hungrily as he was brought closer. On either side of him rose her pale inner thighs, high and sheer like mountain peaks.

'GET TO WORK,' she ordered, releasing him.

Jack clung on to the hood of her clit. Almost at once he felt the hot waxy lips below begin to swallow his legs. He kicked free and dragged himself up towards the safety of her mons.

'WHERE DO YOU THINK YOU'RE GOING, MISTER?' Her finger nudged him back into place. Keeping him pressed to her sex, she began to roll her hips, coating his body with sticky juices. Jack massaged her clit, desperate to please her, terrified of failure. He stroked and petted the strange bulbous head as if it were a beast he needed to appease.

'HAVE YOU STARTED YET?' she called out sarcastically.

Her impatient lips began to draw him inside and an intense sexual musk saturated the air around him, filling his lungs and making him giddy as he worked to please her.

'YOU'RE USELESS,' she cried out in frustration. Taking him roughly in her fingers she rubbed him up and down in the wet channel of her hungry sex, pounding his head against her swollen clit with each deep upward stroke. 'AAAH, THAT'S MORE LIKE IT.' Her hips began a rhythmical circular dance and she dipped him in and out of her insatiable hole – head, chest, waist, legs – like a miniature dildo.

Jack thrashed about madly at the end of her fingers, but there was no escaping her ravenous sex. The inner lips clutched at him eagerly and slurped their appreciation.

'MAKE YOURSELF STIFF,' she growled and thrust him all the way inside, burying her own fingers too. Jack was propelled headfirst down the sticky tunnel of flesh into total darkness. The muscular walls closed tightly around him, trapping him in a hot airless cocoon. He twisted and turned frantically. He pushed and pounded against the walls until his arms went weak. But his efforts were useless against her mighty cunt. Indeed, his wriggling and writhing only increased its hunger and it sucked him deeper inside.

All the while he could hear the selfish pleasure-moans of the giantess. They grew louder and more wanton until the tunnel shuddered and the flesh walls contracted, forcing all the air from his lungs and crushing his bones. The last sound ever to reach Jack's ears was a deep groan of female satisfaction.

For a time all was still. Then slowly the walls slackened and Jack's broken body was expelled. Down the wet shaft it slid until it fell out from between the swollen sex lips with a tiny pop of air and landed on the sheet.

The mattress shook as the giantess rolled over and turned her huge white buttocks towards the discharged male. Soon the sound of her contented breathing filled the room.

The latest poster for the Other World Fashion Company hung on a hoarding above the entrance to a shopping arcade in the high street. It showed a very attractive young woman sitting at a dressing table and applying red gloss to her lips. The dressing table was cluttered with all the usual female paraphernalia, but at the corner, lying among discarded make-up pads, tissues and cotton buds, was a most incongruous object – a tiny naked man, curled up like a foetus. The giantess was smiling to herself (and the viewer) in the mirror. The meaning of that crafty red grin was clear: the three-inch man, like the other items, had served his purpose and was ready to be thrown away.

The dark visual humour was certainly apparent to the two teenage girls who paused to look at the poster as they emerged from Topshop clutching carrier bags.

'I just love these pictures,' said one. 'They're so funny.'

'I know,' agreed her friend. 'And they look so real.'

'I wish I could get a little man like that.'

'Or grow into a giantess.'

'Yeah, think of all the fun we could have.'

4

Heartless

As Jan Angel approached the small Norwegian coastal town, he heard on his car radio that a local girl by the name of Freya Hansen and her footballer fiancé had set a date for their wedding. He drove on deep in thought and his dark eyes seemed to melt. Then, for no apparent reason, he smiled and nodded to himself. He followed the road down into the town, but instead of taking the ferry to Denmark as he'd intended, he parked near the main square and paid for a room at a hotel.

He insisted on taking a room with a view of both the square and the seafront and, since the only one that met these requirements had not been vacated until late that morning, the chambermaid was still making up the bed when he got to the door. He stood silently in the doorway and watched her work.

She was young, with a bob of very straight reddish-brown hair, and wore a traditional chambermaid's uniform consisting of a black knee-length dress with high collars and a white apron. Unaware of his presence, she leant across the mattress to smooth down the sheet and the hem of the dress rose up, revealing the backs of her sturdy stocking-clad thighs.

What a juicy ass, Angel thought wistfully. Enough for me or any man. She must get it pinched a dozen times a day, poor girl! Ah, but how much would she charge me for the privilege of kissing that tempting rump of hers? He stared at it longingly, quite overcome with desire for the innocently proffered backside of the young working woman. His mind raced . . . Name your price, my love, and I'll happily pay it! Just to kiss those lovely bum cheeks, that's all I ask. I won't lay a finger on the rest of your body, I promise. I'll treat you like a princess, like a goddess, like my queen. All I desire is to be your humble ass kisser for ten tiny minutes. I won't hinder you at all. You can go right on making the bed while I pay homage to your royal *derrière*. I'll close the door so nobody else can see us and then I'll get down on my knees behind you and worship that beautiful womanly bottom, which is really much too good for the likes of me. I'll stare at it for a few moments, marvelling at its magical roundness. Then I'll push my head up under your dress and press my lips so gently against the seat of your tights you won't even know I'm down there behind you, adoring you with my whole being. And when you walk to the other side of the bed, your besotted little ass kisser will shuffle after you on his knees, lips puckered and eager to reattach themselves to your big, soft, wobbling mounds . . .

The chambermaid turned around and, catching sight of Angel standing in the doorway, she reddened and nervously straightened her skirt. How he longed to confess to her what she had made him feel just now, but he knew from experience she'd probably run away screaming if he tried.

'Are you Spanish?' he asked.

She looked at him a little oddly. 'Yes, on my mother's side.'

What a pretty face she had: wide cheeks, freckles around the nose, and warm brown eyes which were bold and curious.

'And are you familiar with the films of Luis Buñuel?'

'Never heard of him.' She began to wipe the top of the dressing table with a cloth.

'You don't need to bother with that.'

'Suit yourself.' She dropped the cloth into a bucket and came towards the door. She was not very tall and, as he stepped aside to let her pass, a spicy-sweet fragrance rose from her short hair and teased his nostrils. She walked down the hall with a brisk, nonchalant step and suddenly turned her head around and glanced back. Angel quickly closed the door.

What a waste, he sighed, going over to the window and looking out across the square. A girl like that cleaning rooms for a living. She could have a stable of men to wait upon her hand and foot, if only she knew where to look. It suddenly occurred to him that he might help her. Yes, he definitely would. But how much time did he have to spare?

That evening, as Angel sat in the lounge reading the newspapers, he was joined by the hotel manager. The talkative man was sure he had seen Angel somewhere before but could not remember the occasion.

'I'm sorry to say I think you're mistaken,' Angel said. 'But I do have one of those faces that people always think they recognise.'

They chatted about the hotel business – and the manager found Angel uncommonly knowledgeable on the subject – until a short, slightly built man in a shabby jacket came into the lounge. He walked awkwardly over to the bar, nodding respectfully at the patrons and at Angel in particular.

'Excuse me one moment,' said the manager and he got up and went to where the man was standing at the bar. Leaning over him, he spoke into his ear and the man quickly drained the glass of water he'd been served and sloped away.

'Who was that?' asked Angel when the manager returned.

'We call him Tiny. He cleans the guests' shoes and

does odd jobs for me. He knows I don't like him to come in here in the evening. The patrons complain.'

Nothing further was said about Tiny.

Angel pointed to one of the newspapers on the table. 'I was just reading about a young student who was found dead in the woods near here. Did you know him?'

The proprietor nodded. 'As a matter of fact his mother is an old friend of mine. A terrible waste. He had everything going for him and then all of a sudden he ends up with both his wrists cut. If you ask me, it's got all the hallmarks of a tragic love affair.'

'So you think it was suicide?'

'Can there be any doubt about it? But for the sake of his mother I hope the coroner records an accidental death.'

'Did they recover the knife?'

'They found it thirty feet from the body. It was one of those ornamental knives with an ivory handle.'

Angel reflected for a moment. 'Why would he cut his own wrists and then throw away the knife he'd used?'

'Maybe he wanted to prevent it from being discovered? But who really knows? He was obviously out of his mind. Like I said, I'm sure there's a woman mixed up in it somewhere.'

'What makes you say that?' Angel puckered his brow.

'Let's just say I have my suspicions.'

'Did he leave a note?'

'Yes, of sorts. He was clutching a piece of paper in his hand when they found him. There was a line of poetry scribbled on it.' The proprietor recited the words from memory: ' "Would that thy knife were as sharp as thy final no." '

Angel's face stiffened and then became animated. 'Was the knife blunt?'

'It would seem so.'

'Why on earth didn't he sharpen it, then?'

'It wasn't his knife.'

'No? Well, whose was it?'

The manager paused and then in a reluctant voice he said: 'The knife belonged to Miss Freya Hansen.'

'The one who is engaged to the footballer?'

'The very same.'

'Are you saying he was so madly in love with this woman that he took his own life?'

'They're all mad about her.'

Angel's eyes glazed over, just as they had earlier that day in the car. The manager placed a hand on his shoulder. 'I've given you my private thoughts on the affair and I hope I can trust you not to –'

'I won't repeat a word you've said,' Angel reassured him. And then he excused himself and went back up to his room.

'I think he might be a detective,' the manager told his barman after Angel had gone. 'He didn't say so exactly, but he asked a lot of questions and listened to every word I said.'

The next evening when Angel was in the hotel lounge he saw again the man everybody called Tiny. Wearing the same shabby jacket, the diminutive man came into the room apprehensively and approached the bar. But on catching sight of a particular patron, he quickly turned around and retraced his steps.

'Leaving so soon?' said the woman, laying the document she was reading down on her table. 'You haven't even wished me good evening.' And she beckoned him with a perfectly manicured finger. She was in her late thirties and her mature good looks and confident manner commanded Angel's attention. Her light-brown hair was cut fashionably short and slicked back behind her ears to reveal a pair of expensive earrings. And her tailored business suit, with a skirt that refused to cover her finely shaped knees, made him nod in admiration.

She crossed one stocking-clad leg over the other and her foot pointed at Tiny, who came and stood before her with his head bowed. He glanced down anxiously at the bobbing court shoe.

'You must have a drink,' she said to him and filled an empty glass with wine from the bottle on her table.

'No thank you, ma'am,' he said politely.

'Oh, but I insist.' There was a mischievous edge to her voice and she took a sip from her own glass, her grey eyes smiling. 'It's a vintage Johannisberg Riesling. You ought to be grateful. You couldn't afford to buy a single glass of this stuff.'

'Please, ma'am,' said Tiny in a voice so timid that Angel could only just hear him. 'You know how drink affects me.'

A pair of women at a nearby table began to snigger.

'One drink won't hurt you,' she said. 'And then you can dance a jig for me.'

'Oh, please,' begged Tiny. 'Not tonight. Not in front of all these people.'

'What's the matter with you? You've danced for me before.'

Tiny became flustered. 'I just came in to see if the manager had any more jobs for me this evening.'

She held out the glass to him and spoke bossily: 'Drink. You're starting to annoy me.'

Tiny took the glass in his trembling hand and lifted it to his lips. She watched with satisfaction as he forced himself to swallow. When he finished she tugged at the hem of his jacket with her elegant fingers and tore a hole in the frayed fabric. She laughed at his dismay.

'If you dance for me, I'll buy you a new one.'

Tiny looked at her doubtfully but there was a desperate glimmer of hope in his eyes. 'Do you promise?' he said.

'Yes, yes, I promise.' She took another sip of wine. 'I give you my word in front of all these people that I'll buy you a new jacket if you dance a jig for me.'

For a long moment Tiny was undecided and he even glanced across at Angel as if seeking guidance. Then he slowly put his glass down on the table.

'Very well,' he said, 'I'll dance, but only for a minute. I'm tired. I've had a hard day.'

'Get on with it,' she said impatiently.

Tiny put his hands on his hips and began to hop from one foot to another, kicking out his short stiff legs in a pitiful attempt at a peasant jig. The women at the nearby table immediately doubled up with laughter. He was a man without rhythm or co-ordination and, as he lurched from side to side, it was difficult to tell whether he was dancing or merely trying to keep his balance. It was a truly grotesque spectacle, similar to watching a dog walking on its hind legs or a goaded bear performing at a fairground.

The domineering woman seemed pleased with the performance of her paid male dancer and lit up a cigarette. She casually blew her smoke towards him, her red lips pouting meanly as he coughed and spluttered. At last, out of breath, Tiny halted and stooped before her, wheezing, hands resting on knees. Slow handclaps sounded from a few of the tables.

'Finished so soon?' she said. 'I was just beginning to enjoy myself. Here, have some more wine. You'll be dancing on the table before this evening is over.' She refilled his glass and held it out to him.

He shook his head. 'No more, ma'am, please. I did what you asked. Can't you leave me alone now?'

She put down the glass and from an elegant wallet she plucked out a banknote and laid it on the table. Tiny eyed it covetously and his tongue flicked across his lips.

'It's yours if you drink the wine,' she said.

Tiny shook his head again but his gaze remained fixed on the money.

'What's wrong with you this evening? You used to drink wine from my shoe for fifty kroner.' She slid the

126

banknote towards him. 'There, I've just doubled your wages.'

Tiny looked into her eyes for the first time. His voice shook with emotion as he spoke. 'I won't do it. I'm a man, not your plaything. I won't humiliate myself for a new jacket.'

The woman laughed contemptuously. 'You're a man, are you? We'll see about that.' She took a long draw on her cigarette and casually tapped the ash into his glass.

'Now drink it,' she said, looking at him with her stern grey eyes.

Tiny stared at the wine in horror as the flakes of ash spread out across the surface and began to sink. The women at the nearby table shouted rude words of encouragement.

'No,' he said stubbornly, 'I won't do it.'

'Are you disobeying me?'

'What harm did I ever do to you?' he cried.

Very deliberately, she extinguished her cigarette against the inside of the glass and dropped the crushed butt into the wine. She picked up the glass, swirled the contents around, and presented it to him with a sadistic grin.

'Drink it, little man. Drink every last drop.'

Tiny took a step back and the woman put down the glass angrily and rose to her feet. In her high heels she towered over him and he cringed before her, shielding his head with his arms as if expecting a slap.

But before anything else could happen, Angel sprang up from his chair and came and stood beside Tiny. In a remarkably calm voice he said: 'I'll give you a thousand kroner if you pick up the glass and throw the contents in this lady's face.'

There was dead silence in the lounge and the woman stared at him with a wide-open mouth. Angel reached into his wallet and took out the money.

'Here it is,' he said to Tiny. 'Now all you have to do is throw the wine at her.'

Tiny was in a state of utter confusion. He glanced at Angel, then at the woman and then at Angel again, stuttering incoherently.

'How dare you,' said the woman finally. 'Do you have any idea who I am?'

Angel bowed his head politely. 'Ma'am, whoever you are I recommend you find yourself a man who will teach you some humility and manners. What's more you look the type who would enjoy lying over a gentleman's knee while he chastises you on your bare bottom.'

The woman's face turned very red and her lips began to twitch. She spun around, grabbed the glass from the table and hurled it at Angel's head. But Angel read her movements perfectly and ducked in good time. The glass smashed against an empty table. Wild shouts erupted from all around the room and the manager, who was just then passing by, came running in.

'What on earth is going on?' he cried, staring at the shattered glass and splashes of wine on the tablecloth. 'I won't have a scene in my hotel!'

'I've never been so insulted,' screamed the woman. 'This man is a barbarian and he'll pay for what he said to me.' And with that vague threat hanging in the air, she snatched up her papers and briefcase and stormed out of the lounge.

Angel watched her go. He wanted to run after her but the manager grabbed his arm. 'I can't allow you to insult my guests,' he said crossly. 'Especially not that lady. She's a solicitor in the magistrate's office and could cause a lot of trouble for me.'

Angel apologised to him and took full responsibility for the incident. The manager remained furious for some minutes but was eventually pacified when Angel offered to pay for any damages and bought drinks for all the patrons, many of whom came to his defence. Then, to everybody's surprise, Angel turned to Tiny, who was standing dejected and forgotten by the wall, and invited him up to his room.

'What has happened between you and that woman that allows her to humiliate you in public?' asked Angel when he and Tiny were alone.

'It wasn't as bad as all that,' said Tiny. 'I've got used to it by now. But tonight I was just too tired to do what she wanted. It usually happens when she's had a hard day. She's under a lot of pressure at work. She's only young and she runs the whole department.'

'Hmmm. Doesn't she have a husband or boyfriend?'

'I shouldn't really tell you this . . . though I can't see the harm as everybody knows. Her husband is a doctor. He's very popular, shall we say, especially with his female patients.'

'So, she takes out all her anger and frustration on you?'

'Well, yes, I suppose . . . only I've never looked at it that way before.'

Angel sat back in his chair and reflected for a moment, tapping his chin with a finger. 'How would you like to make some money?' he said after a minute. 'You can't earn much polishing shoes.'

'What do you have in mind?' Tiny sounded wary.

'There's a film I've been longing to make and you would be perfect in the leading male role.'

'Me? Star in a film? But I've never acted before.'

'You won't need to act. I want you to be yourself.' Angel got up, walked across the room and drew the curtains closed, then he stood behind Tiny's chair.

'There are some men who would pay a great deal of money to watch that bossy lawyer tormenting you as she did this evening. In fact, they'd have wanted her to go even further. They'd have liked it if she'd ordered you to get down on your knees and lick those expensive Prada heels of hers. Or if she'd flicked her cigarette ash

129

onto the carpet and made you clean up every flake with your tongue while she rested her foot on your head. There's really no limit to their craving to see snivelling wretches like you being abused by mature and sophisticated ladies. How delightful if she'd told you to remove her shoes and suck her warm executive toes through her dark stockings. And perhaps she could have finished off by slipping on her shoes again – shoes that I'll bet cost more than you earn in a month – and trampling on your worthless body as if you were the ground beneath her feet.'

Tiny wriggled in his chair as Angel spoke and his face became ruddy with embarrassment. 'Stop!' he cried at last. 'This is disgusting. I'd never dream of being in such a film. It's pornography you're talking about.'

'I could pay you handsomely.' Angel opened his wallet, pulled out a wad of notes and waved it in front of Tiny's face. 'C'mon, every man can be bought.'

'The answer's no and it doesn't matter how much money you shake at me.'

Angel dropped the notes in Tiny's lap and the small man stared down at them as if they would burn through to his flesh.

'I am giving you these precisely because you turned down my insulting offer. So, you really do have some dignity, despite your degraded position in this town. But tell me, how did you end up as the manager's lackey?'

'It's a long story,' said Tiny, relieved the topic of conversation had changed. 'I used to work out on the big dairy farm.'

'Wait a minute.' Angel came around to the front of the chair. 'Didn't the student Jungwaert grow up on the dairy farm?'

'You've heard about Jungwaert? Oh what a terrible tragedy. We all miss him.'

'You knew him, then?'

'I knew him very well. I often ran errands for him. The last time I saw him he gave me a letter to deliver.

He said it was too important to trust to the postal service and promised me one of his shirts for my trouble.'

'And was Miss Freya Hansen pleased to receive the letter?'

Tiny jumped in surprise. 'I didn't say the letter was for Miss Hansen.'

'But you won't deny that it was?'

'Yes, it was for Miss Hansen.'

'And she told you not to mention the letter to anyone?'

'Yes. Yes, she did. But how do you know all this?'

Angel appeared agitated. 'Tell me something: is Miss Hansen blonde?'

'Yes, she's blonde and extremely beautiful. Her hair is very long and she usually wears it in a braid. But on special occasions she lets it down and then you think you're looking at an angel from heaven.'

As Tiny spoke, Angel muttered to himself. 'So it *is* her. Why did I ever doubt it?'

'She has amazing blue eyes,' Tiny continued. 'They're so bright they make your stomach flutter. Everybody's in love with her.'

'Do you know her well?'

'Yes ... well, not really ... I mean to say she is always very kind to me.'

'And do you think she'll be happy with her fiancé?'

'Of course, why shouldn't she be happy with him? He's handsome and very successful. It's a real-life fairy tale. He saw her dancing at a nightclub in Oslo and it was love at first sight. They were his very words, printed in our local newspaper.'

Angel nodded and there was a weak smile on his face. 'You're right, it was a silly question. She must be over the moon. I've heard speculation he might be playing in Italy next season: think of all the shopping and the fashion shows ... But tell me, have you seen Miss Hansen again since Jungwaert died?'

Tiny hesitated but the intensity of Angel's gaze compelled him to answer. 'I saw her three nights ago with her friends. They were getting out of a car in front of our local nightclub, Mysteries, and I held the door open for them. Before they went into the club, Miss Hansen gave me the bottle of water she'd been drinking. It was almost empty, but I wasn't very thirsty anyway. The top was red from her lipstick.'

'Did she say anything to you when she gave you the bottle?'

'I can't tell you. I promised.'

'Was it about Jungwaert?'

Tiny remained silent.

'Very well, I won't press you. But just one more thing before we say goodnight: when are they going to bury the young man?'

'Tomorrow at midday.'

As Angel expected, Freya Hansen was present at the burial service. She stood at the edge of the solemn gathering and, with a smile, turned to whisper to one of her girlfriends while the priest performed the burial rites. She was dressed in dark colours and wore a fetching black beret, but her fashionable outfit was not entirely appropriate for the occasion. Her skirt was very narrow with a ruffled hem that reached just below the knee and her sheer stockings gave her calves an eye-catching sheen. Her feet were displayed in black stilettos with very low sides which drew attention to her wonderfully high arches. Her make-up too was calculated to impress – her lips were scarlet and her bewitching blue eyes were framed with darkened lashes.

She glanced at Angel several times, at first with an expression of disbelief and then with a smiling curiosity. At the end of the service she came over to where he was standing, her friends flanking her like ladies in waiting.

Her hips swayed flirtatiously as she walked and Angel forced himself to turn away his eyes.

'I can't believe it's really you,' she said.

She was so close he could taste her perfume and his stomach turned a somersault. Even after all this time, he could still remember the sensation of her body pressing against his, her hot tongue darting into his mouth. Her dazzling blue eyes seemed to dance as she waited for him to speak.

'Congratulations,' he said, fighting to keep his composure. 'You must be very happy.'

She looked at him and her rosy cheeks blanched.

'On your engagement, I mean,' he added.

She brightened at once. 'Thank you. I really am very lucky.'

They spoke a while longer as people drifted out of the cemetery and then her friends dragged her away. As she went she turned her head and said: 'There's a party tomorrow at the club. Why don't you come?'

He watched her walking until she disappeared through the gates. She was even more lovely than she had been in Paris almost four years ago – and she remembered him too, even wanted to see him again. Oh, but what a fool he was being! Playing the moth to her scintillating light and asking to be burned again.

As he left the cemetery deep in thought, he was surprised to see again the woman he had insulted in the hotel lounge the previous evening. She was standing by his car and examining it closely, but she quickly walked away without saying a word when he approached.

Was there ever any doubt that he would turn up at Mysteries? He even arrived before Freya and witnessed her show-stopping entrance. Her hair was down, flowing over her bare shoulders like a heavenly light, and her strapless red dress moulded itself to the contours of her body. A naked leg was proudly displayed through a high slit in the side as she walked. She greeted him briefly and then all but ignored him for the next hour while she went out onto the dance floor. Angel watched her every movement with longing and at the same time he felt a creeping terror.

Not until they found themselves sitting in company at one of the tables did she speak to him again. 'I remember,' she said tipsily, 'how you always used to talk about men worshipping their girlfriends.'

'And I still talk about it,' he said. 'A man will never realise his true self until he has learned to utterly adore his partner.' He had drunk only water and his tone was very serious. Some of the girls giggled.

'That's so old-fashioned,' objected a young man. 'This is the twenty-first century. The sexes are equal now.'

'Of course, she must prove worthy of being worshipped. She has to present herself as a goddess.' Angel glanced across at Freya who was listening with a thoughtful expression on her face.

'And just how should a woman make herself into a goddess?' one of the girls asked.

Angel blushed at the attention he was getting. 'This is all very personal. My ideas are . . . well, rather odd. I'm probably boring you. Dancing is much more fun.'

'Not at all,' she said.

'We want to hear your odd ideas,' the young man chimed in.

'Very well.' Angel straightened his lapels. 'To begin with she must . . . Actually, it would be much easier if I simply told you a story I once read.' And, with the eyes of the whole table upon him, he began.

'This particular young woman was a student at a college in California and one of the jocks – that's what they call the athletes over there – invited her out on a date. After taking her to see a film and then for a meal, he parked his car outside her dorm block, turned off the engine and leant towards her. He was ready for his

134

reward; after all, he'd spend $107 on her. He was optimistic about his chances. She'd dressed rather promisingly in a short white skirt and a revealing tank top. She'd even painted her toenails and was showing them off in thong sandals. (He had been glancing at those feet all evening long and it had not escaped her notice.) In short, his sexy date seemed ripe for the taking, but when he placed a hand on her thigh she pushed it away. Not in panic like a frightened virgin, please note, nor in that affected half-hearted way that is the prelude to seduction, but firmly and looking right into his eyes as she did so with a mature feminine confidence that belied her years.

'"You haven't earned the privilege to touch my legs," she said. He fell back in his seat, confused. It was her calmness and total self-assurance that had floored him.

'"What do I need to do to earn that privilege?" he said after a moment.

'"You can start by getting out of the car and opening the door for me."

'He did so, and even offered her his hand, watching as she swung out her long legs and lowered her feet to the ground. The men at this table will know the condition he was in as he walked with her to the entrance of the dorm block.

'When they reached the door, she thanked him for a pleasant evening and held out her hand to him. "You may kiss my fingers once," she said. He stared at her hand, seeming to wrestle with something in himself, and then, overcome with a passion he had never felt before, he raised her slender white fingers to his lips and planted a deep kiss on them.

'"When can I see you again?" he asked.

'"You can call me." And she went inside the dorm building, letting the door swing closed behind her.

'It was a whole month before she went out on another date with him, although he called her almost

135

every day and left messages when she did not answer. He took her to a Lakers game and then to a downtown nightclub. She was superb company and charmed everybody she met. Once again he found himself staring at her feet at every opportunity. During the basketball game his eyes spent more time on her flexing toes and dangling sandals than on the star players out on the court.

'He drove her back to her dorm and without being prompted he got out of the car and opened her door. They walked across the car park in silence, her perfume in his nostrils, the sound of her clicking heels in his ears. His heart was pounding with anticipation and he could hardly swallow.

'"You behaved like a gentleman this evening," she said when they reached the door of the lighted lobby. "You deserve a reward."

'He looked at her with the eyes of a hopeful dog.

'"You may kiss my toes."

'There they were, down on the ground in front of him, displayed in pretty sandals – long, pale and perfectly formed, the nails painted a brilliant red. He felt dizzy as he looked at them, afraid that if he gave in to his desire there would be no going back.

'"Well," she said, "I'm waiting."

'Slowly, he got down on his hands and knees, lowered his head and touched his trembling lips to her unmoving toes. There must have been something quite magical about that scene in the white light of the porch. Can you picture it? A 220-pound college running back bowed down before a slender girl in a pleated miniskirt.

'"Enough," she said, sliding away her foot.

'Still on his knees, he looked up at her. His face was contorted with desire. "Please," he groaned, "you're driving me mad. I can't take any more."

'She touched her foot lightly between his thighs. "Yes, you can," she smiled and blew him a kiss goodnight.

136

'And so it continued,' said Angel, emerging from the trance he'd fallen into while relating the story. 'He lavished her with gifts and attention and she granted him tiny privileges: her toes, her ankles, her calves and sometimes even her lips. In time she allowed him to help her dress for their dates. She would sit on the edge of the bed while he pulled her stockings over her legs or stand with her back to him while he fastened up her skirt. They dated for three years and only on their wedding night did she finally go to bed with him. But by then he had been so well trained that for him the whole purpose of lovemaking was to give pleasure to his goddess.' Angel hesitated a moment. 'Since I'm in mixed company I won't describe all the ways she taught him to please her. But you can be sure she is one of the happiest young women in America and doing exceedingly well in her career as a contract lawyer.'

'I don't believe a word of it,' shouted one of the men. 'You made the whole story up.' The girls were giggling, Freya too. She tossed her lovely hair and spoke, trying to keep a straight face.

'I completely disagree with you. A woman doesn't want a slave for a husband. She wants a man she can look up to and admire, a man who is strong and masculine.'

'Yes, that's what women have learnt to tell themselves,' said Angel calmly. 'But look how unhappy most of them are when they finally catch their square-jawed hero.'

'She's right,' her girlfriend piped in. 'We girls would much rather have a man like Freya's fiancé than a wimp who kisses our feet.'

'And I quite understand why you feel that way. I've watched him play. He's such a commanding presence on the field. A born leader with sturdy dependable thighs. In former times he'd have been a warrior king leading his men into battle. He doesn't doubt himself for a second and his attention to the game is awe inspiring. For ninety minutes he's single-mindedly obsessed with putting the ball in the back of the net. Such thrusting dedication! And what incredible stamina! When he bounds off the pitch at the end of play he looks just as spunky as when he started the game.'

Freya's eyes dropped and she pressed her knees together. But after a moment she was laughing again. 'Come on,' she said to her girlfriends, 'I've had enough talking, let's go and dance.'

Angel was left alone again and wandered around the club. He considered leaving but he couldn't tear himself away from Freya. She was out on the dance floor, visible through all the other bodies like a red beacon. He watched the snake-like movements of her raised arms, the flowing sway of her hips, and his thoughts went back to Paris, to her bedroom, to her eighteen-year-old thighs shyly parted on the bed.

At the end of the night, she came to him. 'Can you drive me home?' she asked. 'Our driver's got herself drunk and I hate taxis.' She looked at him with her wide, appealing eyes and Angel felt he had a glimpse of his future. He shuddered. At the end of it all there was only desolation and her tormenting smile. She squeezed his cheek fondly. 'I know I can trust you.'

'Why did you change your name?' he asked her when they were in the car.

'Anita is my middle name, but I liked it better than Freya in those days.'

They drove out of the town and up the steep road to her family's farm, where she was staying for the summer. She sat in the seat with her legs crossed, one silky thigh emerging from the split in the dress. She was singing the words of a song she'd been dancing to in the club. Angel forced himself to stare at the road ahead.

'If I'd had sex with you that first night it would have been different, wouldn't it?' he said.

'Maybe.'

'When I just kissed you down there, it lowered your opinion of me, didn't it?'

'I don't know. It's all so long ago. I was only eighteen. I wasn't ready for anything serious.'

'I was in love with you.'

For a while she said nothing and then patted his thigh. 'You're a nice guy. I didn't mean to hurt you. But that's just the way I am.'

They were driving through the woods and for a while the darkness outside was intense, even on this summer night.

'Didn't they find Jungwaert's body somewhere around here?' he asked.

'What did you bring that up for?' she snapped. 'You really know how to spoil a mood.'

'They say he was in love with you.'

'And don't they also say he killed himself because of me . . . with a knife from my house? Can we change the subject please?'

Her mobile began to ring. She took it out of her bag and a second later she was chatting with her friend about the club. While she spoke, she partly slipped off one of her red sandals and let it dangle by the straps from her toes. At one point she burst into laughter and her heavy breasts shook inside the dress. Angel was captivated by her behaviour and could barely keep his eyes on the road. They had just been discussing the death of a man who had loved her and now she was giggling with a friend about a trivial incident in the club. She apparently felt no regret that one of her admirers had taken his own life in desperation. She seemed to regard his suicide as a natural phenomenon, an unfortunate but inevitable consequence of her radiant presence in the world.

They had already reached her house when she finished the conversation and she put her phone in her handbag as he parked the car at the gate. They sat in silence and Angel was gripped by a sudden dread that he might never see her again after tonight.

'Aren't you going to open the door for me?' she asked cheekily.

He got out and walked around to the passenger side. Whether she was just tipsy or did it on purpose he could not tell, but she seemed to stumble as she climbed out and her warm body pressed against him for a second. She went to the gate and turned around. She leant back against it, resting her hands either side of her on top of the wooden frame. She shook her long hair and tilted her head, smiling.

'What made you tell everyone that story? It was the silliest thing I ever heard. We kept laughing about it all night.'

Angel shrugged. 'I get carried away sometimes. I'm sorry.'

'Don't apologise.' A warmth had crept into her voice. 'I like men who get carried away. You know, that's why my fiancé scores so many goals: he never holds himself back.' She fixed him with her blue eyes which sparkled in the moonlight and then threw back her head, laughing. 'But kissing feet – yuck! Who would do such a nasty thing?'

Involuntarily, Angel stared down at her feet. They were planted on the ground in front of her, proudly arched in the red high-heeled sandals. She was aware of the attention he gave them.

'Suppose I said you can kiss my feet as a reward for driving me home, would you do it?'

He swallowed heavily and watched as she flexed both sets of toes.

'Well, would you?' she repeated. 'And by the way, they can't be very clean. I took off my shoes while I was

140

dancing, so the soles will be black. But maybe the toes won't be too disgusting.'

Her words cast a spell on him. He could see himself lying down before her on the stony ground, covering her feet with worshipful kisses and licking around the edges of her soles, hungry for her dirt.

She lifted a foot off the ground and flexed her ankle, drawing a hypnotic circle with her toes. 'I've never felt a man's lips on my feet before. I'm sure it would tickle. I'd probably start laughing and kick him away.' An expression of earnest excitement appeared on her face. 'You've got to promise not to tickle me.'

'I promise,' he said hoarsely.

'And don't use your tongue.'

He could only grunt.

'And don't you dare try to lick my soles. They're so sensitive. The dog always licks them while I'm lying on the couch. It makes me scream.'

She glanced down at the ground. 'But it's so dirty down there and it looks wet too. You'll ruin your trousers.'

'I don't care,' he said, fearing she was about to change her mind. He stepped forward and went down on his knees before her. The ground was hard and cold and the sharp stones dug through his trousers into his skin.

'Oh no,' she said, moving away. 'This is not right. I'm engaged. I can't let another man kiss my feet.'

Still on his knees, Angel closed his eyes in despair. His whole body was trembling. I'm granted less favours than her pet dog, he thought.

'I just meant it as a joke,' she was saying. 'How did I know you'd really do it? I didn't think anyone would actually get down on their knees to kiss my dirty feet.'

Angel got up and brushed the dirt from his pants. 'But now you know that I would, does it mean anything to you?'

'You frighten me,' she said and turned her back to him.

141

'I frighten you yet I'm prepared to obey your every command.'

'Maybe that's why I'm afraid.'

'Why should my desire to obey you make you afraid?'

She turned around. Her eyes had a strange gleam in them. 'You really don't understand women, do you?'

It was not the first time a girl had said that to him. He felt lonely and outcast, as if there was a secret world of women and their bodies that would be forever closed to him.

Freya shivered and rubbed her bare arms. 'I'm getting cold standing here so I'm going to kiss you good night. It's just a friendly kiss though, so you mustn't grab me or try to kiss me back. Promise?'

'Anything you say.'

She came forward and pressed her wet lips against his cheek, giving him another draft of her unique scent. One of her thighs rubbed his knuckles which he held tensed at his side. 'Good night,' she whispered, her hot breath pouring into his ear. Then she turned around and went through the gate and up the drive to the house without once looking back.

Well, Freya, he thought. It's starting all over again: you sending me home at the end of the night with my cock hard and my balls aching for you. And there is that same glimmer in your eyes which says you will sleep very pleasantly tonight in the full knowledge that you are slowly driving a man insane.

The whole of the next day Angel stayed in his room. The only person he saw was the chambermaid, who brought up his dinner.

'What's your name?' he asked from his bed.

'Maria, sir.'

'That's a beautiful name. And please, don't call me sir.' She can't compare to Freya, he mused as he

142

appraised her figure. But she is handsome and has a healthy glow about her cheeks.

'Do you have a boyfriend?'

She blushed and shook her head.

'I don't believe you,' he said with a smile. 'You're too good looking not to have a secret sweetheart.'

'I haven't got time for one. I'm too busy working.'

He picked up his wallet from the night table. 'Here,' he said, offering her a bundle of notes. 'You've been very good to me.'

'I can't accept a tip like that. It's far too much.'

He scrutinised her legs. 'Are those stockings you're wearing?'

'Of course not, they're tights.' His serious face made her smile.

'Sell them to me.'

She was astonished. 'You want to buy my tights!'

'I'll give you a thousand kroner for them.'

'But what on earth do you want my tights for?'

'Does it matter? I'm offering you ten times what they're worth.'

'Why not go to the shops and buy yourself a new pair?'

'You don't understand. I'm not interested in unworn tights.'

'You want me to take them off right here and give them to you?'

'Yes, I won't look. You can even go into the bathroom and slip them off if you're shy.'

She glanced down at her sturdy legs. 'Oh, but it's such a strange thing you're asking me to do.'

'Two thousand kroner,' he said, pulling more notes out of his wallet.

'It's not the money. It's just –'

'Well, at least consider, that's all I ask of you. When you're undressing yourself tonight think about my offer. They would be such a small thing for you to part with. But they would make me very happy indeed.'

The maid left the room looking rather confused but there was no indication she had felt affronted by his request. He laid his head down on the pillow and congratulated himself. She's used to getting her bum pinched but she's never had a request like that before, I'll bet. It's completely thrown her. Now we'll wait and see. But what a charming girl she is! Fresh, wholesome and with such strong principles, despite being so poor that she wears the same flat black working shoes every day.

During the next few days Angel was busy with private affairs and even drove to a neighbouring town and did not return until the evening. On his way into the hotel he met Tiny, who was standing proudly in the lobby wearing a smart new jacket.

'It came this morning,' he said. 'It's a perfect fit. I ran straight to the magistrate's office to thank her but she refused to see me.'

'I'd advise you to say nothing to the lady about this jacket,' Angel said rather sternly. 'By the way, has she caused you any more trouble?'

'None at all.'

Angel nodded and an idea seemed to occur to him. He invited Tiny up to his room and, after making small talk and persuading him to drink a shot of whisky, he said:

'I want your opinion of the chambermaid, Maria.'

'She's a very good girl. Hard working and extremely reliable.'

'And pretty too. Not to mention her ass. It's so round and firm you just want to get down behind her and bury your face in it.'

'Please, don't talk about Maria like that,' objected Tiny. 'It's disrespectful.'

'Don't pretend you've never been tempted. The service lift is very narrow. It must be hard for you not to rub up against her ample bottom when you're

144

squashed in there together. Very *hard* indeed!' He sniggered.

'Don't you make fun of me as well!' Tiny moaned. 'Everyone knows that since my accident with the bull I'm no good for that kind of thing.'

'There's more than one way to please a woman.'

Tiny stared down at the carpet and his fleshy lips quivered.

They talked on until midnight, Angel refilling his own glass numerous times. Even Tiny allowed himself a second shot and at one point he said: 'How strange, but listening to you I can't help being reminded of Jungwaert.'

'Why is that?'

'He used to talk about love all the time just like you do. They even say he was writing a novel on the subject.'

'Ah,' said Angel. 'But if I were to kill myself I certainly wouldn't leave behind a crummy line of verse for the world to remember me by.' He laughed callously. 'How did it go again? "If only your blade –"'

'Why are you talking about killing yourself?' Tiny asked in consternation.

'I've a feeling my death might soon be necessary.'

'But why, in God's name?'

'A beautiful woman may demand such a sacrifice from me.'

'What kind of women would ask a man to kill himself?'

'Miss Hansen is one that I could name. She's an addictive tease and the most shameless flirt I've ever met. What man can resist doing whatever she asks of him? She has already made one of her admirers sacrifice himself upon the altar of her beauty and I'm sure it would flatter her if others were to do the same – myself included. It must be a heady sensation to go to your death with her final rejection ringing in your ears and the image of her bewitching blue eyes guiding you

145

through the darkness. And while you make that heavy journey, she'll be lying between silk sheets somewhere enjoying the rigid attention of her fiancé, who never grows tired or lets his mind wander from the goal. Why should I deny myself such a rich experience? It is perhaps the only real pleasure left to me . . . "He whose eyes behold beauty is already in death's cold grip."' Rather dramatically, he turned in his chair towards the night table, on top of which stood a small glass vial filled with a colourless liquid. 'And when she gives the sign, I know what I must do.'

It was on Saturday that Angel saw Freya again. She had sent an invitation to the hotel inviting him to a party at the house of one of her friends, and although he had torn it up, swearing he wouldn't attend, he found himself amongst the many guests.

She was wearing a short denim skirt and eye-catching high-heeled sandals in a metallic-blue snakeskin print. The spaghetti straps were wrapped around her feet and ankles, creating a crisscross pattern on her creamy skin.

'They asked me to invite you,' she said, coming towards him with a bright smile. 'You were quite a hit with your performance at Mysteries. They think you're a comedian.'

'I'm afraid I won't be telling any stories tonight,' he said, allowing her to lead him by the hand over to her friends. 'I really don't feel up to it.' He did look tired. His eyes were ringed and there was a hollowness about his cheeks.

'But you must,' she said. 'I told them you would.'

And so, for her sake, Angel entertained a small crowd with one of his fantastic stories. When he'd finished, he excused himself and went out into the garden, saying he wanted some fresh air. Freya came out too and stood beside him.

'You see, you can be a superman when you try.' She put a hand on his shoulder. 'And I've heard something else about you.'

His body went tense.

'About how you defended Tiny from that sad old cow who was making fun of him. Didn't you threaten to spank her bottom? That's so funny. I wish I'd been there to see her face.'

'Perhaps I went too far. Besides, Tiny should really stop pretending he's such a victim.'

'What do you mean?'

'I've seen the way he stares at a certain woman. Given half the chance –'

'Oh stop that! He may look a bit creepy, but he's really a little sweetie. He'd do absolutely anything for me.'

'Of course he would. He worships you like everybody else. But if you weren't so beautiful and popular he might reveal a very different side of himself to you.'

They wandered further into the garden and the music from the house became faint. 'I won't deny that I behaved like a bitch back then,' she said as they approached a wooden arbour overgrown with roses and vines. 'I was young. I was still learning about men. I wanted to see how far I could push you and you did nothing to stop me. You let me walk all over you.'

'I used to dream about that.'

'About what?'

'Lying down on the ground while you trampled all over me in your high heels.'

Her perfectly arched eyebrows rose in astonishment and she gave a short nervous laugh. 'You really *are* mad.'

'I just say what's on my mind. But I can assure you that I'm not the only man who's longed to feel your sharp heels digging into his back or the bottom of your sole pressing his face down into the dirt. Do you have any idea what dark cravings a girl as tall and beautiful as you stirs in us poor creatures when you strut about in the type of shoes you're wearing tonight?' They were walking under the arbour and both of them became aware of the sound of her high heels striking the stone path.

'Get down on the ground, then,' she said when they came out at the other side. 'If it really means that much to you, then I'll trample on you.'

He stopped dead and gave an anguished sigh. 'Are you playing with me again, Freya?'

'No, I mean it. What harm can it do? Besides, it might be fun to feel a man under my feet – even if it is only you.'

He needed no further prompting and got down on the ground in front of her. He lay on his back, gazing up in rapture at her towering form.

She giggled and pulled the hem of her denim skirt tight against her thighs. 'I hope this isn't just a trick to get a look at my panties.' She lifted a foot and placed it on his chest. She hardly put any weight on it but he felt the point of her slender heel pressing against a rib.

'What does it feel like?' She was looking down at him, holding her hair away from her eyes. She pressed a little harder. 'Tell me if it hurts.'

He squirmed slightly as her heel dug deeper into his ribs but he did not utter a sound. His eyes were fixed on her sandal-clad foot which stood proudly on his chest. Her naturally high arch was accentuated by the slope of the sandal and the smooth, tight skin revealed the foot's delicate bone structure and tantalising traces of veins. The toes were strong and even and emerged from two crossed straps. The perfect nails were painted a sweet candyfloss pink.

'Are you sure you can take me standing on you?' she said, putting more of her weight onto him and watching the muscles in his face contort.

'Yes ... No, wait.' He grunted in pain. 'Stand on my back.'

She lifted her foot from his chest and he quickly rolled over onto his front. 'Are you sure?'

'Please do it.'

She put one foot on his back but didn't trust her balance. 'I don't want to fall off and twist my ankle. Come on, crawl over to that tree so I've got something to hold onto.' He followed at her heels and dropped down on his belly in the spot she indicated.

A moment later he felt her stepping on top of him. One heel stabbed him between the shoulders and the other prodded the sensitive muscle above his kidneys as she tried to get her balance. He was completely pinned beneath her feet and, just as he'd imagined, the pain was exquisite.

'I'm not too heavy, am I?'

'No,' he groaned.

'That's the right answer,' she joked. 'If you'd said I was heavy, I'd have really made you suffer.' Steadying herself against the tree with one hand, she tried to walk in a straight line along his spine. She swayed from side to side, her ankles wobbled and she had to dig her heels deep into his flesh to stop herself from slipping. 'This is kind of fun actually. I could get used to walking on men. It must be great for toning the calf muscles.'

He bit the grass in agony, yet he would not tell her to stop and made no sound as she walked up and down his prostrate body. She soon perfected her balance and was confident enough to plant one of her feet on the back of his head and push down.

'So there you are, Mr Angel. I'm pressing your face into the dirt. Has your dream come true now?' But before he could answer, her phone, which was in her skirt pocket, began to ring. Still standing with her foot on his head, she checked the identity of the caller.

She quickly stepped off him.

He knew at once it was her fiancé by the excitement in her voice. But she did not walk away to take the call in private; instead, she stepped slowly around his motionless body while she spoke and paused beside his face, giving him a close-up view of her tall blue heels rising from the grass. Her sharply arched feet filled his field of vision and their dominating presence was so overwhelming that he could barely follow the words she was saying into the phone high above him. Her voice was bright and joyful and sometimes she laughed, or whispered almost coyly. For a time, she absently twisted a heel in the grass and then turned around and rested her foot on top of his head while she continued to talk. He lay absolutely still, his cock rigid beneath him and responding to the slightest movement of her foot on his skull.

'He scored the winning goal again,' she said when she hung up. 'The funny thing is, I've never really liked football and I still don't understand all the rules.'

He lifted his face from the grass and watched her begin to walk away.

'I think you've been trampled enough for one evening,' she called back.

Slowly, he pulled himself up until he was resting on his knees. 'Thank you,' he said in genuine gratitude. 'You have no idea how much that meant to me.'

'My God!' She had turned around and was staring at his crotch. 'You've got an erection.'

He smiled meekly and she came closer with a look of wonder in her eyes.

'Show it to me,' she demanded.

'Out here?'

'I want to see it.'

Obediently, he unzipped his fly and freed his engorged cock.

'Gosh. Does it always get that big?'

'Not often.'

'So it's all because of me?'

'Yes, Freya.'

'How long would it take you to finish yourself off?'

His cock quivered, as if it had a mind of its own. 'It would be over before you could count to ten.'

She walked to where he was kneeling. 'Go on,' she said, 'but be quick.' And she began to count. Her feet were planted just in front of him and, gazing down at the slender ankles and painted toes, he stroked his cock. His trapped balls throbbed with a stabbing urgency inside his pants, making him bite his bottom lip.

When she had counted to four she lifted her foot towards the dribbling purple head. 'This is what got you all worked up, isn't it?'

He grunted in acknowledgment.

She laughed and resumed counting, pronouncing each number with a teasing slowness.

'Spit on me,' he begged, slowing his rhythm, trying to delay the approaching climax.

She shook her head saucily and briefly touched the tip of her shoe to his swollen glans. He shuddered and gritted his teeth. He was ready to surrender himself to her.

'Oooh, see if you can hit my foot,' she giggled. Hands on hips and perfectly balanced on one high-heeled sandal, she held her toes a few inches from his cock, ready to accept her tribute. She continued counting but got only as far as eight when he suddenly moaned her name. His hips jerked in a spasm of fierce pleasure.

She jumped back but his warm come splashed over her toes. 'What are you doing?' she screamed. For a second her face became ugly with revulsion.

He stared up at her dumbly, his shoulders twitching as his orgasm subsided.

'You said you would wait until I counted to ten. I was going to pull my foot away before you did it.' She looked down at her foot, pivoting it back on the long heel so her defiled toes were raised. His come oozed over the shiny pink nails and dribbled between the toes. 'Oh my God, I can't believe you really did it.' She bent down, picked up a fallen leaf and wiped her foot furiously. 'Look at you, still holding your prick and staring at me! You idiot! You know I've got a fiancé. You know I'm getting married soon.'

He attempted to zip away his cock, which was still hard, and at the same time he staggered to his feet.

'No! Don't you touch me. I'll scream. I mean it.' She threw the leaf on the grass in disgust and picked up another.

'What? I don't understand,' he stammered.

'Oh, be quiet!'

'But I love you.'

'How can you say that to me after what you've just done?'

She stood up and walked quickly back to the house, where she behaved as if nothing had happened. Angel waited ten minutes before following and soon after that he left the party.

The next morning Angel was informed by a grave-looking hotel manager that Maria the chambermaid had resigned from her job for personal reasons. Angel was racked by guilt, but later the same day he received a note from Maria explaining that her resignation had nothing to do with him – in fact, although she thought he was a bit eccentric, she had become quite fond of him.

It took him two days to track her down to the small room where she was staying. He found her in a forlorn state and with little means of support, but she would not take the money he offered her.

'Then do me the honour of being my guest at the Hollywood Ball at Mysteries.'

'I don't have an outfit,' she said, her eyes moistening.

'Then you have no choice but to let me dress you for the occasion.'

The white gown that arrived for her on the day of the ball was a perfect fit. The silky fabric moulded itself to her broad hips and round womanly ass, and the elegant silver court shoes that accompanied it added three inches to her height. Angel called for her wearing a double-breasted suit, narrow tie and fedora.

'You could be a film star,' she said.

She clutched his arm proudly as they walked into Mysteries. It was her first time ever at the club and she was overjoyed when a waiter served her champagne from a silver tray.

But of course Freya stole the show. In her black velvet dress, spider-web robe and elbow-high gloves, she was the very essence of seductive glamour. And with the added effect of her coiffed blonde hair, flawless white skin and fine features many had the sensation that a 1940s screen goddess was in their midst. Surrounded by a throng of admirers, she occasionally turned her bold blue eyes towards Angel. He resisted approaching her, but when a photographer from the local paper asked them to pose together because their outfits made a perfect match, she whispered in his ear as he stood at her side:

'Are you trying to make me jealous by bringing that chambermaid to the ball?'

Angel stared ahead at the camera lens, his lips forced into a smile.

'If only the poor girl knew what you were really like.'

When the pictures were taken, he looked into her gorgeous face. 'Freya, I'm devoted to you and always will be. Please don't deny me this one small chance of happiness.' She turned her head contemptuously and strutted away on her vintage stiletto heels.

Angel returned to Maria with a sense of foreboding, but the young woman soon raised his spirits. She was enjoying herself enormously and he began to believe that a new life was possible for him. They went out onto the dance floor and he put his hands on her steady hips.

'I'm not a rich man,' he said. 'The little money I acquired will soon be gone. But I'm young and I'm strong and I'm willing to work.' He felt her body pressing against his own. 'I would worship you always, I promise.'

She put a finger over his lips. 'I know you would. But I really don't deserve such a husband. I need time to think.'

'Is there another man?' he asked solemnly.

'Nobody.'

The ball finished in the early hours of the morning and he drove her back to her lodgings. He kissed her and she responded hungrily before pulling away. Her cheeks were flushed and her dark eyes shone.

'I would invite you in, but my landlord –'

'I understand. I'll call for you tomorrow.'

'I'll be waiting.' They kissed again and she squeezed his hand tightly before slipping through the front door.

But he did not return to the hotel. Instead, he drove out to Freya's house and sat in the car staring at her window as he had on so many other nights. He whispered her name to himself, as if trying to invoke her, and pulled out his spurned cock and gave her the contents of his balls one last time. It was morning when he finally got back to his room.

He woke up in the middle of the afternoon and immediately drove to Maria's lodgings, his mind dancing with plans for the future. But she was not at home. He called several more times that day without success and slept fitfully, prey to the darkest fears. The next morning he visited her lodgings again and once more he was disappointed. Finally, he persuaded the landlord to open the door to her room and when he looked inside he discovered that her few belongings had gone.

He walked away devastated. The day was very fine yet everything he looked at – the buildings, the cars, the people – seemed edged with blackness. He wandered about aimlessly and at length emerged in the main street. With no thought to where he was going, he headed along it.

Thirty yards in front of him Freya came out of a shop. She was alone but had her phone pressed to her ear and did not notice him. She walked on slowly, her long golden braid shaking behind her when she laughed. Angel followed, reducing his pace so as not to get too close. She was wearing a pair of tight faded jeans and the lazy sway of her hips was quite hypnotic. Perhaps she is speaking to Maria right now, he thought, and they are laughing at my failure. There was no doubt in his mind that Freya had carried out her silent threat and turned the other girl against him. And she had done it solely out of pride and vanity. She was determined that she would be his only idol, the unobtainable goddess of his dreams.

She sauntered rather than walked, taking firm yet unhurried steps in her sharp-heeled boots and following a meandering path along the pavement, as if time itself would wait for her. He was close enough to hear the excitement in her voice as she spoke into her phone.

Suddenly she stopped and glanced behind her. He ducked into a shop doorway and, after a few moments, he heard the steady clack-clack of her boots as she retraced her steps. He stood with his back to the street, looking into the newsagent's, both hoping and fearing that she would confront him. She strolled past him without showing any sign of recognition and went into a shop a few doors further along. She must have noticed me, he thought. Was she determined to toy with him again? Make him the one to approach her so she could rebuff him in public? He had the chance to walk away, but an inner need for her, even for her scorn, compelled him to wait. He picked up a newspaper from the stand. There, on the front page, was a picture of her fiancé. In fact, his face was staring from the front page of all the papers on the stand. He had just signed a contract and would be playing in Milan next season.

Freya came out of the shop and once more walked straight past him as if he were invisible. Her sporty ass rolled teasingly in the fashionably ripped denim, leaving him in no doubt she knew she was being watched. He put down the paper and followed, loving her for all the studied indifference she displayed. She had bought an ice lolly and licked it as she walked. She was half-turned, looking in the windows she passed, and he watched her slip the plump shaft of ice between her lips. Sucking it slowly, she listened to her phone and spoke occasionally. She ambled at such a leisurely pace that he was forced to keep stopping or he would have quickly caught up with her. At any time she could have turned her head around an extra few inches and spotted him, but she never did. It seemed that her sole intention was to make him obedient to her languorous and sexy gait.

When she got to where her car was parked at the end of the street, she took a last lick of her ice lolly and tossed the stick into a bin. As she did this she glanced back towards Angel. He froze, but her eyes seemed to focus on something beyond him and she turned her head again. Walking on towards the car, she dipped into her shoulder bag, brought out a tissue and dabbed it against her lips. Angel saw the tissue sail to the ground behind her. Had she dropped it deliberately or had it fallen as she'd tried to put it back into the bag? It lay on the pavement behind her shiny black boot heels as she opened the car door.

She did not drive away at once but checked her face in the mirror and touched up her lips. Was she still teasing him? Forcing him to wait before he could retrieve even the crumb she had left in the street? He suddenly feared that a gust of wind would blow in from the sea and carry away the flimsy tissue made forever precious by her lips. She denied him everything: herself, Maria and now this scrap too.

But he was wrong. She put away her lipstick, started the engine and drove smoothly away. As the car disappeared around the corner, he was already stooping to pick up his creased white prize. He put it under his nose and breathed in. It was lightly scented from being inside her bag and reminded him of the intimate smell of her skin. Carefully, afraid of damaging it in any way, he opened it out. In the centre he saw the faint impression of her red lips.

So this was all he would ever get from her? Her final No. For Jungwaert, a blunt knife; for him, a remnant of her heartless smile. He returned to his car and drove out to the woods almost in a dream. Carrying the tissue and staring at the grinning lipstick, he proceeded along a path through the trees. His mind was a squall of recent and distant memories and he cried out in dread as he had a sudden vision of the young student staggering ahead of him. When Jungwaert tore open his veins that evening, what had Freya been doing? Lounging in front of the television, the dog's big tongue licking her feet? Dancing at Mysteries in her latest outfit before a crowd of drooling admirers? It occurred to him that she might be pissing at the very moment he himself laid down his life for her. But instead of revolting him, the image of her sitting nonchalantly upon the toilet seat, panties rolled around her ankles, her golden braid hanging down over one shoulder, only spurred him on.

He sat down against the trunk of a tree, took the glass vial from his pocket and drank the contents in a single gulp. As soon as he had done so, an awful feeling of regret swept through him. While he was alive, surely there had still been hope for him? He lay on the ground and thought despairingly of Freya. She would live on, beautiful and free, enjoying all the sensuous pleasures of the world, long after he had faded from her memory.

After an hour passed, he knew he would not die. Slowly, he reached for the bottle and sniffed it. There was no smell. He closed his eyes, feeling not relief but a cold sense of resignation. He had failed again. There would be no escape for him now. And it was as if he could hear Freya's triumphant laughter ringing from the tops of the pine trees. He would be her living victim, the memory of her beauty feeding and taunting him through all his bleak days.

When he came into the hotel much later that evening, the manager was waiting and confronted him about his unpaid bill. Wearily, Angel took out his wallet and handed him the contents.

'What's this?' the man exclaimed. 'There's only 500 kroner here and an out-of-date ferry ticket to Esbjerg.'

'Tomorrow,' said Angel, 'I will sell my car and you'll have all the money I owe you.' He took out his car keys and surrendered them to the manager. 'Your assurance that I will honour my debts to everybody in this good town.' There was such a ghostly expression on his face that the manager stood aside and let him stagger past.

As soon as he lay on his bed Angel fell into an anxious sleep. But in the middle of the night he was woken by Tiny who had come into his room and was tugging his elbow.

'You!' shrieked Angel, jumping up in the bed. 'This isn't the first time you've let yourself in here with the chambermaid's key, is it?'

Tiny was breathing heavily and he smelt of drink. He said nothing.

'So, you told Miss Hansen about our conversation and she ordered you to replace the prussic acid with water. That was my last chance, you meddler!'

158

Tiny waved his hand drunkenly. 'You'll be thanking me with kisses before the night's over.' He grabbed Angel's arm with uncharacteristic assertiveness. 'Come with me and keep quiet.'

Angel got out of bed and followed Tiny down the hall, all the way to the door of the biggest suite. The little man bent down and pressed his eye to the keyhole. When he stood up he had a lascivious grin on his face.

'Take a look,' he said.

Angel stooped and warily peered through the narrow slit. He could not believe what he saw. Lying on the bed, in clear view, were Freya and her fiancé. They were both naked and kissing one another passionately. Freya's hair was loose and fanned across the pillow.

'They always come here to fuck,' chuckled Tiny.

Angel's eye remained glued to the keyhole. The famous striker was coaxing Freya onto her back, eager to mount her. She needed little encouragement and rolled over with a playful giggle. The striker climbed between her open legs and began to jerk his narrow hips. Freya moaned loudly and wrapped her arms around his back as his thrusts became more vigorous.

Tiny was growing restless. 'I'm going in,' he announced.

Angel held him back. 'Are you out of your mind?'

'Don't you get it? They want company. That's why they leave the door unlocked.' And, to prove his point, he turned the handle and opened it.

Freya and her fiancé did not even notice them come in. The footballer was stretched out on top of her and his sculptured ass jumped up and down like a piston between her thighs which pointed outwards as if in surrender. His technique was efficient but unrefined and he reminded Angel of a daring rustic lad ravishing the parson's virgin daughter on a haystack. Freya's buttocks bounced on the mattress and her hips jumped up to meet her fiancé's thrusting cock. She was shamelessly eager for it. She tossed her head wildly and squealed in protest at what he was doing, but all the while she spurred him on with clutching fingernails and panting excitement.

'Oh yes!' she moaned over and over again. 'Oh yes, fuck me hard!'

As she reached her shrill climax, the striker growled and emptied his balls into her. He lay very still for a moment, the sweat shining on his tanned skin like varnish. Then he rolled off her and stretched out on the bed, arms folded proudly behind his head. Freya's usually pale cheeks and neck were flushed a deep pink and a long musical sigh sailed from her throat. She remained on her back, her legs still open and bent at the knees. Her sex was shaved, the lips rosy and swollen, and her fiancé's seed was oozing from the flaunted gash.

'Which one of you two is going to clean me up?' she asked. Her eyes were big and dreamy.

Tiny was at the foot of the bed in an eye blink. He stretched across the mattress and buried his face in her open crotch.

'Oooh!' she giggled. 'That nasty long tongue of yours.'

Tiny worked away, giving her deep greedy licks, cleaning up the seed which had dribbled down between her ass cheeks as well as slurping it straight from her cunt.

'Get it all out,' she said.

He attached his fleshy lips to her sex and sucked with a gluttonous passion. Angel could hear the sound of his lustful feasting from across the room. The louder Freya giggled the more disgustingly the little man ate. His head nodded between her thighs and his frenzied breathing rasped against her sticky wet crotch.

'Enough,' she said at last. She detached his mouth from her addictive sex and pushed his face down onto the sheet. 'There's a splodge of it down there for you to lick up.'

While Tiny's tongue did its assigned task, Freya looked across at Angel and gave him a teasing smile. 'Sorry, he's sucked me clean,' she said. 'But we can easily make more.' She reached across and squeezed her fiancé's cock. It responded instantly to her crafty fingers, swelling from the base and rearing up like a charmed cobra. 'He can do it as many times as I want and his balls are always full of baby-juice.' Her fiancé winked slyly at Angel, but otherwise his expression remained unchanged.

'Hey, you little monster!' she shrieked suddenly. She shoved Tiny's head away from her buttocks. 'Mind that cheeky tongue of yours. I'm sure none of his juce went up inside my arsehole!'

She climbed over Tiny's head and straddled her fiancé's waiting cock. She eased herself onto the rigid shaft until the whole nine inches had been swallowed by her greedy sex. Her tight inner lips hugged their prize and she slid up and down the smooth length, wetting it with her glossy juices and moaning whorishly.

'Come on, champion,' she coaxed, riding him with increasing abandon. She squeezed his hands against her big bouncing breasts and shook her dishevelled hair. 'Give these two little puppies another shot of your yummy spunk.'

Tiny was standing beside Angel again, running his tongue over his dripping lips. 'What a cocktail! Her sweet cunt cream and his superstar spunk. I could drink a whole bowl of it.'

Freya's fiancé lived up to his billing and delivered a second copious helping of juice. He gripped her hips fiercely and roared. His big balls heaved as his cock injected another load deep inside her prize cunt.

Tiny gasped in awe. 'What a player! He's filled her up again.'

Freya leaned forward and rewarded her fiancé with a long slobbery kiss on his lips. Then she lifted her dribbling cunt off his cock.

Tiny scampered over, tongue lolling from his mouth.

'No! Not you, you greedy little pig! You've had your supper already. It's your friend's turn. He's been waiting four years to get some more of this.'

She crawled backwards across the bed, shaking her bare buttocks at Angel. Her tight little anus, barely a wrinkle, winked as she flaunted her gaping sex. The white jelly leaked from her, falling onto the sheet in big drops. She looked over her shoulder and waved her hips in imitation of an excited bitch. Through a tousle of pale-blonde hair, she teased him with a smile.

'Come and clean my honey pot.'

'What are you waiting for?' yelled Tiny. He gave Angel a nudge. 'This is the best it ever gets.'

She had brought her ass to the foot of the bed and Angel stared at the fabulous cunt, the cunt he had once licked in the musky darkness beneath her duvet and been a slave to ever since. There it waited, oozing its draft of eternal humiliation.

'God save me from you all!' he cried out and in a voice so loud that he woke himself up.

'It's all right, Mr Angel.'

Angel opened his eyes. The lights in his room were switched on and, squinting, he could just make out four figures standing around his bed. One he recognised as the hotel manager, who was furiously waving the bill he had shown him earlier. Another was the female solicitor from the magistrate's office, clutching a file in her hand. The other two figures were unknown to him, but they were large men and dressed in white uniforms. It was one of the latter who had just spoken to him.

'It's all right, Mr Angel,' he said again. 'We've come to take you home.'

Angel threw back the sheets and tried to jump off the bed, but the two big men seized him before his feet had touched the floor.

One afternoon the following spring, Freya and Maria were strolling though Milan's famous Fashion Quadrilatero. They were discussing the gossip from home.

'Do you remember that funny man Angel?' asked Freya.

Maria nodded but said nothing.

'I wonder if he'll ever get better.'

'I doubt it. They say all he does is sit in his cell and stare at the wall.'

For a second, something resembling a smile appeared on Freya's lips. 'What a tragedy. He really was very clever.'

'Do you think so?'

'He saw through Tiny straight away. He even told me the little monster would end up in prison one day. How could he have known? It was months before you revealed all the terrible things Tiny did to you when you worked at the hotel.'

They walked on in silence, looking into the windows of the boutiques.

'I'll tell you a little secret,' said Freya. 'When I was an au pair in Paris he used to have a crush on me.'

'Who?' said Maria absently, and her eyes caught sight of an extravagant high-heeled sandal in a window. It was displayed on a white pedestal in the shape of a crouching male. She grabbed Freya's arm.

'This is the one I was talking about.'

'It's absolutely gorgeous!'

Arm in arm, the two young women stepped into the gleaming showroom.

5

Mistress of the Hunt

Acton had been working at Olympia Hall for scarcely a day when he first laid eyes on the young woman who was destined to change him in a way he could never have imagined. Mounted on a tall chestnut stallion and wearing a dark riding jacket, jodhpurs and knee-high boots, she appeared in the yard as he was sweeping the cobblestones and crossed towards the stables at a slow canter. Her golden-brown hair was tied in a girlish ponytail, a strand dangling loose at the fringe, and her cheeks were flushed pink, as if she had just come from a strenuous cross-country ride.

'Groom,' she shouted and pulled on the reins, bringing the horse to a halt before the stable doors. Acton rested on his broom and observed her. He was not usually an admirer of horsewomen and their quaint outfits, but he had to admit to feeling oddly aroused by this particular rider. She was beautiful by any man's standards: her lips were a provocative shade of crimson and curved sensually at the corners and her eyes were wide and bright. But what impressed him most was her commanding posture in the saddle. She held her shoulders square, her back perfectly straight, and her thighs, clad in the beige jodhpurs, hugged the flanks of the muscular animal in a way that projected authority.

'Groom,' she called out again in a loud and impatient voice.

164

Acton took the opportunity to speak. 'I don't think he's at home,' he joked and put on his most endearing smile. The young woman glanced across the yard, noticing him for the first time.

'Who are you?' she demanded bluntly.

'Acton's the name.' He grinned flirtatiously. 'And who, may I ask, are you?'

As he spoke, the groom appeared at the stable door. He did not look more than forty but his hair was grey and he had a pronounced stoop. He stared down at the ground like a child waiting to be chastised. Forgetting about Acton, the young woman brought her steed forward and turned its flank towards the groom so that his bowed head was level with her thigh.

'Raise your head,' she ordered. The man obeyed and gazed up at the beautiful girl in the saddle. The muscles in his face were trembling.

'I'm sorry, Miss Delia,' he stuttered. 'I'll have the boots ready for you by tomorrow.' As the last word left his mouth, the young woman reached down a gloved hand and fetched him such a slap across the face that he staggered backwards. His fingers went instinctively to his cheek, but he made no other reaction. He came forward again and lifted up his chin, ready to take another blow. Water was streaming from one eye.

'That is your final warning,' she said like a bossy head girl. Then she turned around her horse and rode swiftly out of the yard.

Acton could not believe what he had just witnessed. Leaving his broom, he rushed into the stables where he found the groom standing at a workbench examining the buckles on a harness as if nothing had happened.

'Who was that?' Acton demanded excitedly.

The groom glanced over his shoulder. 'I take it you're referring to Mistress Delia?'

'And who is Mistress Delia?'

'She,' said the groom, picking up a rag and beginning to clean one of the buckles, 'is the boss.'

'She's a bitch.'

'Watch your tongue.'

'I saw her strike you.'

'And what if you did?'

'You've got to make a complaint about her.'

'A complaint?' The groom repeated the words mockingly. 'And why would I make a complaint?' He put down his rag and turned to face Acton. Four long red finger-shaped marks stood out boldly on his swollen left cheek.

'She struck you! I saw the whole thing. Is there a mirror anywhere? Look at the mark she left on your face.'

The groom began to laugh, but it was brittle rather than mirthful laughter. 'Happen I deserved it.'

Acton stared at him incredulously. 'Are you mad?'

'You're new around here, aren't you?'

'That's got nothing to do with it.'

'What did they take you on for anyhow?'

'Kennel hand. Look –'

'Kennel hand, you say?'

'Is there something wrong with that?'

'No, nowt wrong with that at all.' But there was clearly something on the groom's mind as he turned, picked up the rag and resumed cleaning the buckle. 'Now, lad, if you don't mind, some of us have got work to do.'

More than a week passed before Acton had his next encounter with Delia. During that time she had been constantly on his mind. Her performance in front of the stables had left him feeling hostile towards her, but he could not deny her sexual appeal and the memory of her tightly clad thighs provided rich fuel for his nightly fantasies.

166

She rode up behind him on her chestnut as he was pushing a barrow of kitchen scraps across the yard for the dogs, surprising him with the suddenness of her appearance.

'Leave that and follow me,' she ordered.

Acton was prickled by her brusque manner. He was an intelligent young man and resented being spoken to like a flunky. At the very least he expected a few words of explanation when given instructions. But Delia continued on her way and it was clear that he was supposed to drop everything and trot along behind her. She was wearing a waistcoat that morning, instead of a riding jacket, and it was the tempting spectacle of her pert buttocks rising and falling in the saddle and not a desire to show obedience that finally persuaded him to put down his barrow and go after her.

She rode at a brisk pace and Acton had to run to catch up with her. He made a few attempts at conversation but she ignored them all. And so, with his eyes fastened to her lovely bouncing ass, he followed in silence, panting to keep up, as she led the way to the front of the house.

Parked in the driveway were two trucks. Their rear doors were open and a team of men was busy unloading the assorted freight and lugging away crates, trunks and other items. Propped against the side of one vehicle were several rolled-up marquee canvases, and down on the ground next to them men were sorting through a variety of poles and pegs. At the rear of the other vehicle, two men were inspecting the disassembled parts of an old-fashioned pony trap.

Delia brought her horse to a stop and Acton halted too. He stood and watched the men carrying out their various tasks, wondering why she had brought him there.

'What are you standing around for?' she said, turning in her saddle and glancing down at him. 'Get to work.'

This was more than Acton could stomach. He decided it was time the arrogant young horsewoman learnt some manners. He would not let her treat *him* like she treated the groom and the other workers on the estate. But Delia tugged on the reins and rode away at a canter before he had a chance to give her a piece of his mind. Acton was left standing alone before the grand entrance to the house.

The men stared across at him with a mixture of curiosity and resentment as they went about their work. He shuffled his feet and rubbed the back of his head self-consciously. There was a principle at stake, but he doubted they would see his refusal to work in such a noble light. They would put him down as a shirker if he failed to go over and lend a hand.

His help was certainly required. The day was hot and muggy and Acton and his colleagues sweated heavily as they laboured. Perspiration dripped down their red faces and their arms and hands became black with dust. Delia sat on horseback off to one side and observed them like an overseer on a colonial plantation. Occasionally she would ride among them and bark down instructions. Her long hair was tied back in a prudish bun and her pretty face wore a permanent scowl.

'Somebody should give her a whip,' Acton remarked as he and his partner heaved a tea crate onto a cart.

The man seemed not to understand that he had made a joke.

'I mean, she's a real slave driver, isn't she?' he went on, determined to draw a response. 'I can just picture her cracking a whip over our heads.' At that moment Delia passed by on her horse and gave them both a withering glance.

'Hope that taught you,' said the man as she walked out of earshot. He was visibly shaken by the brief encounter and his voice was an angry whisper.

'Taught me what?'

'To mind that insolent tongue of yours.'

* * *

On the Sunday evening Acton joined some of the other hands in the village pub. It was very different from the bars he was used to patronising as a student. There was no music and the only woman on the premises was the landlord's matronly wife. Still, the beer was cheap and strong and Acton's talk became increasingly bawdy as the evening progressed. On his fifth or sixth pint, he jumped to his feet and raised a toast:

'Here's to Delia,' he roared, lifting up his half-empty tankard. 'To Delia and all who want to sail in her.'

A silence descended over the table and the men exchanged uneasy glances. Acton slurped his drink and went on. 'Don't you just love the way her juicy bum bounces in the saddle?' A salacious grin spread across his face. 'I never thought I'd be jealous of a piece of old leather.' The groom, who was sitting beside him, nudged him in the ribs and tried to change the subject. Acton sat down but would not keep quiet.

'C'mon, I bet every one of you jerks off to that cock-teasing ice-queen at least once a day?'

Several of the men picked up their drinks and moved to a table at the other side of the room. Acton turned to the groom. 'What's wrong with them? Can't they handle men's talk?'

'If it's wenches you want to talk about,' said the groom, 'we've got stories that would make you blush. But not Mistress Delia. I've told you before – she's off limits.'

'"Mistress Delia",' said Acton sarcastically. 'You talk about her as if she's royalty. She's only a woman for God's sake! She's got a pair of tits and a hairy little snatch just like the rest of them.' The remainder of the company stood up and walked away from the table. Acton and the groom were left sitting alone.

'You're not making yourself very popular,' said the older man. 'You're lucky they know you're drunk or they'd never speak to you again.' He drained his tankard and rose to his feet. 'Come along, lad, it's time

169

we set off.' The sight of the empty stools around the table had a sobering effect on Acton. It even made him feel slightly depressed. He got up clumsily and followed the groom out of the pub.

'You know,' said the groom as they made their way along the dark village street, 'you don't half remind me of the other lad we had here.'

'Who?' grunted Acton.

'The last kennel hand is who I'm talking about. He was a city boy like yourself. And he was in the habit of remarking about Mistress Delia too. He was in love with her, that's what it was. Men tend to say mean things about ladies they can't get their hands on. You've taken a fancy to the Mistress yourself, if I'm not mistaken.'

'What if I have?' said Acton gruffly.

'Forget about her, lad.'

'Why don't you mind your own damn business!'

'Forget about her. You don't stand a chance.'

Acton swung his fist at the groom but missed by a yard. The older man grabbed his arm and supported him until he had regained his balance.

'Forget about her. That's the advice of a man who wishes you well.'

As they left the village and walked along the lane towards Olympia Hall, whose bright lights they could see shining in the distance, the groom began to explain his view of things to Acton.

'It must be hard for a young chap like you who's used to life in the city to understand our behaviour,' he said. 'But in the country we have a great respect for tradition. And we like things to stay in their place, especially people. As for Mistress Delia, well I can understand how you feel . . . I'm a man too, after all.' He chuckled awkwardly. 'But she's from the gentry class and you're just a commoner. Obey her. Try to please her. But get those other ideas out of your head.'

170

Acton felt his temper rising again. 'Anyone would think you were a serf living in the middle ages.'

'You haven't got over the sight of her slapping me in the yard, have you?'

'I haven't got over the fact you didn't pull her down off that high horse of hers and teach her some manners.' They walked on in silence for a while before the groom resumed.

'I've seen her flog a man,' he announced flatly, 'several in fact.' Acton stopped, visibly shocked, but the groom continued along the lane. 'Come on,' he called back, 'I want to get to my bed.'

'What do you mean by flogged?' Acton said as he caught up with him.

'By flogged I mean just that: flogged. She had them stripped naked and tied by the wrists and ankles to a post in the yard. Some of them she whipped herself. The others were more fortunate as she had the steward administer the punishment while she sat on her horse and watched.'

'Why do you say they were more fortunate?'

'You've never seen Mistress Delia wield a whip, have you?

Acton shook his head dumbly.

'I'll tell you about the last time she gave a flogging. Three of the hands had been caught stealing from the harvest crop so they were stripped and tied to the posts by the steward's men. Their legs were shaking even before Delia appeared and when she rode into the yard, they cried for mercy like little boys. But the mistress doesn't know the meaning of pity. She circled around them – on her high horse, as you like to call it – and let the poor bleeders have it with the longest and fiercest whip you ever laid eyes on. The kind Spaniards use on bulls. It flew at them as quick as lightning, like an evil black serpent that had a craving for human flesh. The crack it made echoed around the yard as loud as gunfire.

The sorry fools were screaming so much after the first couple of lashes she ordered their mouths to be stuffed with rags and then she really had her way with 'em. It was a terrible thing to watch. Calm as you like, she rode around taking aim at their helpless squirming bodies until they were a horrible mess of crisscrossing red stripes from head to toe. When they were finally cut free from the posts, they dropped to the ground like sides of beef. None of them has ever worked again and one old man . . . well, he can't do a thing for himself any more, if you get my meaning.'

Acton doubled up in laughter and clutched the groom's shoulder. 'Flogging. Whipping posts. Crippled old men. You're winding me up, aren't you?'

'Winding you up!' The groom pushed him away in disgust. 'That crippled old man is my father.'

Acton's laughter ceased abruptly.

'Let that story be a warning to you. Guard your tongue while you're working here and don't let me hear any more of your foolish notions.'

'If that bitch ever tried –'

The groom seized him by his collars and threw him to the ground before he could finish his sentence. 'Didn't you listen to a thing I've just been telling you?' He stood over Acton and the pale moonlight illuminated his gaunt face and bristly grey hair. His eyes were wide and anxious like those of a hunted animal. 'There are far worse things she can do to a man than give him a flogging.'

The excess of that evening told on Acton as he went about his duties the next day. His head throbbed and his movements were sluggish. But it was not only the effect of the drink that was causing him to feel out of sorts. Since arriving at Olympia Hall he had experienced unusually vivid dreams and the latest one had been especially disturbing.

172

He had dreamt he was one of the spectators watching the groom's father being flogged. In the dream Delia was dressed in her usual riding outfit and mounted on her chestnut. The old man was naked and tied to the post and she rode around him aiming vicious blows at his scrawny body until his legs gave way and he hung upright by his tethered wrists. Acton had broken from the crowd, which included all the men who were present in the pub, and attempted to wrest the whip from Delia's hand. But she fought back determinedly, raising the sole of her riding boot to his face and kicking him to the ground. As he clambered to his feet he was seized by two burly servants who held him fast. Delia ordered them to rip off his clothes and tie him to a second whipping post. Acton appealed to his colleagues, including the groom, to rescue him; but nobody came to his aid and the two brutes dragged him into position. He was bound to the post by wrists and ankles and left to the mercy of Delia. She was wrathful, her vengeance ferocious and relentless. The whip cracked through the air and ripped the skin from his back. He felt his body burning all over. But it was something other than pain he experienced as she punished him. He had woken up sweating and achingly erect.

When lunchtime came, instead of eating at the communal table outside the kitchen, Acton took his plate to the kennels. He felt the other workers were treating him coldly and was eager to get away from them. Nobody had mentioned his boorish behaviour in the pub but he was sure that was the reason for their guarded attitude towards him. As he ate, he watched the hounds in their pen. They were a boisterous pack, never quiet or at rest. He had still not got used to their innate viciousness, but for the moment he welcomed their company and found their animal enjoyment of life quite refreshing.

All at once the hounds stopped their rollicking and retreated to the back of the pen. Tails between legs, they shivered pathetically against the wall, and some even began to whimper. Acton heard the sound of horse's hooves coming from the yard. He put down his plate and nervously wiped his lips on his sleeve. Outside the kennels, Delia came into view, mounted on her chestnut stallion. Walking beside her was the steward, looking pale and anxious as she spoke to him. She tugged on the reins and the horse halted obediently in front of the compound.

'How much exercise are they given?' she asked the steward in the cultivated accent of her class. The man begged her indulgence and summoned Acton with a quick wave of his hand.

'How often do you take the hounds out, lad?'

'Once a day usually.' Acton came forward and stopped before the imposing stallion. He gazed up at the young rider, entranced by her austere beauty.

'For how long?' she inquired, looking down at him.

'An hour . . . maybe two.'

Delia paled at his reply and the side of her mouth twitched. She lifted her gaze from Acton and addressed the steward. 'Make it two hours twice a day. I don't want fat hounds on a hunt.' With that she tugged on the reins and the horse turned and bore her away. The steward trotted after her, stuttering apologies.

Acton returned to his bench. The encounter had left him shaken and his feelings were in turmoil. Delia was the kind of stuck-up bitch that he usually despised. Her snooty superior attitude offended all of his basic principles. Yet just being near to her drove him wild with desire. She had only needed to glance at him and his cock had begun to swell. He picked up his plate and tried to eat, but his appetite had left him. He walked to the pen and flung the food to the dogs, who were now their lively selves again.

'What in God's name are you playing at?'

Acton spun around to see the steward striding

towards him. The man's face was red with rage and he was waving his arms in the air.

'I ought to send you packing right now,' he yelled.

'What did I do wrong?' Acton held out the empty plate apologetically. 'It was only a few scraps.'

The steward snatched the plate from his hand and threw it against the wall. The fragments flew in all directions. 'Are you a complete idiot? You spoke to the young mistress as if you were talking to the fishmonger's wife.'

'Sorry,' was all Acton could say.

'Didn't they teach you how to address your betters at that fancy university of yours?'

'I never –'

'When you talk to the young lady, you keep your head lowered at all times. And you call her *Mistress* Delia. Understand?'

'I said I'm sorry.'

'Sorry?' The steward spat out the word contemptuously. 'You're lucky she had an engagement or I swear she'd have given you a lesson in respect you wouldn't soon forget.' He looked Acton up and down and walked away shaking his head despairingly. 'And see to it that you do exactly what she ordered. Those hounds better be in top form for the hunt.'

Acton now found himself occupied with the hounds from the moment he got up in the morning until late in the afternoon. And each day he learnt something new about their characters – how one would dominate the others by biting their necks, how another would roll on its back in submission at the first show of fangs. He even began to understand the guttural exchanges of snarls and growls which formed their crude language.

When he was out with the pack he often caught glimpses of Delia as she rode her stallion across the fields and heath land. She was always unaccompanied, a lone romantic-looking figure set against a vast land-scape of rolling hills. The sight of her made him burn with longing and for the rest of the day he would go about with his cock hard in his pants. There were young women among the domestic staff, but they were strictly forbidden to associate with outdoor hands like himself and he climbed into his bed at night with an angry ache in his balls. The pent-up sexual energy fed into his dreams, making them ever more fantastical and so vivid that he sometimes mistook them for reality. Delia featured in every one – mounted, clad in her riding attire and wielding a ferocious whip beneath which animals and men alike cringed in terror.

When Acton called on the groom one afternoon about a matter relating to the forthcoming eve-of-hunt festival, he found himself recounting a dream from the previous night which had left him feeling even more disturbed than usual. The groom's quarters, which adjoined the stables, were only slightly larger than his own and, in addition to a bed, chair and table, there was a workbench built along one wall which gave the place a very cramped feel. On entering, Acton had been surprised to see more than a dozen pairs of tall black riding boots, with boot trees inserted, standing proudly about the floor and on the furniture. Due to lack of space there was even one pair lying on the bed in an open box. They were all ladies' dressage boots with high-cut sides and slim ankles, the style worn by Delia.

The groom was holding up a boot and polishing it as Acton spoke about his dream. His arm was inside the leg and his fingers were pushed deep into the toe. His other hand was busily rubbing the instep with a soft brush.

'I'm afraid I don't quite get your meaning,' he said to Acton with a puzzled look on his face.

'OK, it's like this. I feel as if I've been here before. The landscape seems familiar to me . . .'

'Go on, I'm listening to you,' said the groom, inspecting the supple calf-leather. 'But I do have to get these boots finished or there'll be hell to pay.'

'And then there's Delia . . . Mistress Delia.'

The groom let out a heavy sigh. 'Now I thought we'd agreed –'

'I know I promised I wouldn't mention her, but last night I dreamt –'

'Don't even –'

'Listen to me, will you? Last night I dreamt she was chasing me on horseback, cracking her whip in the air. I was running through the fields, out of breath and scared for my life. I could hear her laughter. It came from all around – the hills, the sky, everywhere. I got to a stream and I thought that if I made it to the other side I'd be safe. I waded across but when I pulled myself out on the other bank she was waiting there for me, sitting on her horse and staring down at me. Only she didn't have her whip any more. She was holding a bow made from gold and aiming an arrow straight at my head.'

The groom shrugged and went on polishing the boot, working the brush steadily up the leg. 'It was just a dream,' he said after a moment. 'The other night I dreamt I was the lord of the manor. But how does that help me now?'

'This morning, when I was out with the dogs, I found the very place it happened – the bank where I pulled myself out of the stream. I recognised it immediately, even though I've never been that way before.'

'In my experience one river bank looks very much like another,' said the groom sceptically. 'Don't let your mind play tricks on you.'

'I found this lying on the ground.' Acton reached into his pocket and produced a coin-sized silver object. It appeared to be a decorative button for a jacket and on the front it bore the raised impression of a female archer in a tunic. The groom looked at it and he stopped polishing the boot.

'In the dream I was carrying it in my hand.'

The groom did not lift his gaze from the button and opened his mouth to speak. But at that very moment his name was called from the yard by a loud and imperious female voice. The two men stared at one another like frightened children who had been discovered in some conspiracy.

The groom was the first to react and quickly laid down the brush and riding boot. He closed Acton's hand tightly around the button. 'Put that away,' he said in an anxious whisper. 'And don't move from here.' He went out of the room into the stables, pulling the door shut behind him. He took a deep breath, then walked towards the entrance, where Delia waited on horseback casting a dark shadow across the yard.

Left alone in the room, Acton paced up and down nervously. He felt disconcerted by all the boots that surrounded him. They completely dominated the groom's small living space and he wondered how anyone was able to eat and sleep among them without becoming oppressed by their dark presence. The inserted trees stretched the leg of each boot, as if it were being worn, revealing its elegant design. To Acton, they appeared proud and contemptuous objects, seemingly imbued with the character of their owner through prolonged contact with her legs and feet.

He picked up a boot and examined it. The sole and heel were spotlessly clean and there was not a scratch or blemish anywhere on the toe or the entire leg section. Yet a slight creasing in the black leather around the narrow ankle area indicated that the boot had often been worn. The high-cut sides were quite distinct and he was sure it was one of the pair Delia was wearing when he had followed her to the front of the house all those days ago. It gave him a strange thrill to be holding it now and inspecting it at his leisure. His hands began to tremble as he brushed his fingertips over the smooth leather and breathed in the potent fragrance of calfskin and polish. It was only a riding boot yet he felt as if he were touching something very intimate. The elegant object seemed impregnated with Delia's essence.

The sound of the door opening shook him from his dreamy contemplation of the boot. He quickly put it down, embarrassed to have been caught in such a revealing activity. The groom came into the room. One side of his face bore the unmistakable red imprint of Delia's long fingers and his eyes were moist. 'Haven't you got work to do?' he snapped. He picked up the boot he had been polishing earlier, slipped his arm inside and promptly resumed his work. 'Well?' he said after a while. 'What are you still hanging about for? Have you never seen a man polishing riding boots before?'

'You were going to tell me something about the button.' Acton was unable to take his eyes off the groom's swollen cheek.

The groom shook his head. His expression was sullen. 'Get back to your dogs, lad.'

Acton did as the groom bid. But as he came out of the stables into the yard, he realised that he had forgotten to ask about the arrangements for the festival. He turned and reluctantly went back to the groom's quarters. Without knocking he opened the door, which was still ajar.

The groom was sitting on the edge of the bed and in his hands he held one of the new riding boots which he had removed from the box. He had the boot in an upright position with the sole cupped in his palms and the rounded toe close to his mouth. Quite unbelievably he was licking it. He carried out the disgusting task with loving care and attention, trailing his long tongue over the shiny surface and working gradually up from the toe towards the instep. He was completely absorbed in his work and unaware that Acton was standing in the doorway just a few feet away, watching him. The tall coal-black boot was an object of devotion for him and he seemed proud of the glistening coat of spittle he was spreading over the leather.

Acton let go of the door handle and walked out of the stables and across the yard. The nauseating image of the bootlicking groom was impressed on his mind. His stomach churned and he went to bed as soon as he had closed the kennels for the evening. He slept badly, waking in a feverish sweat from one nightmare after another.

The festival lifted the oppressive atmosphere which usually hung over Olympia Hall. Villagers from far and wide had been invited to participate and neighbouring landowners were also present, accompanied by troops of liveried servants who added to the colour and pomp of the occasion. Vendors sold their wares noisily from tables and barrows, and acrobats, jugglers and dancers performed to the delight of the crowds. In the marquees food and drink were served at long tables and actors and musicians entertained gleeful spectators. The largest of the marquees was strictly reserved for the aristocratic guests, and there fine ladies in elegant gowns shaded their complexions from the sun and sipped flutes of champagne served from silver trays by waiters in white jackets.

Acton wandered through the crowds, trying his hand at rustic games and flirting with the village girls. He was beginning to feel his old self again; although, even in the midst of the colourful festivities, he would sometimes start thinking about one of his dreams or recall the groom and his sickening worship of Delia's riding boots. He had not spoken to the groom since that afternoon and, when he caught sight of him in the marquee where the pony traps were being prepared, he went inside, determined to confront him.

'So, how did they taste?' he asked bluntly.

The groom gazed at him in bewilderment and scratched his head.

'I saw you. You were holding one of her boots and *licking* it.'

'Make a habit of spying on folk, do you?'

'It's disgusting . . . filthy . . . perverse.'

'Make your mind up,' the groom joked. 'Which one is it?'

'At least I admit I've got the hots for her. But you . . . You say nothing. You tell me to keep quiet . .' Acton's voice was trembling with emotion. 'But in private you get your kicks by licking her boots like a dog. Are the rest of you like that?' He gestured contemptuously to the other men in the tent. 'I bet the whole lot of you are bootlicking perverts.'

The groom gave him a condescending smile. 'So you think I lick the mistress's boots for pleasure?'

Acton nodded emphatically.

'You've got me down as one of those creepy little men, haven't you? What do you call them again? The kind that have a fancy for ladies' shoes and things?' Without waiting for Acton to reply he called over one of his colleagues, an old man with a shaggy white beard and a wrinkled face. 'The lad wants to know the best treatment for new leather boots,' he said to him. 'Tell him what he should do.'

'He should give 'em a good licking.' The old man stuck out his brown-stained tongue and flicked it up and down obscenely. He walked away laughing.

'That doesn't alter a thing,' said Acton. 'You're still a grovelling bootlicker.'

'Aye,' said the groom resignedly and there was a note of sadness in his voice, 'and no doubt I'll remain her bootlicker until the day I die.'

Acton left the groom and made his way to the beer tent. He was deeply confused and no longer felt sure of his own judgment. Perhaps the groom was innocent after all? Maybe it was only his own unnatural feelings towards Delia that had made him react so viscerally to the sight of a man licking her new boots? He drank several pints and tried to forget about the whole incident. Fortunately one of the house servants was working in the tent as a waitress and he struck up a promising, if intermittent, conversation with her as she served the tables. She was a saucy, full-figured country girl and still new to the Hall and its austere regulations. She drank secretly from the beer mugs as she carried them from the bar and soon grew quite tipsy, even whispering to him that she would leave the door to the servants' wing unlocked that evening. Acton was barely able to contain himself and he seized her arm and begged her to come back with him at once. She ran away giggling.

Towards mid-afternoon an announcement was made that the pony-and-trap race was about to begin. Almost at once the marquee emptied and a noisy crowd assembled along the sides of a large quadrangle that had been roped off in the centre of the field. Acton could not understand why the prospect of watching racing ponies should create such a buzz of excitement; but since he did not want to remain in the tent alone and there was no sign of his little waitress, he decided to go and join the spectators. The traps were already in place, lined up at one end of the quadrangle, each one polished and sparkling in the sunlight and flying the distinctive colours of one of the aristocratic houses.

'So where are the ponies?' he asked a man standing next to him.

'Here they come now,' was the answer. Acton failed to see them and the man put a hand on Acton's shoulder and pointed a finger. 'Over there, right in front of your nose.'

At the opposite side of the quadrangle the crowd had parted to create a narrow corridor through which came six handsome young men, each dressed in the colourful livery of the house to which he belonged. Acton watched them enter the quadrangle and walk towards the pony traps. Each man took his place in front of the vehicle that bore the appropriate colours and coat of arms. Then they began to strip, first removing their jackets and then their trousers. Hysterical cheers rose from the crowd. The female spectators, who Acton now noticed massively outnumbered the males, were especially enthusiastic.

'What on earth is going on?' he muttered to himself.

'You don't want your ponies wearing pants now, do you?' His neighbour laughed and continued to cheer with the rest of the crowd.

The men divested themselves of their uniforms, which they handed to attendants, until they were wearing only a pair of tight black running shorts and, rather incongruously, their peaked servant's cap. Each of them boasted a splendid physique and stood as proud and confident as any track athlete before a race. Their lean finely toned muscles glistened in the afternoon sun. More attendants appeared and began to attach these magnificent specimens of manhood to the traps. They took great care that the leather harnesses fitted comfortably over the men's shoulders and around their waists and allowed them to assume the optimal pulling position.

'My money's on the tall blond boy,' said Acton's neighbour. His voice was barely audible above the cheers and whistles. 'Though the curly-haired lad on the far side has got a fiery driver.'

It had not occurred to Acton that these young men would actually be pulling people. But upon each trap was a leather-upholstered seat wide enough for a single rider, and in front of the seat was a metal platform, clearly intended for the rider's feet. If this was not evidence enough that the men were to serve as draught animals, the attendants now set about attaching reins to them by means of a bit which was strapped across their mouths and chins like a gag.

A roar rose from the crowd as six young women filed into the quadrangle. They were dressed in smart equestrian outfits consisting of high black boots, white breeches and a black velvet jacket. Each one wore a black dressage topper – a stylish felt hat that resembled a bowler with a low, flat crown – and carried a long riding crop. After briefly examining the harnessed male that would pull her, each woman climbed up onto her trap and sat aloofly on the high seat, the heels of her immaculately polished boots resting on the platform before her. The pretty young riders took up the reins and tugged, pulling their two-legged ponies to attention. In their other hand, they held the raised crop threateningly.

'This is barbaric,' said Acton, trying to get the attention of his neighbour. 'Why do these men . . .' He suddenly recognised the rider in the far trap and fell silent. It was Delia. She wore her hair in a bun which, combined with the felt topper, made her fine aristocratic features appear even more haughty than usual.

'Aye,' said the man. 'I don't envy these boys, young and handsome as they are, especially not poor curly over there.'

As he spoke, the starter gave the signal and the women, possessed by a fiercely competitive spirit, urged their ponies forward with loud cries. The harnessed men obeyed the shrill commands as if they were brutes and their muscles strained as they struggled to accelerate with their burdens. Their bare feet slipped on the grass and it was not long before some impatient drivers began to apply the crop. The fitter specimens were soon running at a quick jogging pace, but one unfortunate pony was already slackening off the pace and panting for breath before he had gone half the length of the quadrangle. His irate driver, the youngest daughter of a neighbouring countess, rained down blows on his naked back, her cheeks burning with indignation.

The women were racing towards a line of tall poles planted in the ground at the opposite end of the quadrangle and Acton assumed the shameful contest would finish when the first trap reached them. However, the drivers did not stop at the poles. Instead, they used them as turning points for their traps and drove their men-ponies back up the field.

'I don't understand,' he said. 'How does this race end?'

'After six lengths,' replied his neighbour. 'Or when there's only one pony left standing.'

Acton watched the race with growing revulsion. His eyes were drawn to Delia. She was by far the most skilful driver and, though her curly-haired boy was not the strongest of the ponies, he had obviously been well trained for the event. His pulling technique was very efficient and he gave his all for his driver, stretching himself forward in the harness and pumping his arms at his sides. As they came out of the second turn, Delia had opened up a narrow lead over her nearest rival, whose blond animal had not quite found its stride.

The race continued for another length and, urged on by the delirious crowd, the women's cries grew shriller and more vicious. They lashed at their ponies with all the fury of Roman charioteers and their brutal driving soon brought its first casualty. The boy who had been in difficulty almost from the outset, but who had been forced to struggle on by his determined young driver, finally dropped from exhaustion, sinking to his knees in the harness and gasping for breath. The other traps raced on up the field, leaving his young lady in the mortifying position of being the first to go out of the competition. She leaned forward in her seat and flogged the huddled wretch across the back, more out of rage

185

than any belief he would get back on his feet and continue the race. Eventually she climbed out of the trap. She took off her hat and gloves, threw them on the ground in a tantrum and walked away with tears trailing down her pretty face.

One by one other ponies began to drop in the harness and were led off the field in disgrace, their faces haggard, their legs wobbling. Soon only Delia and her rival remained in the race. They were evenly matched and there was nothing to tell between them as they manoeuvred their traps around the posts and set out on the final length. Sections of the crowd clamoured for their favourite and the roar of voices made the air vibrate. The two ponies excelled themselves, still managing even now to pull the combined weight of driver and trap at a jogging pace. Their bodies dripped with sweat and their muscles rippled like the flanks of thoroughbreds. For all the abhorrence he felt, Acton could not help admiring their animal power and determination.

The drivers were locked in a fierce duel and shot hostile glances at each other as they urged the harnessed boys forward with shouts and lashes of the crop. Delia extracted a superhuman performance from her pony and she began to nudge ahead. But the terrible strain showed on the youth's face and it was clear he would not be able to maintain such a level of exertion for long.

Suddenly he stumbled and fell down on one knee. The crowd gasped and held its breath as he pulled himself up. Delia immediately applied the crop to his back and he scrambled forward, losing his cap in the process. The blond boy quickly gained on him but the finishing line was close and, with a final burst of energy, curly carried Delia to a narrow victory.

The crowd broke out in joyous celebration. Caps were thrown up in the air and a band began to play. Delia beamed triumphantly from her high seat and accepted the wild cheers as her tribute. She forced her boy back up onto his feet and, though the wretch had been ridden into the ground, she made him pull her on a lap of honour. Eyes sunken and legs unsteady, he drew the trap around the quadrangle, pausing when she commanded so that her adoring fans could gaze upon her.

Acton could not bear to watch any longer. Shaking with rage, he turned to the man beside him, who was applauding enthusiastically as Delia approached their section of the crowd.

'I've never seen so many grovelling sycophants in my life.'

'Aye, whatever that means.'

'Why doesn't somebody stand up to her?'

Still clapping, the man turned his face to Acton. 'Happen we're just grateful for small mercies.'

'Grateful? Look at the way she's using him. It's an insult to every man here.'

'Not so long ago the mistresses of the house used to hunt a stag during the festival.'

'That's surely better than strapping men to carts like animals?'

'The stag they hunted *was* a man.'

The blunt reply silenced Acton and he strained to listen against the wild chorus of cheers as his neighbour told him about a barbaric custom that was once practised in the locality.

'They would choose a lad from one of the villages and dress him in the skins of a stag. They even fixed a pair of antlers to the poor fellow's head. Then they took him out into a field and turned him loose. He had an hour's headstart and then the ladies would set out after him on horseback with a pack of hounds . . .'

As the man spoke, Acton's head began to spin. The clamour of the crowd became intense and he felt as if he were in the midst of frenzied animals. The faces of the men around him seemed to mutate into hideous caricatures of themselves. Jaws expanded until they were underhung and brutish, or stretched into repulsive baboon-like snouts. Foreheads dropped and brows protruded. The dreamlike vision lasted for only an instant and Acton found himself back in the world he knew, listening to his neighbour.

'. . . If the lad made it to the boundary of the estate they let him go free. But I don't suppose many of 'em ever did. They . . .' The man's voice faltered. 'The ladies . . . When they caught him, they used to cut off his tackle, if you get my drift, and the youngest rider took it as her trophy.'

Acton's neighbour suddenly ceased talking and began to cheer and applaud like a man possessed. Delia was passing before the section of the crowd where they stood and the roar of adulation that greeted her was so great that Acton covered his ears. Never before had he witnessed grown men displaying such fanatical devotion – and all for a woman young enough to be their daughter or even granddaughter. Delia accepted their praise with little sign of gratitude on her proud face. In one gloved hand she held the crop, in the other the reins, and from her seat upon the trap she surveyed the crowd through unblinking blue eyes.

Acton became uncomfortably aware that he was the only person not cheering and applauding her. Squeezed in among the enraptured locals, he felt like an intruder at a cult gathering. He grew nervous and his heart began to drum. Forcing a smile, he beat his hands together in the same devoted manner as those around him.

But his effort to blend in came too late. Delia had already noted his lack of enthusiasm for her triumph. She tugged sharply on the reins and brought her harnessed boy to a halt. The crowd screamed in delight and Acton sensed they would pounce on him and tear him to pieces were she to give the command. She stared at him over the heads of the others, singling him out with her cool hypnotic gaze. An ineffable power radiated from her and his body responded of its own accord, shrinking into itself and cringing in surrender. Her dominance was sudden and absolute, yet her gravely beautiful face showed not a trace of exertion as she steadily subdued him with her will. He felt his knees beginning to buckle under him and in another moment he would have sunk to the ground in grovelling submission, had she not abruptly turned her head and released him from her crushing influence. She jerked the reins and her labouring man-animal staggered forward on his tired wobbly legs.

Acton's body recovered quickly, but his masculine pride had been shattered by the experience. As he watched Delia's slender form being borne away upon the trap, he cursed himself. He had cowered before her, just as he had seen the groom and all the other workers cower before her, and the idea that he had been overwhelmed by a woman, a woman no older than he was, sickened him. A defiant rage swelled up inside him and he wished she would turn around the trap and pass before him again. This time he would show her that he could not to be terrorised like the spineless men around him.

But Delia did not oblige him. Having completed her lap of honour, she received a final chorus of cheers and then steered her trap out of the quadrangle towards the big marquee.

In a sullen mood, Acton drifted back to the beer tent which had already begun to fill up. He found a place at the end of a long table and drank a beer, looking around for his waitress. But there was no sign of her. His thoughts returned to Delia and he brooded darkly on his public display of impotence before a woman whom, despite everything, he still found maddeningly attractive. He dreamed up ways of getting even with her and recovering his sense of manhood.

Acton was woken from his vengeful reverie by the groom. 'Squeeze up there, lad,' he said, putting his mug of beer on the table and sliding onto the bench next to Acton. 'I've been looking for you everywhere since our little to-do earlier this afternoon.'

'Oh,' said Acton and took a slug of beer.

'I think you should leave Olympia Hall.'

'Don't worry, I'm going. I'll be out of this madhouse just as soon as I get the wages I'm owed.'

'You don't understand me.' The groom grabbed Acton's forearm, preventing him from raising the beer mug. 'I'm telling you to leave now.' Acton tried to appear calm, although the groom's urgent tone unsettled him.

'Like I said, I'll get my money first. I don't work for free.' He pulled his arm loose and drank. The mug shook as he held it to his mouth. The groom watched him for a moment and then spoke.

'That button you found by the stream.'

'What about it?'

'The other boy had one just like it.'

'What other boy?'

'The one who worked in the kennels last year. I remember him showing it to me. Swore it was one of the mistress's buttons, he did.'

Acton took the button from his pocket and held it on his palm. 'It looks antique. I reckon it's worth something.'

The groom peered at it and grew pale. He glanced about him anxiously, as if they were a pair of thieves huddled over stolen goods. 'Put it away,' he said.

'What's the big deal? It's just a button.'

'It don't belong to you. You should have left it where you found it.'

'What's got into you?' said Acton irritably. 'So what if it did belong to your precious Mistress Delia? It's mine now.' But Acton felt less confident than he sounded. He slipped the button back into his trouser pocket and pulled the hem of his shirt down over his

190

waist. Once again he had the uncanny sensation that he was dreaming. It suddenly sounded as if the men seated at the other tables were barking and howling rather than talking and their ugly faces mutated to reveal the features of wild animals. Long fang-shaped teeth were exposed as mouths opened in laughter, thick moustaches flared from cheeks like dogs' whiskers and coarse rustic clothes bristled like fur on shoulders and backs.

'He went missing,' the groom was saying, 'on the first day of the hunt.'

'Who went missing?' Acton shook his head to dispel the nightmarish vision.

'Your predecessor. I had to take charge of the dogs myself. Bloodthirsty buggers!'

Trying to keep his hand steady, Acton took another slug of beer. He was afraid to look beyond the rim of his mug in case his eyes started to play tricks on him again.

The groom stood up from the table. 'Get going, lad,' he said. 'Leave tonight, I say. I don't think it's good for you round here. Not safe like. Run and don't look back!'

Acton ordered more drink after the groom departed. The older man's words and anxious manner had left him with an odd sense of foreboding, yet he was determined not to leave Olympia Hall without first receiving his wages. He sat alone at the end of the table and tried to reason away the irrational fears that preyed upon him. He looked about in vain for the buxom young waitress, and the absence of the one woman who had shown him any human warmth in weeks made his sense of isolation all the more acute.

Then a story began to reach his ears. He heard the name of Delia whispered by those around him and little by little he learnt that her victory had been declared illegitimate by the other aristocrats. Her boy had crossed the line without wearing his cap and she had been stripped of her title. Acton smiled darkly as he pictured her humiliation. He wished he had been there himself to witness the 'stripping'. The expression captured his imagination: proud Delia divested by her peers, denuded and disgraced, while another woman, the driver of the blond boy, draped herself in Delia's mantle of victory.

Acton was still relishing Delia's humiliation when he emerged from the tent. The evening was very dark and he was unsteady on his feet from all the beer he had drunk. He had gone only a short way when a piercing scream issued from the woods at the bottom of the field, startling him. The awful sound continued intermittently, rising and falling in volume, until finally it faded away in a long pitiful whimper. Some nocturnal creature – a wildcat or a fox perhaps – had just lost its life among the trees and, though it was not a rare occurrence in the country, it had a profound effect on Acton that evening. He felt utterly vulnerable and once again he had the presentiment that a dark fate awaited him. He increased his pace, eager to get to the safety of his room in the kennels. The groom's parting advice to pack his bag and leave rang in his ears.

As he came to the courtyard, he remembered the sassy young waitress and her whispered invitation. The servants' quarters were just ahead of him and he could see the door next to the washhouse which she had promised to leave unbolted. He recalled the musky-sweet smell of her flesh and delightful sensation of her plump yet firm buttocks between his fingertips. He stood, paralysed by indecision. Fear urged him to retreat to his room; but an equally powerful drive called on him to seize the opportunity that now presented itself. It seemed like an eternity since he had held a woman's body.

He approached the door. He half hoped it would be locked so that he could go back to his room. Slowly he turned the handle and to both his horror and delight the door creaked open to reveal a long corridor with a low ceiling. He took a deep breath and went inside, his blood burning like fire in his veins.

Walking on tiptoe, he followed the directions she had given him, passing through a winding passage and up a flight of narrow stairs. He wandered back and forth through a maze of corridors in search of his shapely servant girl. But either she had played a mean trick on him or in his drunken and excited state he failed to pay attention to where he was going, because he soon became lost, unable even to retrace the route he had taken.

He roamed deeper into the house, leaving the servants' wing and creeping through broad, richly carpeted hallways, anxious to find a way out. Several times he almost ran into a servant who was scurrying on an errand, and only luck saved him from being discovered by a company of lively young ladies as they emerged from a lavishly furnished drawing room.

At length he came to a quieter area of the house and entered a gallery. The room was dimly lit and at first he scarcely noticed the pictures hanging on the walls in their heavy gilt frames. But one caught his eye. It was a full-length portrait of a striking young woman with blue-black hair and ghostly pale skin. Dressed in a cloak, hunting jerkin and tight pantaloons that emphasised her long shapely legs, she was posing in the shade of a leafy glade. She had a quiver full of arrows slung over her shoulder, a bow in her hand, and one boot-shod foot was placed upon a rock. A pair of brawny retrievers gazed up at her adoringly, their long golden tails curving stiffly in the air. A slain deer completed the composition. The sorry creature lay on the ground before mistress and hounds with an arrow buried in the side of its neck, and a thin trail of blood oozed from the wound. Its wide-open eyes stared out from the picture and made Acton shudder. The abject expression on its face appeared almost human.

He gazed around at the other paintings. Slowly they revealed themselves to him in the weak light, each one presenting a variation on the same hideous theme. Most were full-length portraits, similar in style to the first, depicting proud women dressed in hunting attire, some posing with dogs, some with falcons and others sitting astride tall finely bred horses. The quarry of each huntress was displayed like a trophy. There were fox carcasses draped from the branches of trees, glassy-eyed and lifeless as stoles. In one picture, a mighty stag was sprawled across rocky ground like a slain warrior and beside it stood a mounted huntress with a young and petulant face. Another picture showed a wild boar with huge tusks slumped lifelessly at the feet of a tall blonde with strong Nordic features. There was even a gigantic brown bear among the hunting trophies. It lay prostrate on the forest floor, its broad head a pedestal for the dainty boot of its slayer.

Acton wondered who these women were. Some of the paintings appeared ancient, the female figures clothed in strange medieval attire; others were more modern and depicted women in Victorian and twentieth-century hunting dress: waistcoats, jackets and tall leather boots. Were these proud females the former mistresses of Olympia Hall stretching back over the centuries, Delia's ancestors?

All at once he felt stifled. The paintings seemed to crowd in upon him and he walked quickly, eager to escape from the gloomy shrine devoted to female hunting prowess. As he reached the other end of the gallery, a pair of pictures in identical gold-painted frames caused him to halt. One of the canvasses was still incomplete, bearing only a few brush strokes which suggested a human form. The other canvas looked ancient and bore the title *Venatrix*. It depicted a mounted woman charging down a fleeing man – or rather a grotesque hybrid creature. From the chest upward the monstrous thing resembled a stag and a pair of antlers twisted from its enormous furry head. The human lower half was small in comparison and the puny legs staggered beneath the heavy animal burden. Acton moved closer to the picture. Something had caught his eye: a detail on the rider, on the dark jacket she wore. The buttons all bore the motif of a female archer. All at once, the picture seemed to come to life and it was as if he could hear and feel the laboured breathing of the hybrid creature as it tried to escape the huntress.

Acton fled from the gallery. Without a thought of where he was going, he ran down a stairway and through a dizzying succession of corridors. His one desire was to be far away from the sinister room and its macabre paintings. Finally he arrived at a pair of wooden doors. Praying he had discovered a way out of the house, he yanked down the handle and pushed.

The big doors swung open and before him was a magnificent bathhouse. In the centre, sunk into the tiled floor, was a pool of crystal water. Pale marble columns joined by cusped arches stood around its perimeter. Acton felt a cold shiver pass through him. He was certain he had visited this bathhouse before. He wandered in. Everything about the place – the tranquillity, the sense of seclusion, the faint smell of wild herbs – seemed familiar. He shook his head. No, it was not the bathhouse he remembered but somewhere else. He fought to recover the memory and a hazy image of a wood in a vale began to form in his mind. There was a glade, and in the glade a pool . . .

Suddenly he glimpsed a figure at the other side of the bathhouse. He darted behind a column and held his breath. He was sure it was a woman. She had been wrapped in a bathrobe or a long towel, but her face had been turned away from him. Cautiously he peered around the edge of the column and saw the figure for a second time. Now the face was in full view, the beautiful eyes and lips held in a haughty expression even in this unguarded moment. It was Delia, the proud mistress of the house.

She came to the steps at the edge of the pool and tested the water with her toes. Then she brought her hands to the front of the robe and prepared to pull it open. The groom's warning rang in Acton's ears again: *'Get going, lad. Run and don't look back!'* He glanced towards the open door. He could make it there in five strides. But his eyes were drawn back to the glorious sight across the pool.

The robe slid from Delia's shoulders, falling in a crumpled heap around her feet. Acton trembled with fear and delight. Like an animal suddenly catching the scent of a predator, he felt he was in mortal danger, but Delia's glorious naked body held him as captive as any bonds. Her breasts were the kind he always longed for in a woman, conical and high and perfectly symmetrical. Her hips flared from a slender waist with an irresistible womanly curve.

She descended the steps into the pool, the water rising up her long legs until it lapped against the tuft of light-brown hair at the junction of her thighs. Like a nymph in a brook, she paused to check her ponytail, bringing up her elbows to reach behind her neck, and for a few moments her breasts, tipped with pink, pointed nipples, were lifted into tantalising prominence. Satisfied that her hair was firmly tied, she stretched forward her arms and began to swim with strong yet graceful strokes.

Acton watched her supple limbs propel her through the water. He ached with desire for her. Her pert ass cheeks bobbed up and down just beneath the surface. Reaching the middle of the pool, she rolled onto her

196

back, kicking her legs to stay afloat. Her luscious thighs opened and closed without modesty and Acton was given the show of his life.

His hand went down to his fly and fumbled to release his cock, which had grown hard and insistent. Delia, the chaste lady equestrian, lying on her back with her legs spread! He would savour the filthy image to the end of his days. Eyes focused on the mouth-watering pink of her sex, he jerked his cock with crude laddish vigour.

Delia lay peacefully in the water, head back and eyes closed. She kicked her legs lazily, flashing her secretive cunt in its bed of neatly trimmed brown hair, oblivious to the heavy breathing and furious cock-stroking at the edge of the pool. Acton derived a perverse thrill from her innocent display. He was stealing from her and he relished the indecency of wanking unseen in a proud aristocratic girl's bath chamber. He was taking his revenge for all the indignities she had inflicted upon him, possessing the maddening upper-class bitch without her knowledge or consent.

He stared between her thighs and recalled all the times he had lusted after her commanding ass as it bounced upon the saddle. He thought of the other men cringing before her like beaten slaves. He frigged himself aggressively and devoured her exposed cunt with his eyes. He felt joyous, liberated by this furtive violation. His head cleared and the doubts and fears that had tormented him during the long day vanished.

Delia was just a woman. She had tits and a cunt and there was no more mystery to her than that. He knew that somewhere a young man was recovering from pulling her trap like a beast, and that the groom was in his cramped quarters dutifully licking her riding boots like he did every night. But he, Acton, would never be her draught animal or lackey. Never.

His balls tightened and a giddy sensation swept through his body. He beat his cock furiously. Animal

197

lust and a desire for revenge had turned the blood-stiffened tissue into a primed and powerful weapon. He was about to despoil a virgin bitch, violate her in her inner sanctum.

But as he brought himself to the brink of orgasm, Delia rolled lazily onto her front, snatching her sex from his view. He screamed a silent curse and tried to hold back his climax, but it tore through him against his will. Eyes fixed despairingly on Delia's calm face as she swam through the water, he pumped his seed against the cold marble column.

Delia lifted her gaze from the pool, catching Acton in the throes of his frustrated orgasm. She stopped swimming and stared at him, and his blood chilled to ice as the last drips of seed leaked from his cock. He waited for her to scream, to cover her nakedness with her arms, but she simply regarded him calmly from the water. Her haughty features revealed neither shame nor outrage and it was he who felt naked and vulnerable. He had the sensation she was looking into his mind and that all his sordid desires were exposed to her.

He stumbled away from the column, trying to fasten his pants over his cock which was still stubbornly erect. As he backed towards the doorway, time seemed to stand still and he wondered if he would ever make it. Delia followed him with her glowing blue eyes. They made him weak and crushed his resolve, just as they had earlier that day at the race. She seemed capable of anything, of felling him with just her gaze. She was no longer a vulnerable naked woman in a bath but an infinitely superior being with limitless power.

He reached the doorway, turned and ran. But the image of Delia's chillingly beautiful face hovered before him as he made his breathless way along the corridors and then up the stairs. He felt she could see him. He was a rat in a maze and she an aloof female scientist observing his pitiful attempts to discover a way out.

He re-entered the gallery but what he saw on the wall made him stop abruptly. It was impossible. The formerly incomplete canvas was now finished and it looked as ancient as the picture mounted beside it. He moved towards the darkly painted scene and his body turned cold. The figure in the painting was his double and it was fleeing a mounted woman armed with a golden bow. Acton stepped closer and the terrified painted face grew before his eyes until it became a perfect reflection of his own. '*Get going, lad. Run and don't look back!*'

Acton did escape from the house, or so it seemed. He found his way back to the servants' quarters and left by the door through which he had entered. He did not even think of returning to his room to collect his belongings, but sprinted down to the fields and out across open country. Fear gave him inhuman stamina and he ran for miles, guided through the darkness by instinct alone, until, out of breath, he lay down and slept.

It was long after dawn when he awoke. The sky was blue and the morning sun was pouring golden light over the rolling hills. He sat up in the grass. He was free and he was safe. Yet something did not feel right. Sounds that he had never heard before chorused in his ears and his nostrils burnt with the thousand unnameable scents carried on the breeze. Suddenly his ears pricked as a succession of euphoric bugle calls sounded in the distance. His small heart began to pound in his chest.

He started to run. His long body moved swiftly through the dewy grass but the dogs quickly gained on him. Their baying grew louder and soon he could hear the individual voice of each animal as they barked their savage language of curses and murderous threats. They closed in on him from all directions, forcing him to turn in ever decreasing circles until he stopped, exhausted, penned in by a ring of snarling foaming mouths.

From behind the ring appeared a massive chestnut-coloured beast and mounted upon its back was a figure whom even the fox knew to be the invincible goddess of the hunt. The hounds stopped their snarling and waited, tails stiff, for her command. The goddess wore full hunting regalia – riding hat, jacket, tan breeches and high, calf-leather boots. Other riders appeared at her side, all women, their faces flushed with the excitement of the chase. The fox stared up at the goddess with an almost human look in his eyes, searching her austere face for a trace of pity. But the virgin huntress showed pity to neither man nor beast. Without a flicker of compassion, she raised her gloved hand and gave the pack the command to kill.

The groom had just locked up the dogs for the night and was crossing the yard to the stables, when he encountered Delia. He raised his cap and made a deep bow.

'A good opening to the season, Mistress?' he inquired anxiously as she approached on her tall chestnut stallion.

'Satisfactory,' she replied.

He could discern a trace of irritation in her voice and he steeled himself for his punishment.

'But these new boots are too tight.'

'I'm sorry,' he stuttered. 'I –'

'Tomorrow I will wear the pair from Madrid. See to it they are prepared.' She tugged the reins of her horse and continued across the yard, leaving the trembling groom to stare at her shapely and superior ass.

He returned to the stables and, after attending to the horses, went through into his little room and closed the door. He gave a small sigh and shrugged his shoulders. Then he took a tall black riding boot from a box on the table and sat down on the edge of his narrow bed. He brought the toe of the boot to his mouth and with his unnaturally long tongue began to lick the new Spanish leather.

6

Imperatrix

Reclining on a divan in her hotel suite wearing only heels and black lingerie, her dark hair loose to her shoulders, Valerie Sales appraised the three young men who stood before her. She was reasonably satisfied with what she had been sent. Each man was fashionably dressed and the trio closely matched her specifications: there was a blond and two brunets and they were all over six feet tall with athletic physiques. The tallest, however, a Latin-looking brunet, had allowed designer shadow to grow around his jaw and this displeased her. Valerie Sales regarded facial stubble as evidence of sloth and sloth was a failing in the male sex that she would not tolerate. She made a mental note to contact the agency and demand they remove the offending escort from their books. But that could wait until the morning.

'All of you drop your trousers.' It was a clear and direct order and the lack of an immediate response made her mouth twitch in annoyance.

'Which part of "drop your trousers" don't you understand?'

Three pairs of male hands set about loosening belts and unzipping flies. Valerie Sales directed her gaze at the crotches. Although she had seen countless cocks in her twenty-eight years, she was always eager to see new ones. Her mouth watered as trousers and boxers were lowered and the unpacked male organs swung free.

Undressed, the men stood with their arms at their sides, their cocks showing timid signs of arousal. Valerie Sales nodded contentedly: none of them had neglected to shave this part of his anatomy. Their ball sacs were just how she had ordered them, shrimp-pink and scraped to the point of rawness. Balls fascinated her almost as much as cocks. They looked so vulnerable, especially when shaven, the precious male seed protected by only a thin pouch of wrinkled skin. She found it quaint, too, that one testicle always hung lower than the other, sometimes by as much as an inch, and gave the male crotch a comical lopsided appearance.

'Come closer,' she ordered.

Shoulder to shoulder the men shuffled forward, each one instinctively moving his hands towards his bald genitals in a protective gesture, yet not daring to cover them. They were afraid of her and she liked that. But too much fear could make a man impotent, a frequent problem for a woman with the power and status of Valerie Sales.

'Am I not to your liking?' she asked tartly.

The men nodded in unison. 'Yes, ma'am,' they mumbled.

'Then why the big thumbs down?' She picked up a riding crop that was lying beside her on the divan and flicked one of the drooping cocks with the leather tongue on the tip. 'Do you not find me attractive?' she said to the owner.

'Yes, ma'am, very attractive.'

She ran the stiff leather tongue under his hairless scrotum and began to tease the root of his cock with practised skill. Sure enough, the organ began to stir, twitching against the shiny black crop and darkening to purple as the tissue swelled with blood. She smiled to herself. It was true: males always responded to crude and objectifying treatment.

'Take off my shoes, *carefully*, and rub my feet,' she said to the confused young man. As he crouched down at the end of the divan to carry out her order, she pointed her crop at the blond. 'You, get down here and start kissing the top of my thighs, *softly*.' Scowling, she glanced at the dark-haired escort with the incriminating stubble. 'And you, Mr Five O'Clock Shadow, go over to the bar and fetch me a glass of champagne.'

Hands and lips set to work at once. Her expensive black stilettos were slipped from her feet with utmost care and placed beside a briefcase on an ornate table at the end of the divan. Then the kneeling man set about massaging her feet, pressing his strong thumbs against her soles, which shone palely through sheer nylon stockings. The blond was down on his knees too, head lowered towards her reclining body. Obedient to her commands, he planted gentle kisses along the inside of her upper thighs. Valerie Sales felt a pleasant tingle running through her flesh as his lips skirted the tight line of her black panties and brushed the sensitive skin above her lacy stocking tops. Holding the crop in one hand, she used the other to stroke the busy blond head down at her crotch.

'Good boy,' she said. 'Just like that.'

A flute of chilled champagne was brought to her. She took the stem between her fingertips and sipped, leaving the big brunet to stand dumbly before the divan and watch his fellow escorts pamper her body. One was absorbed in the task of caressing her toes through the dark reinforced tips of her stockings, while the other continued to worship her tender inner thighs. She detected envy in the eyes of the redundant escort. His cock had swollen and bobbed stiffly before him, dribbling shiny liquid from the tip.

'Take,' she said, passing him the empty glass, 'and fetch me another.' While he grudgingly did her bidding, she took the blond by the chin, lifted his head from her lap and told him to stand up. The smell of her had aroused him. The head of his cock was deep red and the shaft was traced through with thick purple veins, giving it a knobbly wooden appearance.

She turned her attention back to the big brunet who stood before her with the champagne. She took the glass, sipped from it and then said:

'Get down on your knees.'

'But . . .'

'You're not being paid to argue with me.'

He lowered himself onto his knees at the head of the divan. She knew his type all too well. One of the many photogenic young men who came to London, cocksure they would make it as male models. They ended up working as waiters and barmen or, like this specimen, they signed up with one of the growing number of agencies that provided escorts for wealthy women. He was resentful about his lack of success and having to earn a living in this way – she could see it in his surly manner. Back in his hometown he had doubtless enjoyed a succession of fawning girlfriends; but here in the capital, without money or any marketable talent, with only his body and good looks to recommend him, he was a cheap sex toy for women like Valerie Sales.

'Put out your hand, palm up,' she said to him when he was kneeling down, and she casually placed her half-full glass upon it. He stared at the glass in cold disbelief. She had turned him into her table. His male pride rebelled at the insult and made his whole body shake. But he remained in position, down on his knees, arm outstretched, balancing the champagne glass on his upturned palm.

Valerie Sales looked at the blond. He stood beside his kneeling glass-balancing colleague, his veiny cock pointing stiffly forward. Resting on one elbow, she assumed a more comfortable position from which to study his aroused organ. Erect cocks were simple yet fascinating things, she thought, brute slaves to their single and undisguised purpose. The blond's thick knobbly shaft was quite literally bursting with desire to fuck her. It had begun to weep fluid from the tip and she could clearly see the lumpy veins throbbing under the skin.

She leaned forward and spat on it aggressively, depositing a thick gob of saliva along the top of the shaft. Looking up into the man's astonished eyes, she spread the sticky juice with her hand until his whole cock glistened. The hot slick flesh excited her. She kicked away the escort who was still massaging her feet, sat up and dragged off her panties. Turning around and resting her elbows on the back of the divan, she presented her bare ass to the blond.

'Stick it inside me,' she ordered.

He stepped forward eagerly and guided the head of his cock into the tight fur-lined mouth between her ass cheeks. She whimpered as he pressed himself inside her. The stiff oversized organ stretched her so wide it hurt. But her sex quickly expanded, becoming wet and slippery for him, and her whimpers soon turned into shameless groans.

'Fuck me,' she gasped, looking over her shoulder. 'Fuck me hard.' And she pushed back her strong hips to meet his thrusts. The blond performed well, working for her enjoyment and not his own. He kept the steady rhythm she demanded, filling and stretching her cunt with his bought male organ. She reached a hand between her legs and selfishly stroked her clit as he pumped her.

'Stop,' she shouted after a while. Panting with excitement, she ordered him to withdraw and made him sit down on the divan. His juice-coated cock towered up from his thighs and she quickly straddled him and sank herself upon it. Breathing rapidly, she rode him, her long fingernails clutching his broad shoulders, her breasts pressed up against his face.

She glanced at the man who had served as her foot rubber. He was standing at the end of the divan and stroking a huge erection as he watched her fucking his colleague.

'Get down behind me and kiss my ass,' she shouted.

He hesitated, taken aback by the outrageous command.

'Didn't you hear me?' She rode up and down on the stiff cock and spoke between deep moans of pleasure. 'Come here and kiss my ass. I won't tell you again.'

The man moved behind her and knelt down, positioning himself between the parted knees of the other escort. Her lusty buttocks bounced in front of his face and he leaned forward and chased them with his lips. Valerie Sales felt the warm pressure of his mouth against her fleshy cheeks.

'Kiss me like you mean it,' she shouted down to him.

The man redoubled his efforts, attaching his lips to the bouncing globes of flesh and sucking hard. The noise of his frantic kisses reached her ears and delighted her. The physical sensation caused by his busy lips was pleasant, but it was the very idea of compelling one man to kiss her ass while she selfishly rode another's cock that she found most erotic. She imagined herself a cruel all-powerful empress from antiquity dominating a palace of terrified male slaves.

'Kiss my asshole,' she said viciously.

His lips went into her hairy cleft and found her tight crinkled hole. She was sensitive here and the softest kiss sent a shiver running through her. Purring loudly, she pressed herself down on the cock and slowly rolled her hips. She pushed back her buttocks and parted them with one hand, increasing access to her anus.

'Kiss it harder,' she moaned.

The man began to suck. She felt his lips tugging at her ring as if they were trying to draw nourishment from it. Grinding on the hard cock, she shouted crude words of encouragement and shook her buttocks against his face. He was nothing but her dirty ass kisser.

'Now lick it!' she commanded.

Obediently, he swirled his tongue across her hole. He worked hard, attending to his lowly task even when she resumed bouncing up and down on the trapped cock. Pressing his face into the musky fur-lined furrow, he moved with the rise and fall of her ass, diligently licking and probing her tight salty ring.

She felt the tip of his tongue penetrate her. It twisted and turned inside her ticklish back passage, making her shriek with delight. She felt joyous, proud, spoilt, and her sex began to contract around the big cock. It was not a convulsive orgasm she experienced but a warm melting sensation that rose from her asshole and up through her belly. She fell forward with a moan, smothering the blond in her deep bra-enhanced cleavage. She savoured the sensation of the hard shaft stuffed inside her and the quick sharp tongue poking at her ass crack.

When her moment ended, she pushed the face away from her buttocks and climbed off the still erect cock which dripped with the evidence of her pleasure. She stood before the kneeling brunet, lifted the glass of champagne from his shaking palm and swallowed the contents in a gulp.

'OK, furry chops,' she said, handing him the glass, 'put this on the bar and come right back here.' While he carried out her instructions, she opened the briefcase that lay on the table next to her shoes and took out a bright pink dildo attached to a leather harness. With adroit fingers, she fastened the harness around her hips and between her thighs so the long artificial cock protruded from her crotch. The three men stared at her, their faces expressing wonder and apprehension.

'What? You've never seen a woman with a cock before?' she joked. She ordered her former foot rubber to place her shoes on the floor at her feet and she stepped into them, rising several inches in height, her dark stocking-clad legs gaining length and definition.

'Back down on your knees,' she said to the big brunet.

The beaten man got down into a kneeling position and she stepped towards him, grinning wickedly. With the added height of the heels the shiny plastic cock was level with his face. Placing a hand on top of his head, she wordlessly guided his mouth towards her obscene appendage. Despondently, he took the bulbous tip between his lips and began to suck, his cheeks hollowing as he did so. The sight of his rented mouth moving back and forth over the garish pink shaft made her thighs tremble. Deep down, this one was a true slut, she decided. She would enjoy taking his virgin manhole.

'Swallow it,' she said, pushing her crotch into his face. 'The wetter you make it the easier it's going to be for you.' Holding his skull firmly between her hands, she began to fuck his mouth. He gagged each time the head prodded the back of his throat and tears welled in his eyes, but Valerie Sales continued to thrust her insensitive cock regardless. When finally she pulled it from his mouth, it was coated with saliva.

'Turn around and get on all fours.'

He was reluctant to obey. Not until she had ordered the blond to pass her the riding crop and threatened him with it, did the brunet slowly assume the bitch posture she required. She kicked his knees further apart with her foot and lowered herself behind him, her cock nudging his buttock cleft as she got comfortable. Resting on her knees and using one hand to part his cheeks, the other to direct the cock, she poked the exposed male hole. The brunet yelped and his body recoiled with the first contact.

'Get back here! I'm paying good money for this ass.'

Clutching a buttock, she steadily squeezed home the head of her tool, watching intently as the virgin sphincter split open to receive the intruding object. She relished the weak plaintive sounds that came from her male bitch. Even the toughest men broke when she took them this way. His stretched asshole reminded her of a tiny mouth, open and ready to scream: only it had been silenced, choked full with her favourite prosthetic cock. They were all whores, these vain young men, their precious little bottom holes on sale for a few hundred pounds apiece. She started to screw him, pushing her cock a little deeper with each thrust until half of her length was buried in his back passage. She would make him earn his pay, show him that nothing came easy in this city.

She summoned the other two escorts, one to each side of her, and took their erect cocks in her hands. Holding onto them as if they were handles, she continued to fuck her bent-over boy toy who was moaning into the carpet. She wanked the cocks roughly with her fists, turning her head and sucking on one, then the other. She felt euphoric. She was the mistress of three cocks and the sovereign of a pretty boy's ass.

The leather strap was pulled tight between her thighs and rubbed against her sex as she jerked her hips and punished her ill-groomed man bitch. With each thrust she felt a stab of pleasure. The deeper she penetrated the greater her reward, and she used his ass callously, driven by the animal urges of her clit. Stifled grunts rose from the carpet but these desperate sounds only spurred her on. Releasing the two cocks, she fell on top of her bent-over victim and wrapped her arms around his chest as if there was a danger he might crawl away before she had reached her orgasm. She humped him furiously, the front of her thighs welded to his buttocks, her insatiable cock tunnelling deep inside his back passage.

This time she cried out as she climaxed. She remained buried inside him and rolled her hips languorously, maintaining a constant pressure against her pulsating clit. The man's body began to spasm too. She seldom aimed to make them come, but invariably they lost control, driven to climax against their will by her own selfish pleasure-seeking. She reached down a hand and squeezed his balls as they erupted. She liked to feel men emptying themselves, spending their spoonful of spunk. The male and his pitiful single orgasm.

When he was done, she withdrew her permanently hard cock and stood up. Glowing from her second orgasm, she stepped in front of the crouching man. Standing tall in her exquisite stiletto heels, she waved her pink phallus above his bowed head.

'Suck it,' she ordered.

He raised his face slowly, like a beaten warrior.

'Suck it clean,' she repeated. 'Every sticky inch of it.'

Later, while in the bathroom, Valerie Sales overheard the three escorts talking among themselves as they prepared to leave her hotel suite. It was the usual grumbling of male escorts about abusive female clients. She had no sympathy for them. Why should she pity a whore? They chose this work because it paid more than the other jobs they were qualified to do. A generation ago, few self-respecting males would have sold their bodies for a living. But things had changed. Women were rising to the top in business and the professions and the men they outclassed were entering the labour market to provide for their needs.

'. . . but not as bad as the Russian nympho,' she heard one of the men say.

'Christ no!' said another. 'It would take a team of stallions to satisfy her.'

'The more cock these executive bitches get, the more cock they want.'

Valerie Sales came out of the bathroom. The men immediately stopped talking, like schoolboys caught by a feared headmistress.

'Who are you bitching about, boys?'

'Nobody, ma'am,' muttered the blond.

Fastening her robe around herself, she came closer. 'Don't be shy. You can tell me.'

The men stared down at the floor, intimidated by her bold grin. They knew the agency rule. Under no circumstances were they allowed to pass on information about their clients. Valerie Sales was aware of the rule too, but she also knew that whores were never to be trusted.

'How much is this going to cost?' She picked up her purse from the table, opened it and plucked out a few crisp £20 notes. 'Now, tell me her name.'

The blond escort stretched his hand towards the money. 'Katerina . . . Katerina Dominovna.'

The name Katerina Dominovna was familiar to Valerie Sales from a feature about women business leaders she had recently read while flying back from New York. She remained at home the next day stretched out on the couch with her laptop, seeking more information about this exceptional woman who had inherited an ailing media company following the death of her husband and, in under a year, single-handedly reversed its fortunes. A search using Google returned tens of thousands of results. There were pages of images too, showing her rival in the company of minor celebrities, politicians and sinister-looking oligarchs. She had even been photographed shaking hands with Vladimir Putin, whose cross-eyed gaze was angled down towards her prominent bust. Valerie Sales could not help but admire the statuesque Russian. Her light-brown hair fell in loose waves around her handsome face and her blue-green eyes stared proudly from every picture. Her smile was broad and confident and she was always stylishly dressed, a combination of thigh-high leather boots and an expensive fur jacket her preferred attire for both business and pleasure. *Time Magazine* billed her the 'Czarina' and a full-page colour photograph of her in *Business Week* had the caption 'The Boss in Boots'.

But it was the gossip and rumours about the Russian that Valerie Sales found most absorbing. There were revelations about numerous affairs involving both men and women and reports of sex parties at the many properties she owned in Russia and abroad. Yet the Russian seemed to thrive on her reputation and her business continued to expand, swallowing up its competitors with astonishing rapidity. 'The end of the double standard,' announced *The Times* in a leader that mentioned Katerina Dominovna by name. 'Women have finally achieved equality in the boardroom and the bedroom – and they seem to be outperforming men in both arenas.'

A month later, the two women met in person at a French restaurant in Mayfair. Valerie Sales arrived first, wearing a navy Chanel jacket, a provocatively short pencil skirt and high heels. She cut a striking figure and the other customers, mostly greying businessmen, halted their conversations and followed with their eyes as a bow-tied waiter showed her to the alcove table booked in her name. She lowered herself onto the chair he pulled out for her and sat with one leg crossed over the other, exposing a seductive expanse of smooth stocking-clad thigh. Indifferent to the inquiring glances, she ordered from the wine list and checked her personal organiser while she sipped her drink. Beneath the calm exterior, she was fuming – the Russian woman had dared to keep her waiting.

Katerina Dominovna turned up more than half an hour late, accompanied by a thickset man with a shaved head. Standing over six feet tall in elegant black boots, she coolly surveyed the interior of the restaurant. Valerie Sales experienced a pleasant sense of awe as she watched her. The Russian radiated power and female sexual allure to a degree she found almost intoxicating. But she contained the feelings stirring within her. When their eyes met, she merely nodded politely and allowed a trace of a smile to appear on her lips. The Russian acknowledged Valerie Sales in a more generous manner, the corners of her sensual mouth stretching wide as if she had seen an appetising dessert. She turned to the man who was standing at her side, dismissed him brusquely and crossed to the table.

'I'm so sorry to have kept you waiting,' she said, extending her hand. But there was little conviction in her strongly accented voice. 'I completely lost track of the time, I was so busy. I've been on the job since I arrived in London last night.'

'I'm sure you have,' said Valerie Sales, rising to squeeze the Russian's proffered hand and struggling not to laugh at her confused use of English idiom. They sat down and the Russian ordered a drink from the waiter.

'Your English men are very handsome,' she remarked casually. 'Russian men are bigger but they are not always pretty to look at.' Her sharp green eyes trailed the waiter as he walked away with the wine list. 'That one has such a cute ass, don't you agree?'

'Yes indeed,' said Valerie Sales dryly, 'but I do believe he is Algerian.' And she raised her glass to her lips and smugly sipped her drink.

The tone of the meeting had been set. The two women spoke politely and put on plastic smiles as they discussed business, but there was a deep hostility between them. They sized up one another like matriarchs of rival dynasties, silently comparing hairstyles, jewellery and manicures. When the Russian interrupted the conversation to take a call on her mobile, Valerie Sales had to fight the urge to reach across the table and slap her face.

'Now that we've made our positions clear to one another,' she said as Katerina Dominovna slipped her

213

phone back inside her handbag, 'I would like to suggest we conduct our negotiations in more cordial surroundings. There is a private club not far from London which caters exclusively for women like ourselves.'

'Women like ourselves?' the Russian asked.

'High-earning executive women who are not afraid to express their desires.'

'Tell me more about this club.'

'Our male counterparts have always mixed business and pleasure. They frequently close deals in strip clubs and massage parlours. But I think you would agree, our needs are more complex than theirs.'

'Absolutely.' Sipping her drink, the Russian cast a lustful glance at the young waiter as he walked past their table. 'My needs become more complex every day.'

'At the club there are no limits to what you can experience and discretion is assured. I can even arrange it so that we have the place entirely to ourselves.'

'Just the two of us?'

'There will be staff there, of course, and menwhores too, as many as we require.'

The Russian wriggled on her chair. ' "Menwhores". I have never heard that expression before but I like it. I like it very much. But what do you have in mind, Ms Sales?'

'A contest, Ms Dominovna.'

'Are you challenging me?'

'You have quite a reputation. They say you can exhaust six strong men in a single evening.'

The Russian smiled. 'Thank you. I have also heard tales about you, my darling. And to think, your poor old husband is still alive! He must cry into his pillow when you climb into bed smelling of your nighttime adventures in hotel rooms.'

'Then we understand one another.'

'Perfectly.'

'This is what I propose. My driver will take us to the

club this evening and whoever exhausts the most men by morning can claim victory.'

'A fucking-contest?'

'Aptly put, Ms Dominovna.'

'And how are we to determine when a man has been exhausted?'

'Simple. When his balls have been emptied he counts as exhausted. That is generally the case with men, don't you find?'

The Russian grinned. 'This competition is going to be very easy for both of us. I think we will lose count of our exhausted boys long before morning. It will be like milking cows.'

'I expected a little more imagination from somebody of your renown, Ms Dominovna. Any girl can milk a cock. But it takes a truly superior woman to exhaust a man with a cock of her own.'

'Continue, Ms Sales, I'm listening.'

'I'm sure you are aware that men have a special place inside their asses. I think nature put it there for the benefit of women like ourselves. If you have the skill to excite this male joy-spot, as I call it, the owner's balls will erupt whether he wills it or not.'

'Ah, so it is we two who shall be doing all the fucking?'

'Until sunrise.'

'And the prize?'

'Whoever has exhausted the most men by morning will gain possession of the other's business.'

The Russian fell silent and reflected, but she retained her relaxed and confident demeanour. Finally she spoke: 'You play for high stakes, Ms Sales. And with the livelihood of your employees too. But I accept your challenge. Your public relations company would be very useful to me and I can't think of a more enjoyable way to get hold of it than by fucking my way through a line of your pretty English menwhores.'

* * *

215

The club, a former hunting lodge, was located in the Chilterns in tens of acres of undulating land and hidden from the road behind a wall of trees. After gaining admittance through a pair of tall iron gates, the chauffeur followed a winding drive to the front of the main house, where Valerie Sales and Katerina Dominovna were greeted by a conservatively dressed young woman who would serve as their hostess and referee. Leaving the chauffeur standing beside the car in the falling dusk, the three women went inside the club and discussed the evening's arrangements over drinks at the bar.

'All the men have accepted your terms and conditions,' said the hostess. 'Initially some were reluctant to take part in such a competition, but the financial compensation you're offering proved irresistible. You can expect silence and complete obedience from every one of them.'

Valerie Sales nodded her approval. She was impressed by the red-haired woman's efficiency and forthright manner and considered poaching her for her own staff.

'Their balls, crotches and arseholes have been thoroughly shaved and they have all been given enemas as you instructed. Cleanliness is guaranteed.'

'I can hardly wait to begin!' cried the Russian, wriggling on her stool.

'The Ottoman suite has been prepared for you,' the hostess continued. 'I shall wait in the hall outside and send in men as required. They will be naked and each will have a number stencilled on his right buttock for identification purposes. Your colour is black, Ms Sales, and yours white, Ms Dominovna. I shall keep a tally of those you exhaust according to the definition you have given me.' She paused briefly and in a matter-of-fact voice inquired: 'Do you require cocks or have you brought your own?'

Valerie Sales and the Russian looked at one another and then down at their briefcases. Both grinned girlishly.

'I seldom travel anywhere without mine,' said the former. 'High heels, an Italian handbag and a strap-on cock are *de rigueur* for every serious businesswoman.'

'How true,' agreed the Russian. 'Though I would add a fourth item to your list: a personal assistant with a long and flexible tongue!'

The three women laughed and sipped their drinks.

'But to return to our business,' said Valerie Sales, addressing the hostess, 'I did request a riding crop for myself and my Russian friend.'

Apologising profusely for her forgetfulness, the young woman left the bar and quickly returned, carrying a pair of short black riding crops wrapped in a velvet cloth. She presented one to each of the guests.

'You think of everything, Ms Sales,' said the Russian, and she flexed the slender rod between her hands, nodding approvingly.

'I rarely have use for one,' said Valerie Sales, brushing her fingertips along the smooth length of cane. 'But it is a useful accessory to carry on an occasion such as this. It shows a man who is in charge and lets him see from the outset what kind of woman you are. Men are such unsubtle creatures. Crude symbols of power like crops and whips work wonders on them.'

The Ottoman suite lived up to its name. Panels of embroidered silk hung before the walls and the floor was a mosaic of richly coloured rugs. Lamps burned in the corners and a dizzying fragrance, a blend of jasmine flower, cloves and other exotic spices, rose into the nostrils of the women as they entered.

'A harem!' said the Russian, gazing about the room in delight.

'But in this harem,' said Valerie Sales, 'it is the men who wait patiently in scented twilight, and distinguished female guests who come to satisfy their jaded appetites. It is my favourite of all the fantasy rooms.'

A pair of men approached. Each was naked and boasted a lean and well-defined physique. Their chests and crotches were hairless and their smooth oiled skin reflected the amber light of the lamps. Bowing respectfully, they took the briefcases that were handed to them, turned around – each man displaying a large number 1 on his right buttock – and led the women to their respective corners. Other naked men awaited them, squatting around broad mattresses scattered with cushions.

Holding her crop at her side, each woman allowed herself to be undressed by her stable of male attendants. Jackets and blouses were removed with great care and threaded onto hangers; skirts were eased gently over hips and neatly folded. A kneeling man unzipped the Russian's tall boots, freeing her calves and feet while she rested a hand on his head for support. But Valerie Sales would not permit her high-heeled shoes or black lingerie to be removed.

'How modest you are,' remarked the Russian, noticing the other woman's attachment to her lacy underwear. She herself had been completely undressed and was slipping her arms into a satin robe that an attendant held open for her.

'Not at all, Ms Dominovna. I find that properly fashioned lingerie enhances female nudity.' She glanced down at a male who was kneeling on the rug in front of her. His face was level with the mound of her panty crotch and his eyes were riveted to the dark welts at the top of her sheer stockings. 'It also has the advantage of exciting men.'

'I do not require such an advantage,' retorted the Russian, and she reclined on the mattress like a model posing for a French painter. The front of the untied robe fell open to expose a swathe of pale flesh running from her neck to her thighs.

Valerie Sales felt a surge of admiration for the body of her competitor. She had well-formed shoulders,

218

heavy yet beautifully shaped breasts and broad maternal hips. Between her solid thighs was a bushy triangle of fur, a shade darker than the hair on her head. Like Valerie Sales, the Russian trimmed but did not shave her sex, preserving its primitive and slightly uncouth appearance.

Resting lazily on her elbows, the Russian stretched out a leg and flexed her toes sensually. 'You,' she said, pointing to the nearest man. 'Suck them.'

The man stepped forward and dropped to his knees with surprising willingness. He cupped the heel in his palm and with a peculiar relish sniffed along the pale wrinkled sole, which moments earlier had been enclosed in the tight leather boot. Sighing loudly and shutting his eyes, he took the large big toe between his lips.

'No hands,' she said, glaring down at him. Immediately the man took away his hand, but he kept the toe in his mouth, sucking it like an infant animal nursing on a long teat.

'I have more than one toe,' she complained, forcing open his jaw and squeezing her other toes inside. He gurgled passively as his mouth was invaded. His lips stretched grotesquely to accommodate the big knuckles at the end of her foot.

'Keep sucking! I didn't tell you to stop.'

The role of female pasha came naturally to the Russian. While her toes were being sucked, she nibbled dates from a platter that a kneeling attendant held for her. The man down at her feet never wavered in his devotion. He surrendered his mouth to her restless toes, bending almost to the floor as she gradually lowered her leg over the edge of the mattress.

'Enough,' she said finally and pulled her foot away from him.

But the man clutched desperately at her ankle. Grunting, he chased her wet toes with his hungry wide-open mouth.

'Enough, I said!' She gave his face a shove with her heel. It was powerful enough to send him sprawling onto his back.

He did not attempt to get up, but lay motionless on the floor, eyes glazed over, an inane grin on his lips. Valerie Sales saw with dismay that white goo was dribbling from his short chubby cock and big blobs of the same viscous substance were soaking into the rug near the spot where he had been kneeling.

The Russian saw the mess too and gave a throaty laugh. She had exposed a footslut, a foot-obsessed male submissive. Such men were the bane of every male escort agency and their numbers seemed to increase just as quickly as the female client base grew. Valerie Sales encountered them with a monotonous regularity and always made her dissatisfaction known. But on this occasion there was more than an evening's entertainment at stake. The Russian had been given a headstart. The degenerate footfreak would be added to her tally of spent males.

'I had no idea your English menwhores would be so easy to milk,' she said condescendingly. 'I think I can afford to take my time.' She stretched out on the mattress and parted her legs. The bottom of the robe fell open around her hips to reveal her pink sex in its nest of hair. Glancing at a member of her harem, she calmly issued an order:

'Come here and lick me.'

Without hesitation, the man got down on all fours at the side of the bed. Buttocks raised to reveal a white number 2, he buried his head between the Russian woman's thick creamy thighs and worked his tongue vigorously, exploring the hairy folds of her sex. Her face twitched suddenly and she tensed, her thighs closing possessively around the man's ears. Sighing, she laid her head back on a cushion and wound her fingers through his mop of curly hair.

Valerie Sales was in no mood for foreplay. The future of her company was at stake and her own reputation too. She grabbed the arm of the man who was kneeling in front of her and steered him towards the bed.

'Open the case,' she barked at another man. 'And give me the cock.'

In no time at all she had strapped the fearsome device to her hips. The big plastic shaft, the colour of doll-skin and complete with balls, projected from the crotch of her black panties, a burlesque imitation of the real thing.

All that mattered to her now was beating the Russian. She allowed the cringing man a few seconds to moisten the end of her phallus with his mouth, then she turned him around and bent him over the edge of the bed so that his bare buttocks were raised towards her.

'Please,' he gasped, 'use some lubricant.'

His voice angered her. This whinging male and his fellow whores stood between her and victory. 'Quiet,' she growled, pushing his face down between a pair of cushions. 'I've paid for this ass.' She spread his buttocks forcefully and directed the head of her cock towards the exposed crack. His ass recoiled and he clenched the muscular cheeks together, defending his virgin anus from her attack. She shrieked in frustration and struck his buttocks hard with her palm.

'Give me your arsehole, you cheap slut! Give me your fucking arsehole or you'll never work for any agency ever again.' The threat produced the desired result. It seldom failed. Trembling, the handsome young escort unclenched his bum cheeks and surrendered his virgin hole to the imperious executive woman. Indifferent to his shame, she parted his glutes to reveal the hairless orifice buried between them. The sight of the bared male rectum excited her. It signified weakness and vulnerability. The man was only a few years her junior. She and he could be lovers. Yet here he was, forced by circumstances to sell his body to her and submit to this most degrading of acts.

Holding her cock with one hand, she drove forward, splitting open the tight crack. She squeezed the bulbous head into the narrow slot, savouring the deep male grunts that she forced from her victim's throat.

'Be still,' she ordered as if talking to an animal. She took a firm hold of his hips and advanced her brutal pink cock inch by inch up his back passage. His anal lips distended around the invading object and he pressed his face into the cushions to mute his cries. Virgin assholes were springy and stubborn and their resistance was prized highly by connoisseurs like Valerie Sales. She pushed the dildo hard and the leather harness strap squeezed against her excited clit, richly rewarding her efforts.

The other men in her stable watched in fear as she made use of one of their number. The man's asshole soon slackened sufficiently for her to fuck him properly and she began to jerk her hips with a steady rhythm, sliding her tool back and forth with a laddish swagger. She enjoyed showing them how expertly she could use a cock and make a big man squeal beneath her like a teenage girl. Her dark hair fell loose and she arched over his back, a cruel conquering she-animal. Gripping his shoulders, she pulled his body towards her thrusting cock. Her large breasts, cradled in the low-cut bra, swung back and forth as she humped him with all the strength in her broad female hips.

The man began to whimper. She put a hand between his legs and felt for his cock. It was stiff and dribbling juice. 'Come for me, you little slut!' she growled against his neck. 'I know you love it.' She changed rhythm and, keeping the cock buried inside his ass, she ground her hips in a circular motion. His cries grew louder and more abandoned as she stirred and stretched his bowels. Altering the depth and angle of her penetrating cock, she controlled his every sensation.

From the other bed she could hear Katerina Dominovna's loud moans of pleasure as the curly head busied itself between her fleshy thighs. The noise distracted Valerie Sales and made her even more determined to beat the arrogant Russian who had the effrontery to indulge her own cravings during a competition.

She turned her attention back to the man skewered on her plastic shaft. Again she reached down for his cock like a farmer checking the readiness of a stud bull. It felt thick and warm between her fingers and was oozing copious amounts of sticky fluid. She could have wanked him off in seconds, but she would not stoop to cheating. Still arched above him, she slid her shaft in and out of his now gaping asshole, urging him to come. He bit into a cushion and clenched his fingers, fighting back the strange sensations stirred in him by her plunging cock. But his virgin ass was no match for her relentless precision fucking. Repeatedly she nudged against his spot until he lost all control. His balls tensed involuntarily and he shouted out in denial as their liquid contents foamed up through his cock and spurted across the sheet.

Valerie Sales' performance roused the Russian from her complacency. Shoving the male head away from her thighs, she rose to her feet and discarded the robe, revealing her voluptuous naked body.

'My briefcase,' she said, pointing her finger.

She snatched the case from a trembling male hand, opened it and took out an enormous black phallus attached to a pair of latex bikini briefs. The size of the artificial cock astounded everybody, Valerie Sales included. With all eyes upon her, the Russian put on the device, pulling the briefs up her long sturdy legs as nonchalantly as a woman slipping into a pair of panties. The shiny black latex clung to her hips like a second skin and nestled in the valley between her heavy buttocks. She made a quick adjustment to the cock, pointing it forward at the angle she required.

Valerie Sales stared across the room in wonder. It was the biggest cock, real or artificial, she had ever laid eyes on. Like a club of polished ebony, it bobbed menacingly from the Russian's latex crotch, making a striking contrast with her snowy thighs. Clutching the base in her fist, the imposing woman stepped to where the man marked number 2 was cringing on the rug next to the mattress.

'Put out your tongue,' she ordered, holding the thick black shaft in front of his face. She was staring down at him, blue-green eyes glinting wickedly above high cheek bones. 'I said tongue out!'

His jaws parted slowly and out crept a pointed tongue one centimetre at a time until it hung fully extended, a tender pink offering to her eagerly poised cock. She cock-slapped it repeatedly, flicking her wrist with focused aggression. The sound of dense phallus beating against moist flesh was loud enough for Valerie Sales to hear.

'Now suck,' she said.

The man forced his lips around the head of her thuggish tool and sucked. Standing with hands on hips she watched him fellate her and issued instructions. He worked diligently, swallowing her shaft like a true bought slut, choking and spluttering as it knocked against his tonsils.

'Enough!'

With a wet popping noise she pulled her cock free of his lips. Despite his desperate efforts, he had managed to wet only an inch or two around the plum-shaped head.

'Over the bed,' she said curtly.

'Oh God!' he cried. 'Please, no!'

'What's wrong? You've taken a lady's cock before. I can tell by the way you sucked me.'

'But never such a big one, ma'am. And it's still dry.'

'Wet it then,' she said impatiently and presented her cock to him once more.

He set to work, diligently running his tongue up and down the mighty shaft, struggling to cover it with saliva. But fear had made his mouth dry and his attempt to lubricate the long device was pitiful. The Russian laughed at his frantic efforts.

After watching him for a while, she bent her head and dribbled a long line of spittle down onto the cock. The man showed his gratitude by quickly rubbing his mouth through her foamy contribution, spreading it along the shaft. The Russian made several more donations, all equally generous, and he received them eagerly. With his tongue and lips he smeared her woman-spit over the plastic as soon as it landed, fearful of wasting a single precious drop of lubricant.

'That will do,' she said when her whole cock was varnished with saliva. She instructed the man to bend over, elbows on the mattress, and arch up his backside. 'Higher! Higher!' she shouted as she took her position behind him. Parting his buttocks with one hand and guiding the big cock with the other, she butted the soft undefended target. On her third attempt the man let out a scream. Incredibly, she had broken into his hole with her prodigious phallus. Valerie Sales felt another twinge of envy. The Russian had judged correctly. The man was one of the agency's dildo sluts and possessed a loose and accommodating asshole. Her competitor was having all the luck.

She grabbed another man from her stable and bent him over the bed as the Russian had done. She wetted her forefinger in her mouth and then squeezed it slowly into his anus until all but the last knuckle was buried in his passage. He protested weakly as she twisted it around inside him, opening up the tensed muscles, readying them for her cock.

225

The noise coming from the Russian's corner was terrific. The man was squealing like a stuck pig and Valerie Sales could not stop herself from glancing over. The poor male bitch was sprawled face down across the mattress and the powerful Russian was stretched out on top of him, her forearm around his neck. Her fleshy latex-clad ass jerked up and down with animal vigour. As she screwed him, she shouted words in Russian, short harsh utterances intended to goad and command, just like a jockey spurring on a horse.

Valerie Sales inserted a second finger into her man's anus, determined not to be intimidated by the bravura performance of her competitor. With her two experienced digits, she reamed his hole sufficiently for her cock to enter. Taking a cue from the Russian, she spat, directing gobs of her thick spittle into the gaping male orifice. Then she slid herself inside.

Once she began to fuck, she forgot about the Russian. There was nothing she enjoyed more in life than taking a helpless male up the ass. She was feared in the boardroom and ran her ageing husband's company with an iron hand, but her desire to dominate – and dominate men in particular – found its fullest expression in her sex life.

Panting with exertion, she leaned forward, pressing her large breasts against the young man's back, and brought her mouth down to his ear. 'Who owns your ass?' she growled, thrusting her rigid cock deeper into his rectum.

'You, ma'am,' he sobbed.

That was what she liked to hear, the pathetic submission of a bought male slut. His asshole would recover from the violation in time, no matter how roughly she took him, but the effect on his morale would be everlasting. As she poked the gaping red hole, she mused about using the same technique to cow her workforce. The idea made her wet between the legs. She imagined herself striding through an open-plan office wearing a slutty skirt suit and stiletto heels, surveying the ranks of men bowed over their computers. Each one cringed when she passed, trembling in his most private region as he recalled the terrible sensation of her stern and unnatural cock.

The women settled into their stride, each one fucking her man with a punishing rhythm. Clustered around the beds, the other marked men watched in silent dread. The Russian soon cock-speared number 2 to an ear-splitting climax and, even before he had crawled away, she had seized her next victim. Her fair skin was flushed pink and her big bare breasts rose and fell in time to her excited breathing. Pressing herself against the muscular body of the new man, she sucked and licked his lips and ran her fingers proprietarily over his cock and balls, urging a response. Then she turned him around, like an object she had purchased, and pushed his head down into the cushions on the mattress. Taking up position behind him, the insatiable black cock bobbing in anticipation, she gave his numbered buttock a hard slap.

Valerie Sales dragged one of the men from her pool, a big dark individual with thick hairy limbs. Undaunted by his size, she ordered him to lie on his back and spread his legs. She climbed nimbly onto the mattress and knelt between his thighs, pushing back his knees with her hands so that his shaved ass crack was peeping up at her. He turned his head away in shame, yet continued to eye the lurid pink cock that was poised to assault him.

'What a marvellous idea,' exclaimed the Russian, glancing over her shoulder as she steadily fucked her own male. 'You're going to take him like a pretty virgin bride.'

The 'virgin bride' was over six feet tall with a jutting chin and the body of a field athlete. His pumped-up muscles and dark manly features impressed Valerie

Sales and her unchallenged gaze devoured him, moving over his square shoulders and beefy pectorals down to where his cock lolled between his open thighs. Even in its unaroused state it was thick and meaty.

She slid forward and rubbed the head of her own cock over the shaved bridge of flesh between his asshole and balls. Her skilful teasing quickly yielded results and his heavy cock stirred and began to grow, its animal nature taking over. She fixed her gaze on his face, which remained turned to one side, and nudged her slippery pink phallus against his arsehole. Holding it in place with a hand and steadily increasing the pressure on the clenched ring of flesh, she managed to squeeze the plump tip inside. His doleful expression fascinated her. It seemed the bigger the man, the greater his despair at being violated by a woman.

She stretched over him, leaning on her elbows, her face held just above his, and fucked him with careful contempt. He lay still, frigidly so, legs raised and knees bent. His eyes watered with pain and humiliation, yet he was excited by the abominable thing she was doing to him. She felt his cock stiffen into a flesh truncheon beneath her belly. It rubbed against her as she moved back and forth, wetting her skin with its liquid confession of joy. He was an easy slut after all.

She thrust a dozen more times, carefully directing her cock to intensify the tormenting pleasure in his ass, then she swiftly withdrew, sensing his climax was approaching. She sat on her knees between his legs and watched his convulsions. His big balls heaved and with a few rapid contractions they surrendered their contents, the white goo spattering up across his hairy torso.

Were it not for the number stencilled onto each man's right buttock, Valerie Sales would soon have lost count of her conquests. With her skilful technique and brute determination, she forced climax after climax. She took her victims from the front and the rear, sometimes standing, sometimes kneeling and sometimes lying above them on the bed. For hours, the Ottoman suite echoed with the cries of dildo-impaled men and the sheets and rugs were bespattered with the sticky evidence of the women's success. Standing at the door with her clipboard, the hostess ticked off the vanquished and sent in a steady stream of replacements. The naked men huddled in their respective corners, waiting to feel the cruel and indefatigable cock of the woman who had bought them.

Valerie Sales was in her zone. The adrenaline surged through her veins and gave her a feeling of limitless power and energy. Her head was blissfully clear, her breathing deep and rhythmical. She glanced across at the Russian who, like her, was crouched over a prone male body, her cock stuffed deep inside his arse. As she watched the Russian perform, her wet sex rubbed against the strap between her legs. It was herself she saw across the room in this unbridled display of female libido and she felt a sudden sisterly bond with the other woman.

The Russian sensed something too and turned her head, but as she did so her man squirmed off the end of her punishing black cock. She crawled after him, seized him by the neck and re-entered his well-reamed hole with a single savage thrust. It was a compelling display of sexual dominance and Valerie Sales tingled with loving admiration for the other woman. She had been affected by a similar sensation on first seeing her come into the restaurant, before her strong competitive instinct had taken over.

But now that tender emotion would not be suppressed and she made the decision to act. She pulled her cock from the slackened asshole and walked over to the Russian, leaving the discarded man confused and moaning on the bed. The other woman turned her head as she approached and her eyes lit up in recognition of the changed state of affairs. She likewise shoved her man off her cock and tilted back her head as Valerie Sales bent to kiss her and within seconds each woman was sucking passionately on the other's tongue. Their trembling hands roamed over breasts, hips and buttocks, and all hostile feelings floated away.

'You're so right about the lingerie,' said the Russian breathlessly. 'It does wonders for you.'

'And you,' said Valerie Sales, 'have a body to die for.'

They laughed and kissed again, forgetting about the men around them, who looked on in envy and confusion. At last the Russian pulled her lips away. Red gloss was smeared around one corner of her sensual mouth, giving her pale face a debauched appearance.

'Let's play,' she said.

'Oh, yes! Let's play,' echoed Valerie Sales.

The Russian picked up her crop and pointed at one of the men in her stable. 'You,' she said, 'come here and get down on your hands and knees.' And she tapped the rug next to the bed in a peremptory fashion. As soon as he was in position, she stood up and pushed her cock into his face, ordering him to suck the now rather greasy-looking object. Wincing in disgust, he nevertheless stretched open his mouth and swallowed the head of the black shaft that had been driven into countless men that evening.

As he sucked her, the Russian addressed her new girlfriend in a camp executive tone. 'The applicant for the new position is a good little cocksucker,' she said, glancing down at the kneeling escort. 'But I wonder how well he can multitask?'

Biting her lip to stem the laughter, Valerie Sales stepped briskly behind the cock-sucking male, squatted down on her stocking-clad legs and sought out his defenceless anus with her stiff pink prick. Inch by inch she penetrated the tight passage, forcing muffled grunts from the owner's cock-stuffed throat, until he was impaled both front and rear like a hog on a spit. Down on all fours, the helpless male gobbled on the dark tool of one female executive and took the thrusts of the other in his ass. For the next ten minutes they fucked him methodically, moving their strong hips back and forth in unison, each woman pushing her cock far inside its respective orifice as if she hoped to meet the other's cock in his middle.

'Kiss me, beautiful,' said the Russian and bent her head towards Valerie Sales. The two women pressed their glossy lips together and noisily sucked tongues. The man beneath them was forgotten as they caressed one another's shoulders and breasts. Their hips moved mechanically, driving the cocks deep into receptive male flesh.

They were taken by surprise when the man came suddenly and loudly. Choking on the fat black phallus buried in his throat, he emptied his balls onto the rug as Valerie Sales continued to stoke his ass.

'Half a point each,' joked the Russian.

They shooed him away and fell back on the mattress laughing, their lady-cocks pointing up from their crotches, stiff and ready for more action.

'My pussy is aching for tongue,' said Valerie Sales.

'Mine too.'

Spontaneously they began to remove their strap-ons, Valerie Sales unbuckling her harness, Katerina Dominovna dragging the latex briefs down over hips. Reclining on their elbows, thighs shamelessly parted, they appraised the naked men and discussed their preferences.

'That one,' said the Russian, finally making up her mind, and she summoned the leanest of the bunch with her finger.

'I'll take you,' said Valerie Sales, pointing to a youth with a promisingly wide mouth. She pulled aside the

231

crotch of her black panties and exposed a luxurious dark bush.

The two men approached and were told to place their faces between the open legs of the women. Dutifully, they lay belly down across the mattress and began to lick the hairy sexes. The women, still reclining on their elbows, chatted freely.

'In my Moscow office I keep a man under my desk for this very purpose.'

'What an excellent idea! I'll try that myself.'

'And when I'm travelling, my bodyguard has the honour.'

'Really? That bald brute you brought to the restaurant?'

Katerina Dominovna threw back her head and laughed. 'Boris is as gentle as a pussy cat with me. And he has a miraculous tongue. I'll lend him to you if you like. But you must promise not to poach him for your own staff, Ms Sales.'

The women instructed the men to turn onto their backs. Without a pause in their conversation, they lowered their asses over the upturned faces as nonchalantly as two friends settling onto stools at a fashionable wine bar.

'There is very high male unemployment in my country,' continued the Russian, wriggling her buttocks into a more comfortable position and entirely smothering the trapped face. 'Men are grateful for any work they can get. I even have an ex-soldier on my staff whose sole purpose is to massage my feet during long meetings. It is becoming quite fashionable back home for executives like myself to employ handsome young men as office objects such as footrests, coat stands and even rubbish bins. We Russians do not have the same inhibitions as you in the West. And in our lawless land money rules absolutely.'

A crude rasping sound made Valerie Sales glance down towards the Russian's big oval buttocks. Only the top of the man's head was visible beneath the curvaceous mounds of pale woman flesh and his arms were pinned against his sides by her heavy thighs. The noise grew louder as he fought for breath under the soft suffocating sex, until at last Katerina Dominovna leaned forward and raised her buttocks an inch to allow air to reach his gasping mouth. Her puckered asshole hovered rudely above his face and the parted lips of her hairy sex waited impatiently while he gulped oxygen into his burning lungs.

The sight thrilled Valerie Sales. It was a glorious display of female mastery. The Russian's pink and open sex seemed insatiable, the head captive beneath it nothing more than a device to give it pleasure. She watched as the big proud round buttocks were lowered once more and the male face was squashed into its service position – the nose pressed tight into her asshole, the mouth buried in her sex.

'Imagine what we could achieve if we joined forces,' Valerie Sales said.

'My thoughts exactly,' replied the Russian.

'We could build a media and public relations empire.'

'And have the time of our lives doing it!'

While the women made plans to merge their companies, the men, faces hidden beneath the heavy globes of flesh, tirelessly licked and sucked the dominating sexes of their powerful executive clients. At intervals they were allowed an inch to breathe before being smothered again in the humid and pungent channels.

Queening her man with a regal posture, Katerina Dominovna pointed to his cock, which lolled half-erect against his thigh. 'Technology has long been capable of producing a superior version of the male organ,' she remarked. 'For a small price, a woman can buy a manufactured penis that meets her exact specifications and is permanently hard.'

'Yes,' agreed Valerie Sales, dragging her moist panty crotch further up over her ass cheek and grinding her sex hard against the labouring male face. 'Cocks are easy to improve upon, but there will never be a manmade equivalent of a pussy. And when you combine a pussy with the whole woman – our beautiful breasts, our curvy bottoms, our way of moving and dressing – how can men compete with us?'

'Their time is over and they know it.'

Turning to one another, the two women kissed lovingly, while down in the airless darkness beneath their buttocks the menwhores obediently did their job.

After being dismissed from the agency following a complaint about his facial grooming, Raoul Davies made up his mind to leave the male escort business altogether. Some weeks later, when his meagre savings were exhausted, he saw an advertisement for the position of personal assistant to the president of an international media and public relations company. The salary was high, frequent foreign travel was guaranteed and, amazingly, the only requirement was that the applicant should be photogenic and flexible.

On the day of the interview, he found himself in a plush waiting room in the company's London offices along with three dozen other candidates. They were all handsome young men like himself with gelled hair and dressed in fashionable off-the-peg suits.

Raoul was among the last to be summoned and his stomach ached with anxiety as he was led to the elevator by a pretty redhead from Human Resources. He wanted the job badly, yet he was troubled by a personal detail he had been asked to provide on the application form. Why should a company president want to know the length of her assistant's tongue?

They emerged from the elevator on the top floor and, as they approached the entrance of a grand-looking office, the redhead took what appeared to be a stopwatch from her jacket pocket. At the far end of the room Raoul could see the figure of a woman sitting behind a wide desk. Her face was silhouetted against a bright window and she was leaning back in her chair, hands folded behind her head. Something about her seemed familiar and his gaze dropped beneath the desk to her long stocking-clad legs and shiny black stilettos.

She opened her knees wide, pushing back the hem of her short skirt to the top of her thighs. 'Crawl to me,' she commanded. 'And start licking.'

Raoul heard a beep as the stopwatch was activated.

nexus

The leading publisher of fetish and adult fiction

TELL US WHAT YOU THINK!

Readers' ideas and opinions matter to us so please take a few
minutes to fill in the questionnaire below.

1. Sex: Are you male ☐ female ☐ a couple ☐?

2. Age: Under 21 ☐ 21–30 ☐ 31–40 ☐ 41–50 ☐ 51–60 ☐ over 60 ☐

3. Where do you buy your Nexus books from?

☐ A chain book shop. If so, which one(s)?

_____

☐ An independent book shop. If so, which one(s)?

_____

☐ A used book shop/charity shop
☐ Online book store. If so, which one(s)?

_____

4. How did you find out about Nexus books?

☐ Browsing in a book shop
☐ A review in a magazine
☐ Online
☐ Recommendation
☐ Other _____

5. In terms of settings, which do you prefer? (Tick as many as you like.)

☐ Down to earth and as realistic as possible
☐ Historical settings. If so, which period do you prefer?

_____

☐ Fantasy settings – barbarian worlds
☐ Completely escapist/surreal fantasy
☐ Institutional or secret academy

- ☐ Futuristic/sci fi
- ☐ Escapist but still believable
- ☐ Any settings you dislike?

_____

- ☐ Where would you like to see an adult novel set?

_____

6. In terms of storylines, would you prefer:

- ☐ Simple stories that concentrate on adult interests?
- ☐ More plot and character-driven stories with less explicit adult activity?
- ☐ We value your ideas, so give us your opinion of this book:

_____

_____

_____

7. In terms of your adult interests, what do you like to read about? (Tick as many as you like.)

- ☐ Traditional corporal punishment (CP)
- ☐ Modern corporal punishment
- ☐ Spanking
- ☐ Restraint/bondage
- ☐ Rope bondage
- ☐ Latex/rubber
- ☐ Leather
- ☐ Female domination and male submission
- ☐ Female domination and female submission
- ☐ Male domination and female submission
- ☐ Willing captivity
- ☐ Uniforms
- ☐ Lingerie/underwear/hosiery/footwear (boots and high heels)
- ☐ Sex rituals
- ☐ Vanilla sex
- ☐ Swinging
- ☐ Cross-dressing/TV
- ☐ Enforced feminisation

☐ Others – tell us what you don't see enough of in adult fiction:

_____

_____

_____

8. Would you prefer books with a more specialised approach to your interests, i.e. a novel specifically about uniforms? If so, which subject(s) would you like to read a Nexus novel about?

_____

_____

_____

9. Would you like to read true stories in Nexus books? For instance, the true story of a submissive woman, or a male slave? Tell us which true revelations you would most like to read about:

_____

_____

_____

10. What do you like best about Nexus books?

_____

_____

11. What do you like least about Nexus books?

_____

_____

12. Which are your favourite titles?

_____

_____

13. Who are your favourite authors?

_____

_____

14. Which covers do you prefer? Those featuring: (Tick as many as you like.)

- ☐ Fetish outfits
- ☐ More nudity
- ☐ Two models
- ☐ Unusual models or settings
- ☐ Classic erotic photography
- ☐ More contemporary images and poses
- ☐ A blank/non-erotic cover
- ☐ What would your ideal cover look like?

_____

15. Describe your ideal Nexus novel in the space provided:

_____

_____

_____

_____

16. Which celebrity would feature in one of your Nexus-style fantasies? We'll post the best suggestions on our website – anonymously!

_____

THANKS FOR YOUR TIME

Now simply write the title of this book in the space below and cut out the questionnaire pages. Post to: Nexus, Marketing Dept., Thames Wharf Studios, Rainville Rd, London W6 9HA

Book title: _____

NEXUS NEW BOOKS

To be published in December 2007

BUTTER WOULDN'T MELT
Penny Birch

When Pippa is accepted as a trainee at a city law firm, she fondly imagines a life both cultivated and intellectual, rather than the crew of sleazy ambulance chasers she ends up with. Worse still, they know rather more about her private life than she would have liked, leaving her little choice but to accept some deeply humiliating duties and help them out in areas which involve very little legal know-how and a great deal of having her knickers taken down. Then there's AJ, notorious diesel dyke and boss of a motorbike courier firm, who regards Pippa as her private property, and American businessman Hudson Staebler, who has his eye on Pippa's little sister.

£6.99   ISBN 978 0 352 34120 4

UNIFORM DOLLS
Aishling Morgan

This is a story straight from the heart of a lifelong uniform fetishist and conveys the sensual delight to be had from wearing uniforms and enjoying others in uniform. Whether it is the smartness and authority of military dress, the sassy temptation of a naughty schoolgirl, or the possibilities offered by an airhostess, policewoman or even a traffic warden, it is all described here in sumptuous and arousing detail, along with unabashed accounts of kinky sexual encounters.

£6.99   ISBN 978 0 352 34159 4

If you would like more information about Nexus titles, please visit our website at www.nexus-books.com, or send a large stamped addressed envelope to:
  Nexus, Thames Wharf Studios,
  Rainville Road, London W6 9HA

NEXUS BOOKLIST

Information is correct at time of printing. To avoid disappointment, check availability before ordering. Go to www.nexus-books.com.

All books are priced at £6.99 unless another price is given.

NEXUS

☐ ABANDONED ALICE	Adriana Arden	ISBN 978 0 352 33969 0
☐ ALICE IN CHAINS	Adriana Arden	ISBN 978 0 352 33908 9
☐ AQUA DOMINATION	William Doughty	ISBN 978 0 352 34020 7
☐ THE ART OF CORRECTION	Tara Black	ISBN 978 0 352 33895 2
☐ THE ART OF SURRENDER	Madeline Bastinado	ISBN 978 0 352 34013 9
☐ BEASTLY BEHAVIOUR	Aishling Morgan	ISBN 978 0 352 34095 5
☐ BEHIND THE CURTAIN	Primula Bond	ISBN 978 0 352 34111 2
☐ BEING A GIRL	Chloë Thurlow	ISBN 978 0 352 34139 6
☐ BELINDA BARES UP	Yolanda Celbridge	ISBN 978 0 352 33926 3
☐ BIDDING TO SIN	Rosita Varón	ISBN 978 0 352 34063 4
☐ THE BOOK OF PUNISHMENT	Cat Scarlett	ISBN 978 0 352 33975 1
☐ BRUSH STROKES	Penny Birch	ISBN 978 0 352 34072 6
☐ BUTTER WOULDN'T MELT	Penny Birch	ISBN 978 0 352 34120 4
☐ CALLED TO THE WILD	Angel Blake	ISBN 978 0 352 34067 2
☐ CAPTIVES OF CHEYNER CLOSE	Adriana Arden	ISBN 978 0 352 34028 3
☐ CARNAL POSSESSION	Yvonne Strickland	ISBN 978 0 352 34062 7
☐ CITY MAID	Amelia Evangeline	ISBN 978 0 352 34096 2
☐ COLLEGE GIRLS	Cat Scarlett	ISBN 978 0 352 33942 3
☐ CONCEIT AND CONSEQUENCE	Aishling Morgan	ISBN 978 0 352 33965 2

NEXUS CLASSIC

NEXUS CONFESSIONS

NEXUS ENTHUSIAST

---------- ✂ ------------------------

Please send me the books I have ticked above.

Name   ....

Address   ....

                ....

                ....

                .... Post code ....

Send to: **Virgin Books Cash Sales, Thames Wharf Studios, Rainville Road, London W6 9HA**

US customers: for prices and details of how to order books for delivery by mail, call 888-330-8477.

Please enclose a cheque or postal order, made payable to **Nexus Books Ltd**, to the value of the books you have ordered plus postage and packing costs as follows:

UK and BFPO – £1.00 for the first book, 50p for each subsequent book.

Overseas (including Republic of Ireland) – £2.00 for the first book, £1.00 for each subsequent book.

If you would prefer to pay by VISA, ACCESS/MASTERCARD, AMEX, DINERS CLUB or SWITCH, please write your card number and expiry date here:

....

Please allow up to 28 days for delivery.

Signature ....

Our privacy policy

We will not disclose information you supply us to any other parties. We will not disclose any information which identifies you personally to any person without your express consent.

From time to time we may send out information about Nexus books and special offers. Please tick here if you do *not* wish to receive Nexus information.   ☐

---------- ✂ ------------------------